Beneath The Lie

Fabulous Five Series

Virginia C. Hart

ISBN-10: 149280259X
ISBN-13: 9781492802594

For my husband, my daughter and my son...you are my life and I share this dream come true with you all.

Chapter One

(Present Day)

Pulling my car into the driveway, I can't believe how hot it already is for the beginning of April. Of course, I just drove from the cool ocean breezes of Garden City, into the arm pit of hell, lovingly referred to as Columbia, South Carolina. The capital city is the hottest place in our great state. Luckily, I won't have to endure this heat much longer. I will graduate from the University of South Carolina in early May and spend the summer at our Garden City Beach home looking for a job, that is, unless I manage to qualify for the Ladies Professional Golf Association, which would put me on tour and bring all my dreams to fruition. Becoming a professional golfer is not a dream; it is my goal in life. I learned long ago that most dreams don't come true and can easily become your worst nightmares. I gave up dreaming when my innocence was crushed by the cruel people who invade this earth. The one and only silly dream I have clung to and allowed myself to indulge in for the last four and a half years will fade away with the scorching temperatures at the end of this summer and reality will once again crush the fantasy inside my head. Shaking my head to bring myself back to the present, I get out of my car and stretch from the two and a half hour drive. Chloe's car is in the driveway and I know she has made it safely home from visiting her family in Charleston over the Easter holiday. I grab my purse from the passenger seat and my luggage from the trunk and start to walk towards the porch of our rental house. The door opens and I'm immediately greeted by my overly dramatic roommate and best friend.

1

"Welcome home, darlin'," Chloe shouts in her overly exaggerated southern drawl.

"Hey Chloe, how was your holiday weekend in Charleston? Meet any cute surfer dudes?" I ask. Chloe's dad's family is originally from Charleston and they spend the majority of holidays there visiting with her favorite aunt, Tina and her husband, Aiden. Tina and Aiden retired on Folly Beach, purchasing a second row beach cottage that is the most wonderful place to get away and escape reality. It's also a great spot to check out the local surfers and get our hottie fix.

"I barely had time to get to the beach and ogle the eye candy with all the family drama. My sister was there with her not- so- likable boy-friend, my mom was hitting the sauce pretty frequently, and dad just played golf for an extended number of hours with uncle Aiden. So I chatted it up with Aunt Tina which I enjoyed every minute of and did some studying. How about you? Did you enjoy your time with your fam-ily in Garden City?"

Before I unload the details of my 'not so exciting weekend', I pull my luggage into the den and throw my purse on the kitchen table, immediately grabbing a bottled water from the fridge and holding it up to my head, reveling in the cooling temperature against my skin. "God, did we leave the air conditioner off while we were both out of town? It is scorching in here!" I sigh. Chloe walks down the hallway to adjust the thermostat while fanning herself with her hands.

"Yeah, we did. But it was in the mid sixties last week. I didn't realize a heat wave would occur during the Easter weekend bringing temps like it's mid July. And stop avoiding the question, how was Garden City?" I know what she is really asking in her not so round-about way. She wants to know if I saw anyone from home. Not just anyone, the only someone that makes my heart race and break all at the same time. *Patrick.* I stroll back to the kitchen table meeting her staring gaze that is letting me know that this conversation cannot be avoided.

"No, Chloe, I didn't see Patrick and the future Mrs. this weekend! Not that it would matter if I did," I state bluntly. Chloe gives me another knowing stare before speaking.

"I don't remember asking whether or not you saw Patrick and his future bride, but since you bring him up..."

"Don't," I beg. I just can't have this conversation so close to finals. I can't go down that dark path leading to nowhere, when the only thing it will bring is sadness and grief. "Mom and Dad are fine. They are busy planning European vacations that will correspond to Flynn's soccer schedule and check out a couple of his games this summer."

My brother, Flynn, is the most awesome soccer player to come out of the great state of South Carolina. He is currently a junior at the University of Alabama, Dad's alma mater, and has been selected to play overseas this summer. If he shows promise, the European scouts may offer a professional contract which would delay his college education and leave broken hearts all over the southeast. But, Flynn's soccer career has always over shadowed my golf aspirations and our relationship has suffered due to jealousy. Don't get me wrong. I love my brother dearly, and we maintain a very close friendship, speaking often. However, whenever we are both in the presence of our parents, that's when the green monster rears his ugly head and my overall demeanor parallels that of a three year old.

"Was Flynn at the beach house for the holiday?" Chloe asks, not hiding the fact that she has been infatuated with my brother since high school. Although she vehemently denies it, secretly she would love for a relationship to happen between them. I would love for Chloe to be a legal part of my family, even though she is like a sister to me and another daughter to my parents already. However, I will protect Chloe's heart from Flynn until he decides to mature and not be the 'man whore' of the South that he currently is.

"No Chloe. You know I would have told you if Flynn was in town. He had soccer conditioning and couldn't make the trip back for such a short weekend. He will be at the beach house after graduation for a couple of weeks before heading overseas. You know you are welcome to come and drool!" I laugh knowing she wouldn't pass up the opportunity. I just hope she keeps her heart guarded.

"Now, enough about family drama and the like. What do you have going on tonight?" I ask observing that she is showered and dressed in a cute spring sundress with a yellow pair of wedges. "I know you didn't dress up just to welcome me back!"

"Well," she says, "remember that guy from my historical theater class? The cute one I told you about? He called over the weekend and asked me out. We are going to get a bite to eat downtown and maybe grab some cocktails afterwards. You and Wyatt should meet us for drinks."

Oh great, another wanna be actor that Chloe has decided she can sink her teeth into. I wince at the thought of having drinks with a theater geek. "I haven't spoken to Wyatt and I'm not sure what he is doing tonight. I'll give him a call after I go unpack and get through this stack of mail my mom sent back with me. Text me the name of the bar y'all go to after dinner and maybe we will meet you there," I say only half heartedly, knowing that may be the last thing I want to do tonight. Chloe and I have been best friends since we started taking golf lessons at the young age of nine. Chloe was very good and could have gone anywhere on a golf scholarship. Even the University of South Carolina offered her a full ride to play, just like me. But, her heart wasn't in it. Chloe was never one not to follow her heart and her dreams. So, to the dismay of her parents, she turned down the scholarship and opted to study drama, which is her passion. She is very good at what she does and I don't doubt that she will be famous one day. I pray that happens, since she more than likely will have to pay back the hefty tuition her parents give the university since forgoing the full ride.

"Sure I'll text you, but you better come and not give me some lame excuse. Plus, I know Wyatt is dying to see you. He already called and left you a message to give him a ring once you're back in town. Come on Suzy Q, this could be fun, and you could spend some time with Wyatt, since y'all are getting closer to 'sealing the deal'," she snorts.

"Sealing the deal? Is that your new phrase of the week referring to having sex? Look, you know my feelings for Wyatt are complicated. We have been such good friends for so long. I just don't want to risk losing that if things don't work out romantically. You and Wyatt are the only two people that know the real reason I dropped everything and moved to the beach to finish my senior year of high school. I just don't want those lines to cross and mess up things for a lot of people." She knows exactly who I am referring to without making me say his name. Those memories of my senior year were the best and worst of my life. If things turned physical between Wyatt and myself, and didn't last, I'm afraid of what that would do to my already broken heart. A heart that wasn't whole to begin with and might possibly never be again.

Chapter Two

(Present Day)

As I am unpacking my duffel bag, separating the clean clothes from the dirty ones, I hear the doorbell ring. Then, I hear the click clack of Chloe's yellow wedges hitting the hard wood floors as she makes her way to the door. Our house is a small, two bedroom duplex in the nice neighborhood of Forest Hills. Lucky for us, we found this house as soon as it went on the market a couple of years ago. I was more than thrilled to move out of the ancient dorm room I had been living in my freshman and sophomore years. Chloe was too, only having to endure dorm life her freshman year. Forest Hills is a very desirable neighborhood, so we had to move fast to get the place. My parents were looking for investment opportunities at the time and it just so happened I convinced them that this would be a great one. Long story short, they bought the entire building and rent to us and the tenants who occupy the other duplex apartment. The neighborhood is more of the family type so my parents made Chloe and I promise that we wouldn't hold any wild college parties. We stick to the rule with the exception of the occasional out of town USC football game in which we invite a few friends over. The location is extremely convenient to our classes and the downtown bar life, and is only a fifteen minute drive to the golf course on which I practice with the other Gamecock lady golfers who make up our team. I love living here and I'm going to miss it when I graduate. Chloe is begging me to try and find work around the Columbia area so she doesn't have to find another roommate. However, I really need to get out of this town and away from the prestigious University of South Carolina law school before next year. I can't chance running into Patrick and his lovely bride once they settle here in Columbia while he attends law school and she does whatever it is she does.

I hear Chloe in her most charming southern accent inviting her date in the house for a drink before dinner. I know it would be rude for me not to go out and introduce myself, even though I look like shit from the long drive from the beach. I finish separating the clothes and try to straighten out my windblown hair, with little success. I exit my bedroom and walk down the hall to meet the 'date of the week'. Chloe hears my approach since these hard wood floors are so unforgiving to footsteps of any kind and turns to me with a smile. She looks stunning all dressed up for her date. Her dirty blond hair is styled in its natural wavy state, sitting right above her shoulders in a stylish bob. Her makeup is subtle, since she has the most gorgeous olive skin year round. The only makeup she usually wears is some earth tone eye shadows and mascara that showcases her beautiful brown eyes. Only standing a mere 5'4, she has curves that rival those of Scarlett Johansson and makes men notice. Her most striking feature, however, is her smile. When she flashes those pearly whites, men lose their ability to speak and just start drooling. As I approach, her smile has obviously put her date under the same spell because he doesn't even notice that I have walked into the room. Chloe breaks her spell by introducing me. "Brian I'd like you to meet my best friend and roommate, Suzanna. Suzanna, this is Brian Westwood." Brian politely, but not so eagerly, turns from the fabulous view of Chloe to acknowledge my presence. I walk closer to the couch and offer my outstretched hand.

"Hey, Brian. It's so nice to meet you."

He kindly accepts my hand, but instead of the obvious hand shake, he gently raises my hand to his lips and deposits a soft kiss on the opposite side of my palm. Then in his most charming voice, he replies, "Hello, Suzanna, the pleasure is all mine."

Oh, my. Chloe may have met her match in the charming department. I really seem to like this guy so far and his southern charm. Also, Brian is very easy on the eyes. He towers over Chloe, standing close to six feet in height. He is thin, but lean with broad shoulders. Dark, almost jet black hair frames his chiseled facial features, accentuating his big blue eyes. He is definitely a looker! Chloe is beaming, excitement lighting up every inch of her face. After the introductions, Chloe and Brian settle onto the couch and I in the chair opposite all enjoying a glass of wine before they leave for dinner. Come to find out, Brian is originally from the Charlotte, North Carolina area. He was a gold medal swimmer in high school and could have attended any of the state colleges or universities on an athletic scholarship, but just like Chloe, followed his passion of theatrics and decided to enroll at USC for its drama program. He is, also, in his junior year like Chloe and they share a couple of classes. I can tell from our brief conversation that Brian is extremely bright and passionate about his field of study. Although he doesn't mind being in front of the cameras, his ultimate goal is to be behind the cameras, as director or producer of some big production. As we finish our wine, Chloe and Brian stand and start heading towards the door to leave for dinner. I grab the empty glasses and walk towards the kitchen. "Y'all enjoy dinner and have a great time!"

Chloe turns and pleads to me with her eyes before her voice starts. "Think we might see you and Wyatt later for after dinner drinks? Please. We would love for you guys to join us and it would give Brian a chance to meet Wyatt." What is it with Chloe that she has to have an entourage with her for a dinner date?

"I'll think about it. I still have to finish unpacking and do laundry and then go through that huge stack of mail. Remember? Just text me when dinner is done and y'all decide where you are going for drinks. I'm not promising anything."

Chloe sighs, "Oh my gosh, Suzanna. You sound like an old hag. Laundry, really? Just put that off 'til tomorrow and come have some fun. I haven't seen you all weekend. Plus, this will give you a chance to catch up with Wyatt, and also, get to know Brian some more." Brian looks like he is using all his acting skills to perfect the perfect pout that mirrors the one Chloe is now displaying all over her pretty face. I laugh and *finally* give in.

"Okay, but I have to at least get through this mail first. I'll call Wyatt to see if he's up for drinks. Text me. Now go, get out of here!" Chloe and

Brian both smile and then head towards Brian's car to leave for dinner. I shut the door behind them and take their empty wine glasses placing them in the dish washer before refilling my glass and walking back to the kitchen table to attack the stack of mail. Most of the mail is junk mail related to credit card offers or magazines subscriptions that need renewing. Some of the letters are from junior golf academies across the state offering me summer employment to work with the junior golfers and camps. Making some head way, I finally make it to the bottom of the pile. The next letter I open has my heart soaring. It is an invitation to the qualifying round for the Ladies Professional Golf Association being held in early August in Hilton Head. This is just a regional qualifying round that takes lady golfers from the Southeastern states. If I make the cut, it would guarantee me a spot for the national qualifying that would be later in the fall. I am ecstatic! All my hard work and lessons and golf rounds were finally paying off. I would have to practice every day, playing 18 to 36 holes, to get ready. But, I can't wait. I also can't wait to tell Chloe and my family. They will be thrilled! Jumping up and down, squealing like a school girl, I almost forget about the last unopened piece of mail. I glance back at the table and pick up the impressive envelope with my name and home address beautifully written in calligraphy. Very fancy I think. There is no return address, and in all my excitement with the previous letter, I really am not thinking what's in this pretty piece of mail. When I open the letter all my excitement and happiness from earlier disappears as I look down at the picture of the love of my life and a very attractive brunette. Tears sting my eyes and immediately blur my vision of the lovely couple and the words that appear around the picture, in the beautiful bold script. I wipe a stray tear away to take a better look at the most gorgeous face I have ever seen of the boy I have known since I was eight years old. His big blue eyes sparkle and dance showing his happiness. His blond hair is still as blond as ever, making his eyes even bluer. He looks like his skin has been kissed by the sun, golden and radiant. His smile is breathtaking showcasing his straight white teeth. He is just too beautiful for words. I trace my damp finger over his face and feel a warm sensation flow through my body. Then, the sensation turns to extreme pain when I realize that Patrick isn't looking back at me in the picture. He is lovingly looking at the gorgeous brunette that shares the photo on the invitation. His head is cocked towards her as his arm wraps around her shoulders in a tight embrace. She is looking right back at him with the same goofy happiness spread all over her pretty face. In the picture, they seem like America's sweetheart couple. Realization then dawns on me and a loud sob breaks through the silence of the empty house. Unable to control my breakdown, I clutch the invitation in my hand and slide to the floor. Leaning against the kitchen chair and still crying, I continue to torture myself by staring at the happy couple. I don't know how long I sit on the floor giving in to my breakdown. Finally, when I don't think I can shed any more tears, I try to read the words on the card stock. With each word, I feel like a voodoo doll being stabbed by pins repeatedly.

Please Join us to Celebrate the Engagement of Patrick Miles and Katelyn Bostick Saturday, May 10, 2013, at the home of Dr. and Mrs. David Jones, Garden City Beach

The invitation is real. It is happening. Patrick is engaged and getting married. Married to some girl named Katelyn. No, he is not supposed to marry Katelyn. He's supposed to marry me. We promised each other. Even though we were young and in high school, we vowed to each other that we were destined to be together forever. I remember it like it was yesterday...

Chapter Three

(Summer Before Junior Year of High School)

We had been dubbed *The Fabulous Five*. It sounds cheesy, but Landon's dad gave the five of us the nickname because he is a Michigan University grad and loves their basketball program. Years earlier, Michigan took the college basketball world by storm with a group of very talented freshman. Although they didn't win the National Championship, they came close two years in a row. Since the five of us (me, Chloe, Patrick, Landon and James) were inseparable since the fourth grade, spending the majority of our time on the golf course, the name stuck and our parents and friends have been calling us the Fab Five ever since. We had all been friends since the fourth grade. Patrick, Landon, James and I were the same age and Chloe a year younger. Regardless of our ages, we did every-thing together. We became close friends because our parents threw us into golf lessons at the local country club where our families all belonged. Once old enough to go out on the course alone to play nine holes without adult supervision, it was guaranteed that that's where you would find us after school and during the summer. During the summers, we spent every weekday morning at the club on the course and afterwards, when the heat was unbearable, we'd all change into our swimsuits and race each other across the driving range to the club pool. That is precisely what we are doing today. The sun is already scorching bringing the temperature to the low nineties by noon. Hot and sticky from a round of golf this morning, Chloe and I are in the ladies locker room peeling off our sweat soaked golf clothes to change into our swimsuits.

"I played like crap today!" I yell to her from my dressing area over to hers.

"We all played like crap today. It was just too damn hot! Who could even see that little white ball with the sweat running down our faces and into our eyes, blurring our vision?"

I agree with her, "Yeah, you've got a point. But, relief is coming soon. Hurry up and change. I can't wait to jump into the pool, although, it will probably feel like bath water." We quickly change and put our clubs and other golf gear into our lockers. I grab my beach bag and start to head out the door in the direction of the men's locker room to meet up with the boys.

"Hey, wait for me!" Chloe yells. "I can't have you walking around half naked and getting all of our guys' attention by yourself!"

"Oh for Pete's sake, Chloe, you know I don't think of any of our guys that way. We are family. That would be weird. Besides, I assure you, I don't have anything they would be interested in," I say with a sigh. Chloe stares at me like I have two heads. "What?" I demand.

"Have you not looked in the mirror lately? You have matured this summer. You're filling out that bikini like nobody's business."

I look at her like she is crazy. "Please! I don't have anything you don't have. Come on. Let's go. I'm really hot and can't wait to jump in the pool." It is the end of summer before my junior year in high school. I have always been scrawny and petite, although my small frame is toned from playing sports. Up until this summer, I guess you would consider my physique more boyish and athletic. But now, I have developed some curves around my hips and my breasts have doubled in size since last school year. Mom and I actually had to go purchase me some new bras to accommodate the ladies. So, yeah, I guess I have *matured*, as Chloe put it. But, I didn't think our best guy companions would take notice. Our relationships are strictly platonic. Chloe, who had developed in early middle school, brings her already curvaceous figure towards the door and we then bounce arm in arm down the hallway to meet up with the guys.

It is always a spectacle watching us race each other across the driving range to the pool. We manage not to get hit by range balls running as fast as we can, laughing hysterically. By the time we make it to the pool, we are all out of breath from the run and our laughter. Standing at the entrance of the lifeguard hut, I notice that Patrick is looking at me differently, almost like he is seeing me for the first time. His gaze focuses on my body and then slowly makes its way up to my face. Our eyes lock then, and an uncontrolled blush comes over me. Seeing how I have been affected by him, he quickly turns away and takes off towards the deep end of the pool to take a dip. Landon and James follow, never noticing the strange moment that just took place. If only Chloe hadn't been so darn observant.

"See, I told you that hot bod of yours was gonna get noticed," she boasts. Feigning ignorance, I shrug my shoulders like I have no idea what she is talking about. "Oh come on, Suzanna. You'd have to be blind and stupid not to notice what just happened with you and Patrick. If he hadn't escaped to the pool, he'd be standing here in a puddle of his own drool. Girl, I think he is enamored!"

"Enamored? Chloe, spare me the dramatics! Come on. Let's go cool off." Secretly, she has no idea how badly I need to cool off. Although Patrick looking at me differently brings a variety of emotions my way, the one at the forefront now is pure *heat*. And this *heat* isn't due to the summer sun.

After a quick dip in the pool and some horsing around, we are all starved, so we head over to the snack bar. Landon grabs us a table, giving James his order. We all take turns at the window placing our lunch orders and getting our drinks. While we are waiting at our table for the food to be ready, James starts telling us about his date this past weekend with a girl named Abby. Landon is giving James a hard time and asking crude questions that is none of our business. James only laughs and jokingly punches him in the arm. Usually Patrick would be giving James hell also, but he seems more quiet and reserved today and he is still trying to steal glances of me. Occasionally, I catch his eyes roving over my body, but I quickly look away not wanting him to know that he has been caught. The fact that he is in essence "checking me out" makes me feel strange. But a good strange...I think I kind of like it! We have always been close but no one has ever crossed that line between friendships.

I love our group and the way we are together. We always get along and have each other's back. I don't think a romantic involvement between two members of the Fab Five would go over well with the others. But I can't shake the other strange feeling I am having...I am enjoying Patrick looking at me differently than just his golfing buddy. When he looks at me the way he is today, my whole body tingles, leaving me shivering despite the increasing temperatures. I am jolted from my dirty thoughts when I hear my name being called alerting me that my food is ready. Scooting my chair back and swinging my legs to the side to stand up, my knee accidently brushes Patrick's leg and my skin feels like it is on fire. Patrick, who had been in conversation with Landon about pre-season football polls, snaps his head to face me and stares at me again. This time instead of quickly looking away, I hold his gaze. In this moment, I don't see my golfing buddy or one of my dearest friends from childhood. No, in this moment I see a beautiful man who makes me feel things I have never felt. In this moment, I see a future with Patrick not just as friends, but as more. Not wanting to break our intense connection, but not wanting the rest of the table to notice, I quickly stand up and put my hand on his shoulder.

"Sorry Patrick, I didn't mean to nudge you." My voice comes out more high pitched than normal. He glances at my hand on his shoulder, turns to face me looking me dead in the eye, and smiles the most gorgeous smile I have ever seen.

"No problem, Suz, you can *nudge* me anytime." I laugh at him and walk away carefully, since my knees are weak, to pick up my food order. Glancing back over my shoulder, I see that Patrick is still watching me from the table. I dare to think that he is having the same type of reaction to whatever has changed between us. But secretly, I wish he is feeling something remotely close to what I am feeling. If so, it is going to be an interesting junior year.

Later that afternoon, I am tiring of the sun and the pool. James and Landon are busy playing a game of ping pong, and Patrick is waiting to take on the winner. Chloe and I are lounging in the sun, working on our outrageous tan lines. We both have great tans from golfing every day, but our feet never see the sun unless at the pool. We try really hard to even out our tans, even going as far as rubbing a tanning accelerator on our feet while sun bathing. I am enjoying the warmth of the sun, relaxing with my eyes closed when I hear Chloe's cell phone start to ring. She answers in her sweetest southern drawl and continues a conversation using her best manners, as all I can hear is her frequent use of "yes 'ma'am". When she clicks end, she sighs.

"I have to go now. Mrs. Jones is in need of sitter pronto. She sounded so urgent on the phone, I felt like I couldn't say no." I was thinking what could be so urgent as to not arrange a sitter ahead of time. As if Chloe is reading my mind she says, "She probably saw a gray hair and has to immediately go to the salon for a root job!" I laugh, knowing that Chloe may be correct since Mrs. Jones is the neighborhood hottie. Although well into her forties, she doesn't look a day older than twenty-five. I bet her cosmetic procedures cost a small fortune. Considering we had raced over the driving range leaving our cars in the parking lot, I start to stand with Chloe to walk her back over. But, before my feet hit the pool deck, Landon walks over, obviously the loser in the ping pong game, and starts getting his things together. Seeing that he may be leaving, Chloe asks if she could catch a ride to her house. He obliges and we say our goodbyes.

"Later Suz," Chloe calls out before racing Landon back across the golf course, giggling and distracting the few golfers on the course who are brave enough to bare the ungodly temperatures and humidity. Laughing, I wave goodbye and recline back in the lounge chair to resume my relaxation. I close my eyes and try to drown out the squeals of toddlers and babies splashing in the pool. I try really hard to clear my mind and enjoy my solitude, but my mind is constantly replaying the moment that Patrick and I shared earlier by the snack bar. Has he really noticed me as someone other than a golfing buddy or friend? Has he started to see me differently, more as a woman than some silly teenage classmate? God, if he only knew how long I had secretly been crushing on him. How long has that been...since the day we met? And what exactly would I do if he did have feelings for me? Do I follow my heart and cave in to the desires of wanting him, not just as a friend? Or, for the sake of our cherished friendship and the friendship of the Fab

Five, can I risk getting close to him and it not working out romantically? That could put a strain on all of us. As my mind continues to be consumed with all things Patrick, my body feels the slightest shiver. That is strange, since I am lying in the scorching sun. Then the shiver escalates to a tingling sensation that runs the length of my entire body, when I feel the warm touch of someone's hand on my arm. Slowly turning my head and squinting my eyes to avoid the sun, I see the most beautiful sight lying right next to me in the lounge chair that Chloe has vacated. *Patrick.*

"Hey Suz, were you napping?" Was I? Maybe this is a dream and Patrick is its star. Maybe I am hallucinating from the extreme heat and Patrick is a figment of my imagination. I slowly start to bring my body to a sitting position, fearing if I move too fast, I just might faint.

"Oh, hey Patrick. I don't think I was sleeping, just in deep thought. What's up?" I ask nonchalantly like it is no big deal for us to be lying next to each other in lounge chairs this close together.

"Nothing much. Just thought I'd come keep you company, since the rest of the gang took off earlier." I guess during my semi-sleep state, I did not notice that James was no longer at the pool. My face frowns slightly as I digest what Patrick just said. Everyone else is gone and I am the only one left for him to spend time with. Ugh, the feeling of being his consolation prize is depressing! I guess my assumptions of romantic interest on his part, based on his earlier actions and our eye contact during lunch, is way off base. Patrick must sense my sudden sullen mood because he immediately starts back pedaling.

"I didn't mean it like that. Like you are the last person here, so I *have* to talk with you. I, uh, I hoped that we would get a chance to talk today...alone."

"Oh," is all the response I can muster. A nervous silence hovers between us until I bravely ask, "What did you want to talk about?"

Patrick smiles, but is hesitant with his question. It seems like he is trying to find just the right words. Moments that seem like days later, Patrick finally asks in a whispering tone, "Suz, would you like to go out to dinner with me tonight?" Okay...dinner. What is the big deal and the mysterious lead up to ask about going out to dinner? We do this sort of thing all the time. I mean, just the other night the five of us went to the movies to watch the latest summer blockbuster.

"Yeah, sure. That sounds fun. Where and what time? Do you want me to call Chloe and you call the boys?" Patrick looks slightly offended and I wonder if I have said anything that would have upset him. Turning in his chair and looking straight into my eyes, Patrick continues.

"Well, as much as I love the boys and Chloe, that isn't really what I had in mind. I was hoping it could be just you and me tonight. You know, like a date." I start to blush and hope that the redness that has overtaken my neck and is sneaking up to my face can only be mistaken as sunburn. I am so taken aback by his forward revelation that I just sit there and look at him.

Looking at him is so nice. I take a moment to enjoy the view of this very handsome creature. I notice Patrick has done some maturing of his own this summer. His broad shoulders lead down to his now defined chest. My eyes dip lower to the rippling of his abdominal muscles. In a complete state of lust, I gaze even lower to check out the narrow hips and waist. Since everything is covered by his swim trunks I can only imagine what is beneath the waistband that my eyes are now glued on. Suddenly, feeling very dirty, I whip my head back up to concentrate on his facial features. Wow, what a glorious sight! Strong cheek bones and a chiseled nose are the foundation of his beautiful face. His lips are full, and when stretched wide in a smile, show off his dazzling pearly whites. Not to mention the lone dimple on the left side of his cheek. I think I would like to lick that dimple. Whoa, where did that come from? I move my focus from the dangerous dimple to his eyes. I have never before seen a pair of eyes the color of the Caribbean Sea. It's not just the color of his eyes that makes them so mesmerizing. It's the way they are encased by long thick blond lashes that would make any girl jealous. Completing his model look is his hair, blond and sun streaked to perfection. Women pay thousands of dollars to get his natural highlights. Altogether, the package is amazing. I could sit here all day and enjoy the view. I am completely entranced, and I nearly jump out of my skin when Patrick places his hand on my shoulder.

"Suz, are you okay? Do you need some water? Are you overheated?" Yep, that's what it is. I am definitely overheated!

"No, I'm fine," though I am anything but fine at the moment.

"Okay, well I guess I'll see you around," Patrick says as he starts to stand and walk away.

"What? What about tonight?" I blurt out. Patrick turns back to me looking a little stunned at my sudden outburst and, also, a little surprised that I had mentioned tonight.

"Well, I thought you might not want the same thing I want since you asked about Chloe, Landon and James joining us. I don't want this," motioning between the two of us, "to be uncomfortable for you." He is giving me an out before this, whatever it is, really even begins. I guess he has the same concerns about our mutual friendship and the friendship of our group also. But this boy, that I have secretly crushed on since we were introduced, is asking me out on a date, a *real* date. I can't let this opportunity slip away because we are both scared of what the future holds. I honestly believe our relationship, as friends, is strong enough to handle the risk if something more is there. And, I believe it can survive even if we discover that friendship is the only thing between us. But really, who am I kidding? I would risk it all for the chance to go out on a date with Patrick. So, feeling slightly brave and a little giddy, I grab Patrick's hand and look him straight in the eyes.

"Patrick, I'd love to go out with you tonight." Patrick's eyes widen and he smiles the biggest smile that makes my heart swoon.

"Great! I'll pick you up around 7:00 and we can go get something to eat. This will be fun, Suz, I promise." Seeing how excited he is makes my heart flutter. I have definitely experienced some new sensations throughout my body today. I start to collect my things to head back to the golf parking lot where my car is parked.

"It's a date!" I say, loving how the words roll off my tongue. I can barely contain my excitement. Noticing the late afternoon sun, I know I need to head home now and start getting ready. Patrick is still grinning ear to ear and that's when I notice that our hands are still laced together. He pulls me beside him and out through the life guard shed, exiting the pool. Just as we are about to cross over the gravel road that leads to the driving range, big rain drops begin to fall. Looking towards the sky, I know we don't have long until the bottom falls out and we get soaked. Patrick comes to the same conclusion and we start running, still holding on to each other's hand and race across the range. Only about twenty yards from the clubhouse, I think we are going to make it. But, then the heavens open and Patrick and I get drenched. The rain falls so hard that each drop feels like a bee sting on my skin. We continue to race to shelter, making it only to the golf cart shed. Laughing hysteri- cally, we make our way in the shed to escape the downpour. My eyes are having a hard time adjusting to the dim lighting of the shed as I push my wet, flattened hair away from my face. Patrick shakes his head side to side, trying to get the extra wetness from his hair before gliding his hand through it and slicking it back so that I can finally see his face. Our laughter subsides and the moment suddenly feels very serious. Patrick starts to walk closer to me. Soon we are toe to toe with each other. I glance down knowing where this might be heading, but feeling some- what nervous and a little uneasy. Patrick puts his finger under my chin and raises my face forcing our eyes to meet. As if in slow motion, Patrick leans in and places a feather light kiss to my lips. My eyes automatically close as I push every thought out of my head, just concentrating on the sensation of Patrick's lips pressed against mine. All too soon, Patrick pulls away breaking the sweet kiss.

"Suz, I'm not sure what I'm feeling right now because I've never felt like this before. You mean the world to me as a friend, but I'm not just having friendly feelings toward you anymore." My heart is racing and I am sure he can hear it beating loudly during his brief silence. He starts speaking again. "If there is even the slightest chance that you might feel the same, then I think we should give this a shot. But, if you just want to remain friends, then that's okay, too. I just want you to know that I want something more, but will settle with what we already have to keep you in my life." Seeing the sincerity in his eyes and feeling his breath brush across my skin as his words leave his lips, I know then and there that I want more too, much more. Letting him know that I am willing to take the next step in our relationship, even if it means risking our friendship, I bring my lips back to his and seal this new phase of our relationship with another soft, yet exquisite kiss. Realizing that I am indeed on the same page as him, Patrick wraps his arms around my waist, pulling me closer and kissing me deeper. We kiss until the rain quits and the sun starts to shine again.

"Suz?" Patrick asks as we walked out of the golf shed together toward our cars.

"Yeah?" I respond with insecurity, wondering if he is suddenly regretting our impulsive make out session.

"This is gonna be great! I can just feel it. I'll see you at 7:00." And with that, Patrick climbs into his jeep and drives away, leaving me with a silly grin on my face, butterflies in my stomach, and what could possibly be love in my heart.

Chapter Four

(Present Day)

I don't know how long I sat on the floor, clutching the engagement invitation in a blubbering mess. It could have been minutes, hours or even days for all I knew. My world stopped spinning the moment I opened the engagement invitation. Is this a cruel joke? Does Patrick still hate me that much that he is willing to throw his engagement in my face? The thought of Patrick hating me and loving another, intensifies my sobs. I didn't even know my body could produce the number of tears that I have cried, but they continue to stream down my face. I wipe away a tear with the hand that has been locked in a death grip to the invitation when I notice my fingers are smudged with black markings. First thought is that the invitation is printed with cheap ink, and that almost puts a smile on my face, only wanting the worst to come from this engagement. I wish the engagement would melt away and disappear just like the words from this piece of cardstock. But upon closer inspection, the engraved words on the front are still intact, reminding me that Patrick and Katelyn are still the happy couple. Flipping the invite over to the back, my heart stops at what I see. Written in the chicken scratch penmanship that belongs to Patrick himself, is a personal note addressed to me. Not caring if my ink stained hands transferred to my face, I wipe away more tears to focus in on his words.

Dear Suz, I know it has been four years since things ended so badly between us. But I have put the past behind me and I'm moving forward. I am really happy, Suz. It just wouldn't be right not to share my happiness with my best friends. You have always been a friend and I would love for you to share in this special time in my life. Please, come and join the others so the entire fab five can help me celebrate. I hope to see you there. With love, Patrick.

Reading the personalized invite over and over, my heart breaks into a million little pieces. Not that it was whole to start with since things ended between me and Patrick years ago. But the fact that he is ready to move on seems so final. Almost like a death. I guess I had still been holding on to that last dream of mine with the hope that one day Patrick would resurface in my life and we could find our way back to each other. Although that would require an explanation of why I left and then lied about it, an explanation that I am willing to take to my grave to keep from hurting him. How can he really want me to attend his engagement party? Does he really think that our history together could be so easily forgotten and we can just go back to being friends? I wonder if Katelyn has any idea that Patrick has personally invited his ex-lover to their engagement party. Maybe Katelyn doesn't even know I exist. I am a wreck just receiving this emotional piece of mail. How the heck would I even function if I attend their party? Seeing the happy couple plastered on a piece of cardstock is one thing, but having to see them in person would be unbearable. I can't go and share in an event that is supposed to be a happy occasion when it is anything but to me. Selfish or not, I don't care that Patrick has personally asked, when he has never asked anything of me except for my love. I will not go and that is that! I can't be a part of this so called happy celebration.

I must have ignored my cell phone during my pity party, because not much longer after reading the invite for the hundredth time, Chloe bursts through the door almost angry. Seeing me in my slumping form on the floor, face reddened and eyes swollen from hours of crying, her expression changes from anger to panic.

"Oh God, Suzanna, what's wrong?" she asks as she hurriedly rushes to kneel down before me taking my hands in hers. The paper I have been holding onto so tightly crumples in her hand as she looks down to read it. Immediately, understanding flashes in her eyes as she wraps her arms securely around me. "Suz, I'm so sorry. It's going to be okay," she keeps whispering in my ear as she holds me while my body is rocked with more uncontrollable sobs. She holds me until I finally stop shaking and the tears are manageable. Sensing that my body might be able to function again, I pull away from her giving her a small smile, that doesn't reach my eyes. I untangle her arms from around my shoulders and start to stand.

"Thanks, Chloe, I'll be fine. It just still hurts so much." My voice sounds foreign because it is quivering so much. Just then I notice Brian is standing a few feet away from us, probably wondering what kind of crazy roommate Chloe lives with. "What are y'all doing back so soon?" I ask. Chloe looks at Brian and then back to me.

"Suz, it's almost 11:00. I texted you and called you several times after we left dinner. When you never responded or answered the call, I got worried. Thank heavens I got here when I did. I'm so sorry I wasn't here to help you." Now I feel even more terrible if that is even possible. My breakdown over an old boyfriend has caused Chloe to cut her date short with Brian because she was worried about me. Looking at Brian and Chloe, I try to apologize.

"Don't be sorry, Chloe. I'm the one who should be sorry. I feel so stupid for not hearing my phone. I hate that you guys came home early to witness my near breakdown, but really I'm going to be fine." Feeling extremely guilty I continue, "I'm just gonna go to my room and get some rest while y'all try to enjoy the rest of your evening. Brian, again, I'm so sorry. It was really nice meeting you. Maybe next time we can all hang out some. Goodnight guys. Chloe I'll see you in the morning." I head down the hallway to escape my humiliation in search of some much needed sleep.

It isn't long before I hear a soft knock on my bedroom door. Before I have the chance to ignore it and fake sleep, Chloe turns the knob and slightly opens the door.

"Hey, can I come in?" she asks hesitantly. I roll over on my pillows to look her way and motion for her to enter. She slowly walks over to the bed and sits beside me, comforting me by rubbing her hand down my hair. She exhales loudly before speaking, "Suz, I know you are hurt-ing, but you knew this was coming, right?" Of course she is right. Even though Patrick and I severed ties a long time ago, being from the same small town means word travels fast when one of their own plans to marry. I had heard months ago that Patrick was engaged, and although it bothered me at the time, I subconsciously didn't really believe it. But, the invitation today has made it believable and very real. Trying to con-trol more tears that threaten to slip out, I sigh.

"Yeah, I guess this just made it official to me. Now, I have to finally accept it." Seeming to understand, Chloe nods in agreement.

"Are you going to attend the party?" she asks. Looking at her like there are snakes coming out of her head, I reply rather harshly.

"NO! Why would I put myself through that? You saw what the invite did to me tonight. How could I possibly torture myself and see them together in person?" Never taking her eyes from mine and not reacting in the least to my harsh response, Chloe surprises me.

"Suzanna, I really think you should go." Sitting straight up, my despair turning to anger, I narrow my eyes and yell.

"What? Have you lost your mind? How many drinks did you and Brian have?" Suppressing a laugh, Chloe continues with an air of confidence.

"I know it sounds crazy now, but Suz, you have to have some clo-sure. You have been moping around the last four years. Yeah, you've done the college thing, been to parties, hooked up with a few guys, even been on some dates. But, you have never let anyone, other than me and Wyatt, get close to you. You've got to move on, let Patrick finally go, in order for you to be happy."

"If you remember correctly, I did let Patrick go, four years ago. You were there!" I respond anger spilling out through each word. Chloe continues to look past my anger and goes on.

"You may have let him go physically, pushing him out of your life, but Suz, we both know you never let him leave your heart." Not wanting to hear the blunt truth of the matter, I turn away from her, lying back down in my bed.

"Chloe, I'm really tired. Please leave so that I can get some sleep." Knowing that she is being dismissed, Chloe stands from the bed and starts walking to the door. Before exiting the room she stops and turns to face me, although I don't look her way.

"Good night Suz, I love you. We will talk more about this in the morning." Chloe slips out the door, closing it behind her, leaving me alone for what is sure to be a sleepless night.

As I watch the first rays of sunlight peeking through my bedroom window, I feel relief wash over me. I can finally arise from the worst night of non-sleep I have yet to experience in my lifetime. I stretch my body, suddenly regretting that decision. My body seems to take revenge and ache with each movement I make. I feel like I have been run over by a MAC truck! I don't know if the pains and aches were caused by my extended stay on the hardwood floors while sobbing uncontrollably, or the tossing and turning that consumed my night. The few hours that I did find sleep were short lived due to vivid dreams. I was dreaming of Patrick. He was walking down the beach, blond hair blowing in the wind. He was dressed in an untucked button down white linen shirt which fell loosely over his khaki chinos. He was barefoot, carrying his Sperry dock shoes in his hand. His skin held a beautiful golden tan that set off his ocean blue eyes. His smile was breathtaking and he looked like he couldn't wait to meet his destination. He continued to walk closer and closer in my dream, giving me ample opportunity to admire all of his exquisite features. It felt like he was looking straight into my soul, his eyes filled with passion and love. When I thought that he was about to walk straight into my arms, my delicious dream turned into a nightmare. Viewing the entire picture, I could see that Patrick wasn't walking towards me anymore. He changed his direction and walked right into the arms of a pretty brunette woman. The woman wrapped her arms around him and then turned to face me with the most wicked smile on her face. She said nothing, but her actions did all the talking for her. She had laid claim to my Patrick and he had chosen her.

Shaking my head to try and forget the vivid details of the nightmare, I get out of the bed and walk to the bathroom. I don't recognize the woman staring back at me from the mirror. She is frightening! Her face is splotchy and her eyes are red and swollen. Dark circles appear under her eyes as a result of very little sleep. Her hair is a mess, stringy and tangled. But, the worst part of the woman in the mirror is her sadness. Her expression screams that what little hope she had, is now gone. Not wanting to look at her another minute, I quickly brush my teeth, wash what little makeup is left on my face from the night before, and try to tame my tangled hair into a ponytail. Exiting the bathroom, I head into the kitchen to brew a pot of coffee. Maybe caffeine will do the trick and take away all my physical and emotional pain that met me this morning. Waiting for the coffee to finish brewing, I am surprised to hear footsteps coming down the hallway towards the kitchen. A few seconds later, Chloe stands facing me looking as fresh a flower considering it is the break of dawn. She walks over to the cabinet to fish out two coffee mugs and a few packets of Splenda. Next, she opens the fridge to get our favorite flavored creamer from the shelf of the door. By then, the coffee has finished brewing and Chloe is making both of us a cup. Placing my mug in front of me, Chloe sits down in the chair beside me. A silence hangs in the air, until Chloe finally speaks first.

"Suz, how are 'ya this mornin'?"

Laughing, I look at Chloe and in a dramatic fashion sure to impress her, motion from the top of my head to the bottom of my toes. "Well, from the looks of me, how do you think I'm doing Chloe?"

Resisting a laugh herself, she says, "You must feel like shit, because that's how you look!" Both of us busting into giggles, Chloe immediately puts me at ease making light of the elephant in the room. After our giggling fit, Chloe becomes a little more serious. "Suzanna, are you ready to talk about your mini-breakdown that took place last night?"

Realizing that she isn't going to let me avoid this heinous topic any longer, I sigh, "Yeah, I guess we can discuss it".

Starting off the question and answer session, Chloe begins with a tough one. "Do you still love Patrick?"

I spit the last sip of coffee I had taken right across the table. "Wow, Chloe! You're not gonna make this easy for me, are you?"

In her dramatic flair, Chloe says, "Who said love was easy? Besides, you don't even need to answer that question, I already know the answer," she states with confidence.

"Oh, really! Well, what is the answer?" I ask curious of her psycho-analysis of my feelings toward Patrick.

"Let's be real, Suz. You have loved Patrick since the day you met him. You fell head over heels for each other during high school and would probably still be that mushy, gushy couple had you not left. Of course you still love him; otherwise that invitation last night would not have affected you so much." Looking at Chloe I know she is right. I never really quit loving Patrick. I just let him believe that I did.

Nudging Chloe in the arm, I ask, "When did you get so smart, huh?"

She smiles, "It doesn't take a genius to recognize the love you still have for him. Come on, Suz. You just need to admit it to yourself."

I glance over at her, tears stinging my eyes, "I have admitted it to myself. I still desperately love Patrick. The fact that he loves someone else is killing me inside. I could live with my lie and let him think I was a horrible person, but I never considered he could love another, not like he once loved me." As if getting the words out of my mouth somehow triggered a switch that controlled my eyes, they immediately start tearing up and I can no longer hold them back. They slip from my eyes, sliding down my face hitting the top of the kitchen table. Not really caring about the crying, I continue to rant. "What I am going to do Chloe? I have held onto the sliver of hope that maybe one day we would find our way back to each other. I know that sounds silly, since I hurt him so much, but I really thought that love would conquer all, or some crap like that." Chloe laughs at my random words not caring if I am making any sense or not. "I don't know if I can handle this, Chloe. I don't think I am strong enough." I place my head down on the table letting another sob escape. Chloe rubs my back, just like she had done last night to try and comfort me. We sit in silence for a few minutes letting my admission of still loving Patrick sink in. Suddenly, Chloe surprises me with her next words.

"Maybe there is still hope." Lifting my head up to look at her with my very puzzled expression, she explains. "Maybe Patrick still feels the same way that you do."

Exasperated, I fling my hands in the air. "Really Chloe? He is engaged to another woman. I seriously doubt Patrick feels anything for me."

She looks at me like I am a complete idiot. "Suz, he feels something. Why else would he personalize his engagement invitation almost begging you to come? Maybe he is feeling nostalgic and just misses your friendship, like he misses the good ole times of the Fab Five. But maybe there is something more. Maybe he really needs to see you again, to know for sure. Maybe this marriage may not be a sure thing." Considering everything she said, I still very much doubt that Patrick would be so callous as to ask someone to marry him without being completely in love. But, Chloe does have a point. Why is he reaching out now, after four years of no contact? Did he need to see me to assure him that he is making the right decision to marry Katelyn? What if I didn't show up at all? Would he just marry that girl anyway, not being as sure as he should be to make a lifelong commitment? My mind is reeling with the idea that maybe Patrick does need to see me and that maybe there is still some small chance to reconnect. Suddenly I am starting to feel a little sympathy for the woman in my nightmare that has become an instant villain. If she doesn't know I exist, she might think that Patrick is hers and only hers. But my love for Patrick outweighs any slight sympathy that I am feeling for his *fiancé*. If I have any chance for happiness, I have to find out if Patrick is still harboring any type of feelings towards me. Pulling myself together, I look right at Chloe and crack the first real smile since my return to Columbia.

"Chloe, let's go shopping!" Slightly taken aback, not fully comprehending my 360 degree mood swing, Chloe looks bewildered.

"Huh?"

Pushing myself from the table and holding my head up high, I say again, "Come on Chloe. We've got some shopping to do. I've got to look fabulous for an engagement party I *will* be attending." Chloe finally catches on and gives me a devilish smile before following me down the hallway to get ready for our excursion.

Patting me on the back, she says, "That's my girl!"

Chapter Five

(Fall Junior Year of High School)

Patrick and I have been together since August. Our first date was incredible. He picked me up promptly at 7:00 at my house. I played it cool around my parents and Flynn, letting them believe that Patrick was picking me up just as a friend, never once mentioning to them that it would be just the two of us without the rest of the gang. At first, we were a little nervous around each other, but eventually we eased into a relaxed conversation between old friends. It was almost natural, except for the occasional touches and frequent glances toward each other. Like on the way to the restaurant, Patrick reached over to hold my hand. When he walked me into the restaurant, he placed his hand on the small of my back guiding me to our table. At dinner we sat side by side, shoulder to shoulder. Our legs brushed against each other under the table. With each touch, my skin heated and tingled with sensations I had never felt, other than during our first kiss in the golf cart shed. It was so easy to get lost in his eyes, the way he looked at me and the way he touched me. We enjoyed every single moment together that we got to spend with each other, alone. Our *alone* time was short lived; even our first date got crashed by Chloe, James and Landon. Patrick was bombarded with texts from the guys and Chloe was constantly texting me. So, reluctantly we invited them to join us.

Before they all arrived, Patrick and I decided that we would keep the status of our new relationship a secret from our dear friends. Patrick was hesitant at first, saying it was no big deal. I wasn't quite convinced and wanted to test the waters first. I didn't like keeping things from our friends, but I wasn't sure if they would understand. We were all so close, and the fact that two of us had ventured off into something more wouldn't be taken lightly. Plus, I still feared that if what Patrick and I were experiencing now, somehow didn't develop, it would put a strain between the two of us which would trickle down to the group. So, we kept our relationship a secret from Chloe, James, and Landon. It was hard, but we were always coming up with ways to spend time together. Whenever we would go out for a round of golf, we made sure we were paired together and the other three played ahead of us. We would hold hands in the golf cart and seek out other tender touches between each other. When the three of them were well ahead of us on a hole, we would sneak sweet, tender kisses. After a round, when we would all arrive at the golf shop, Chloe and I would go to the ladies locker room to change and store our clubs. The boys would do the same in the men's locker room. Patrick and I would always plan to *forget* something so we could meet back up in the hallway, embracing each other and kissing more passionately. A few times we almost got caught, but were quick with an excuse that seemed to pacify the person who had come so close to the truth. But eventually our luck ran out.

It is early November, and we just attended the last football game of the season, the rivalry game between the two big high schools in our area. This year, our team was victorious, and everyone is ready to celebrate. Mindy Hyler, one of the varsity cheerleaders and her twin brother, Mark, who plays on the football team, are hosting a party at their house since their parents are out of town. Everyone from school will be there. The Fab Five decides to attend after swinging by the club to grab beer from Wyatt. He is going to meet us there when his shift ends. Wyatt is always willing to be our designated driver, never needing to experiment with alcohol like we do. I guess it is the age difference. As soon as we drive up in the driveway, we all hop out of the car, popping open our first beer. The party is in full swing with drunk, horny teenagers scattered on the lawn and throughout the house. We make our way into the kitchen, stopping briefly here and there to say hello to a friend or two. Once in the kitchen, we join the drinking game "quarters" already in progress. The object of this game is to bounce a quarter off the table and land it in a cup. The cups, which are full of beer, are placed in a circle with one cup also filled in the middle. If the quarter lands in one of the outside cups, then the person who that cup belongs to has to drink all of their beer. If the quarter lands in the middle cup, then everyone has to down their beer, and the last to finish also has to drink the middle cup. It is a punishing game, sure to get anyone drunk. I'm not a big drinker, and have never been good at chugging beer. But everyone else wants to play, so I join in, not wanting to be far from Patrick. I notice, Leslie, the co-captain of the varsity cheerleading squad, has joined the game. Leslie is a beautiful girl, but has a bad reputation. It is common knowledge that Leslie is more advanced than the average high school girl when it comes to boys. Gossip is rampant about what she is willing to do to get her man. I have always been nice to her, feeling bad that people talk about her behind her back, even though she brings it on herself. But tonight, I notice that she is particularly interested in Patrick, so much so, that she maneuvers her chair right beside him.

"Room for one more? I love this game!" she says to everyone, but only looks at Patrick. He kindly makes room for her to scoot in beside him and the game resumes. Everyone is drinking and laughing, especially James who unfortunately has been the unlucky guy when the quarter landed in his cup three times in a row. Of course, we all had to drink at least one cup full during the duration of the game. As the game progresses, I focus less on it and more on Leslie's hands practically groping my boyfriend under the table. She occasionally rubs his arm, when she thinks something is funny, laughing and slinging her head back in dramatic fashion. At one point, she even once hugs Patrick when he lands his quarter in her cup. Faking the innocent act, she stands and starts drinking her beer letting a few drops drip down her mouth and neck. Once she finishes, the table erupts like she has just cured cancer, and she wipes the excess liquid from her lip with her tongue, very seductively, eyeing Patrick the entire time. Since no one really knows the deal between me and Patrick, I can't really blame her for trying, but even if she did know the truth, I'm not sure it would stop her. Everyone else around the table seems fine with the excessive flirting as I grow more irritated by the minute.

"Ugh, can you believe her?" I whisper in Chloe's direction.

Chloe laughs. "Yeah, I can. This is Leslie we're talking about. I think Patrick may get lucky tonight."

"Ew, he wouldn't touch her. Would he?" My insecurities are starting to get the best of me. Plus, Patrick is doing nothing to stop Leslie's advances, but he isn't encouraging her advances either. So far, he hasn't initiated anything with her that I know of.

Bringing me back to reality I hear Chloe say, "Well, she is willing to probably give him more than he's ever gotten from a girl." Patrick and I have yet to get beyond kissing and a few stops between second and third base. Does he expect more? He has never pushed for more intimate moments with me, not that we ever get that much alone time. Would he be willing to look elsewhere just to keep our relationship a secret? He was the one who wanted to go public and let everyone know we were dating. I was the one who was scared and begged him to keep our little secret. Deep in thought, I barely notice that Leslie and Patrick are now whispering to each other, heads close together, almost touching. An emotion streaks through my body like a lightning bolt. Jealousy! I am filled with it and anger is starting to bubble to the surface. I hear some of the other guys at the table egging Patrick and Leslie on, with rude comments like "Hey, man, y'all should get a room" or "Wish I were in Patrick's shoes now. He's gonna be feeling fine real soon!" Before I can stop myself, I stand abruptly from the table, causing the cups to shake and spill beer over the rims. Maybe it is my alcohol induced state or my protectiveness towards Patrick, but I'm not about to let Leslie get her claws into what is mine. And Patrick is mine, and the rest of these people are about to find out. Patrick shifts towards me, when he feels me stand from the table.

Looking up at me, placing a friendly hand on my arm, he asks, "Suz, you feeling okay? Are you gonna be sick?" Obviously, he thinks I am reacting to the alcohol that is seeping through my veins, but he is so wrong. My actions, although fueled by jealousy, are also spurred on by the love I feel for this man. The love I am no longer willing to hide from everyone else, no matter what the risks. Grabbing his hand from my arm, I pull him up so he is immediately standing in front of me face to face. With my boldness still in control, I wrap my arms around his shoulders and place an opened mouth kiss on his lips. At first he is stunned and I feel like he might reject my advance, but then he begins to relax and deepens the kiss, our tongues dancing with each other. I completely forget that there is a room full of other people. All I care about in this moment is Patrick and me and how we feel about each other. Eventually, I hear some catcalls, whooping and hollering, and then some shocked OMG's. Never wanting the kiss to end, but having to come up for a breath, our lips separate but our embrace remains intact.

"Well, Miss Suzanna, I guess our secret is out of the bag!" he whispers looking mischievous. I blush realizing our audience.

"You're right, but I couldn't wait a minute longer to tell everyone that you are mine!" I say with the most confidence I have ever felt. Hearing Chloe clear her throat, I turn slightly and watch her narrow her eyes at me.

"You two have some explaining to do, now." Without another word, she, James and Landon start walking from the table to exit the party. Feeling a little nervous, I glance at Patrick. He shrugs his shoulders breaking our embrace. He grabs my hand and starts leading me to confront our friends. Before we completely leave the kitchen, I turn slightly to glance back at the table and see Leslie shooting daggers at me with her eyes. I look right back at her and smile, feeling victorious, just like our team was tonight.

When we return to the car, Chloe, James, and Landon are in deep conversation, like they are ambassadors at a world summit trying to establish world peace. Hearing our approach, they stop their discussion and look our way. I can't read their expressions because of the dim lighting. My heart is beating fast as we slowly approach hand in hand. Having Patrick beside me, displaying the physical attachment between us, I relax a bit. Landon is the first to speak.

"What the hell was that Suzanna?" Taken aback at his harsh question, I don't have time to respond before Chloe pipes up.

"Yeah, you guys holding out on us or was that just some stunt to get attention?"

Feeling guilty for keeping something from my best friend, I start to try and explain. "Um, I... we..., I'm sorry..." I am a stuttering mess.

Coming to my rescue, Patrick speaks up. "Suzanna and I have been seeing each other since August. We wanted to tell you from the beginning, but we also wanted to wait to see how our relationship would develop. We have feelings for each other that go beyond friendship. I hope you're not too mad at us for keeping you all in the dark, but we didn't want to mess up our friendships." Looking down at me with soft eyes, he smiles that gorgeous smile that makes my insides go all mushy. I smile back, mouthing a silent "thank you" for explaining our relationship to our friends. Now, it is a waiting game to see how they will react.

No one speaks at first but, then, James breaks the ice. "Well, if you two are happy together, then I'm happy for you." Feeling relief rush through me, I hug James fiercely.

"Thank you James, so much. I'm sorry we didn't tell you to begin with." James nods and smiles sharing again his acceptance to our relationship.

Chloe is next with her two cents. "I'm so freaking mad with you Suz! How could you have kept this from me? But, I can tell you two are happy together. I mean, that kiss said it all!" Then she laughs taking some of the tension away. "We're gonna have a nice long talk, just me and you. You're not getting off so easily with me, girly!" I know I will have to go over every detail with her, but I will be more than happy to since there is no longer anything to hide.

Landon remains quiet, deep in thought. Patrick walks over to him giving him a small nudge. "Hey man, you're okay with this, right?" Landon shrugs like it is no big deal, but we can all tell that it seems to bother him.

"Whatever. I'm fine. Just don't screw this up!" That comment is directed straight at me. I know that it is his way of saying that if something goes wrong, if I ever hurt Patrick, Landon will choose sides. His loyalty will always be with Patrick, not me, and I will lose his friendship forever. Feeling like I need to reassure him, I join Patrick by Landon's side.

"Landon, your friendship means so much to both of us. We wouldn't have jumped into a romantic relationship with such causality and risk losing you in the process. I assure you, this," moving my hand between me and Patrick, "is real. I don't ever want it to end."

With that, Landon's facial expression softens and he begins to accept that Patrick and I are an official couple. "Well, are we done here at this party, or do y'all want to go back in and piss Leslie off some more?" Landon jokes. We all double over in laughter and decide that our party of five is all we need. We leave the party that night to go home, closer than ever.

Chapter Six

(Present Day)

Both Chloe and I quickly get dressed and leave the house in route to the nearest mall. Chloe drives us, chattering on and on excitedly about the possible reunion of two of her best friends. The bravery and determination I was feeling earlier is slowly becoming a blur, just like the trees and traffic that I look at through the passenger window. Realizing that she is doing the majority of the talking, and I am slipping into my thoughts, Chloe suddenly says, "Hello, earth to Suz! Whacha thinking about so hard over there?" I exhale loudly, releasing a small amount of frustration throughout her car.

"I don't know Chloe. I was all gung- ho about twenty minutes ago, ready to go get my man back. But now I'm having doubts. I don't know if I should interfere or even go to the party. What if he really does love this girl?"

Pulling into the parking lot and finding a space close to the door, Chloe parks the car. She looks at me and very seriously says, "Suz, if you don't do this, you'll never really know. You have to decide if you can live with not knowing or you can live with the truth, whatever that may be. Going to this party will either give you hope or break your heart. Regardless of the outcome, I think you have to go in order to move on with your life." Taking in all she just said, I know she is right. However, there is more at stake than just me and Patrick.

"What about the rest of you? I was lucky to have you when everything ended in disaster. But Landon and James have never forgiven me for leaving. I don't know if they are mad because of Patrick and all that brotherly love stuff, or because our close circle of friends exploded into pieces. How will they react to my being there?"

Chloe responds carefully. "You left because you had to. You were protecting Patrick."

"I know that, you know that and Wyatt knows that! But they don't. They think I'm a bitch who treated Patrick horribly in the end," I say in frustration. "Landon will barely speak to me or even acknowledge my presence, and James, although he speaks and is polite, it's only because his mama makes him. You know how close my mother and James' mother are. She wouldn't let him be mean."

Chloe chuckles, "Yeah, I know. But they will come around. Why don't you let me talk to them, feel them out?"

"No! Chloe you can't tell them what happened," I beg.

"I wasn't going to tell them anything about that night. I was just gonna tell them that Patrick really wants all of us, including you, to be there for him. If they know about his personalized invite, I think they will be okay with it. I might even convince them that we could all go together. Wouldn't that be fun? Four of the Fab Five coming to the party arm in arm. What a sight to behold!" Chloe starts giggling and I can't resist holding in my smile. She actually has lightened my mood.

Reluctantly, but feeling a tad better about things, I say, "Okay, Chloe, talk to James and Landon. See what their take on my attendance will be. But, don't push your luck thinking we will be all buddy-buddy arriving together at the party."

Chloe smiles her most charming smile. "Suz, don't ever underestimate my power of persuasion. Come on, we've got some shopping to do."

Hours later, we pull back up to the house our hands loaded with bags carrying our lute from the shopping excursion. It was fun and Chloe and I found the perfect outfits to wear to the engagement party. Taking my bags to the bedroom to put them away, I hear my cell phone ring. I struggle to find the phone in my purse before it goes to voice mail but unfortunately I am too late. Looking at the screen, I see that the missed call was from my mom. Suddenly, I remember some exciting news that I need to share with her and my dad. For that matter, exciting news I have failed to share with anyone since the invitation caused me to forget everything but Patrick. The golf qualifications...I made the cut for the southeast regional qualifying rounds for the LPGA. Throwing my new purchases in the closet, I sit on the bed and call my mom.

"Hi Mom, sorry I missed your call earlier. I couldn't get to my phone fast enough."

My mom's sweet voice fills my ears. "Oh honey, I'm so glad you called me back. When we didn't hear from you yesterday about you arriving safely back to Columbia, we got concerned. Is everything okay?" Do all moms have a sixth sense? How can she possibly know I'm not quite okay, especially when we are miles away?

"Sorry Mom for not calling, but everything is fine. Chloe and I got to talking as soon as I walked in the door and it just slipped my mind to call you and Dad," I explain hoping she won't ask anymore about my well being.

"Well, good. How is Chloe? Did she have a nice time in Charleston with her family? Tell her she has got to come visit us at the beach this summer. I know Flynn would enjoy seeing her." My mom, the ultimate match maker. She has been trying her best to get Chloe and Flynn together since forever. I have never told her how much Chloe would love to entertain that idea. I guess I don't want to get either of their hopes up should Flynn never change his philandering ways.

Ignoring Mom's matchmaking skills I lead into my exciting news. "Actually Mom, there is something I need to ask you about the beach house. I was wondering if I could use the house to live there this summer, since I'll be practicing golf everyday to prepare for the LPGA qualifying round."

There is complete silence. I almost think I have lost the call until I hear my mom, squeal. "Suz, did you just say the LPGA qualifying round? Did you get invited to play in it?"

I giggle with pride. "Yes, Mom, I opened the letter yesterday. It was in the stack of mail you sent back with me. The round is in Hilton Head in early August and I would love to live at the beach to play all the surrounding courses to prepare."

"Oh Suz, I'm so proud of you! Of course you can stay at the beach house. I can't wait to tell your father. He is going to be so proud of you, too. Wait. Why are we just hearing this news today if you found out yesterday?"

Oops, I didn't mean to let that little piece of info slip. "Well, I just couldn't believe that I had made the cut. It just took a day to set in. You are actually the first person I have told." Hearing some relief in her voice I know she has bought that small white lie. I don't want to let her know that I put my good fortune on the back burner to brood over Patrick's engagement. She would definitely worry about my mental health. Hell, I'm worried about my mentality!

"Well, I couldn't be happier for you. When do you plan to move to the beach to start practicing?" she asks.

"I think I need to get started right after graduation. Since I graduate on Sunday, I was planning to arrive at the beach mid week. Plus, I have a party to attend the following Saturday night in Garden City." Now there is another moment of silence. I guess I have successfully made my mom speechless in less than ten minutes.

"Mom, are you still there?"

I hear her sigh before she speaks. "Suzanna, what party are you attending on Saturday night? Would this be Patrick's engagement party at the Jones'?" I am so busted.

"Uh, yeah." No use in trying to hide it. She probably thinks I'm pathetic.

"Do you think that is a wise decision to attend his engagement party? I know that you ended things years ago, but do you really want to celebrate his engagement?" she says a little stunned.

"Well, I wouldn't have considered it, but he specifically wrote a personalized invite asking me to come. He wants all his friends, especially the Fab Five, to be there for him during this special time. It will be hard for me, but I think I owe him that," I say silently praying for a subject change.

Mom's voice gets more forceful as she continues. "You don't owe him anything. I will never understand why he broke your heart, only because you decided to move to advance your golf career." I love how protective she is of me, but feel a tinge of guilt knowing that I too had lied to her. Not wanting her to think I was the bad guy, I told my parents that Patrick had broken up with me when I decided to spend the second semester of my senior year at the beach to play golf under one of the best junior coaches in the state. I told so many lies to so many people my senior year that they all ran together.

Trying to make her understand and convince my mom it is not a big deal, I go on. "I think it will be fun to see the old gang. I promise it's not going to bother me, Mom. I have so moved on. Plus, Chloe, Landon and James will all be there. I have to go to round out the Fab Five."

She isn't totally convinced, but decides to let it go for now. "If this is what you want, then okay. We were actually invited as well, but will be out of town attending a conference for your dad's work. I have already regretted, although I hate to miss it. The Joneses always give the best beach parties. So I guess you and Chloe can use the house, and I'll be down later that week to help you get settled in for the summer."

"Thanks, Mom. I can't tell how much I appreciate you and Dad letting me live at the beach this summer. It will really be convenient to play as much golf as I can before qualifying." We chat a few minutes longer before she has to go get ready for some garden club event. Always the social butterfly. "Love you mom, we'll talk soon."

"I love you, too, Suz. Again, I'm so proud of you. Your dad will probably call you as soon as I tell him your news so keep your phone handy." When our call ends I realize Chloe and I had shopped through lunch and I am starving. By now it is close to dinner time. Figuring we could celebrate my good news over pizza and beer I waltz into her room to ask if she will come with me. She is on the phone with Brian. Yikes! Brian, the sweet guy from Charlotte whose date I ruined because of my breakdown. Grabbing the phone from Chloe's hand while she is in mid sentence, I interrupt their conversation. "Hi Brian, this is Suzanna, Chloe's roommate. I'm so sorry for ruining your date last night. Are you busy now? Good. Why don't you meet me and Chloe at Sharkey's for beer and pizza, my treat! I have news. No, I won't cry! Great, see you in about thirty minutes."

Chloe is looking at me very suspiciously. "What's going on?"

Smiling and grabbing her hand to lead her out of the door, I say, "Well, I feel badly about cutting your date short. Plus, I have amazing news that I forgot to mention last night. It's worth celebrating!"

Still not sure if I am completely crazy, especially since my mood swings are all over the map, Chloe hesitates, but finally concedes and we head to Sharkey's to meet Brian. On the way there I call Wyatt to invite him to meet us there, first, because I don't feel like being Chloe and Brian's third wheel, but also because I haven't seen or spoken with Wyatt since last week, before the holiday break. Wyatt is a good friend. Even though I have known Wyatt since high school, we never attended school together. He is three years older than me. We all met Wyatt when he worked as a bartender at the country club. After a round of golf, we'd all go to the lounge to order snacks and get a soda. Wyatt was always there and if it was only us in the lounge, he would sometimes serve us alcoholic beverages, mostly just beer. He became a good friend to both me and Chloe and the guys. Sometimes we'd meet him after he got off work and head over to the 17th golf hole to have our own small party. He was always able to get a cooler of beer, somehow charging it to our parents' accounts. Our parents never noticed since they were all regulars at the country club bar. Out of all of us, Wyatt and I had the closest bond. He was there for me when I needed him most, always willing to give and never asking anything in return. We remained close even when I moved to the beach, which was more difficult for him than for me. After he finished Francis Marion University, he quit his job at the club and moved to Columbia for graduate school. He still works as a bartender at a fancy restaurant in the vista area called The Blue Marlin. We usually get together once every week or two to catch up, talking on the phone more often than that. I will always feel indebted to Wyatt. He saved me from a very bad situation that could have been much, much worse. Because Wyatt and I have maintained our friendship, many people assume that there is more between us. Sometimes, it is easier to just let people think that. But I have no romantic feelings for Wyatt, even though, if I open that door, I think Wyatt would come in. I have sensed on several occasions that what Wyatt feels for me goes beyond friendship. Chloe is sure of it, and even pushes me to pursue more with Wyatt. But my heart isn't in it and from my past history, I don't have the best track record when it involves friends becoming lovers. I don't want to ruin what Wyatt and I now share.

Wyatt agrees to meet us at Sharkey's and I can't wait until he arrives so that I can finally tell them my good news. Chloe and I grab a booth and wait for Brian and Wyatt to show up. The waitress comes by to get our drink order. We order a pitcher of beer and some appetizers to start off with. Brian is the first to arrive. He immediately sees us and gives Chloe his megawatt smile. She smiles right back and waves him over to join us. When he reaches the table, she jumps out of her side of the booth and gives him a big hug and kiss on the check. She sits back down sliding toward the inside of the booth and he slips in beside her.

"Hey, Brian. Thanks for joining us tonight. And again, sorry about last night," I say.

He looks at me with genuine concern. "Thanks for having me, Suzanna. Are you alright?"

I laugh, thinking he probably thinks I'm a crazy person, getting ready to burst out in tears. "Yeah, I'm fine. Just had a bad night. But, today is much better. In fact, once Wyatt arrives, I have some fantastic news." Brian looks relieved that my spirits have miraculously done a one-eighty. He looks at Chloe, thinking she might clue him in on what is going on.

"Don't look at me. I have no idea what she is talking about. If Wyatt doesn't get here soon, I'm gonna have to get her drunk just to get it out of her. I can't stand waiting!" We all laugh and continue to wait for Wyatt. Brian orders another pitcher of beer, since we have already finished the first. We are each finishing our second beer when Wyatt finally arrives. I see him first, as soon as he enters the door. Man, he is good looking. Why no woman has snatched him up by now, I will never understand. Wyatt has dark brown, wavy hair that he wears a little longer than the average preppy guy. Kind of like one of my favorite golfers, Bubba Watson. His hair style frames his handsome face which features strong cheek bones. His eyes are an unusual shade of hazel, with green flecks scattered over each iris. A flawless complexion is enhanced with the golden tan he sports year round. Tonight he is wearing a pair of low slung jeans paired with a fitted t-shirt that shows off his rugged, well defined physique. He looks simply amazing. Observant as always, Chloe notices that I have been staring towards the entrance and focuses her gaze in the same direction. Then she smirks at me, letting me know she caught me ogling our friend.

"Hey, is Wyatt here?" Before I can answer her, Wyatt approaches our table. Damn, I didn't realize I had been staring for that long!

Breaking out of my lust filled Wyatt trance, I say in greeting, "Hey Wyatt, glad you could join us. Come, have a seat," I say while patting the seat beside me as I slide to the other side of the booth.

"Hi girls! I've missed you!" he says, always the charmer. Chloe gushes, lavishing the attention.

"Well, we missed you too. You should come by more often and we can just avoid missing each other." We all laugh. "Wyatt, I'd like for you to meet Brian. Brian, this is our dear friend, who we miss terribly, Wyatt."

"Hi Brian, it's nice to meet you," Wyatt says and extends his hand to Brian.

Brian shakes Wyatt's outstretched hand. "Likewise, man. Here grab a beer." Now that Wyatt has arrived and introductions have been made, Chloe isn't about to wait another minute for my announcement.

"Alright, girl. It's time you spill it! I can't take another minute not knowing what this secret announcement is. It's killing me."

Wyatt chimes in, "Yeah, Suzanna, you don't want to kill your roommate, so what's up?"

Taking another sip from my beer, I look at their faces washed with anticipation. "Well, I got a letter yesterday," I start. Chloe immediately looks unnerved, thinking I am referring to the engagement invite. Even Brian, who walked in during my meltdown, looks a little unhinged. Seeing them so uncomfortable, I immediately correct their assumption. "No, not that letter! I did tell y'all this is good news right?" I joke. Wyatt is completely lost with no knowledge of any letters that I have received. Before Chloe can open her big mouth about the sad letter, I quickly tell them. "I got a letter from the LPGA. They invited me to play in the southeastern qualifying round this summer in Hilton Head."

Chloe starts clapping like a cheerleader on drugs, whooping and hollering. "Oh my God! Suz, that is great news! Congrats!"

Wyatt pulls me in for a hug. "Way to go, Suzanna. I always knew you were so talented. I'm so happy for you!" Seeing the look in his eyes, I know he is genuinely happy for me.

Brian voices his congratulations and calls the waitress over. "Miss, could we order a round of tequila shots, top shelf please. We might have the next lady Tiger Woods in our presence and we need to celebrate." Smiling and nodding to Brian, but definitely checking out Wyatt, the waitress walks back to fill our drink orders.

Chloe starts in on me with a hundred questions. "So when is it? Where? Can I come?" Blah, blah blah...

"It's the first week of August in Hilton Head, the ocean course, where they play one of the men's tournaments. And yes, you can come. You better be there to cheer me on!" I tell them of my plans to live at the beach after graduation to practice daily. Our shots arrive and Wyatt starts to make a toast.

"Here's to the best damn lady golfer in the state of South Carolina, and the entire U.S. of A! Congrats to you sweet Suzanna, you deserve this!"

"Here, here," Brian and Chloe chime in and then we all do our shots in unison.

After more beer and another round of shots, courtesy of Chloe this time, I start to feel the effects of the alcohol. Since we have been talking all night about my news, we completely forgot to order pizza. We only ate the few appetizers from hours ago. But we are all feeling good, me especially, and I really need this. I drag Wyatt out to the dance floor, once Chloe and Brian start making goo-goo eyes at each other. We dance to some fast paced music until we are sweating. It feels so good to just be happy and enjoy this without thinking about Patrick and his soon to be wife. The music suddenly changes to a slow ballade, and Wyatt pulls me in close to dance. His hands hold me around my waist while my hands slide up and latch around his neck. I lay my head on his shoulder and we move in sync to the music. I feel so safe in his arms. He has always been there for me and here he is again, sharing in this very special moment with me. Other than Chloe, he has always been with me through the good and the bad. I start to picture Patrick and realize he isn't here for me, and hasn't been in four long years. Not that I can blame him since I was the one who pushed him away. I guess I just take for granted the fact that Wyatt has been here all along. Maybe it is the alcohol, but I suddenly feel very tingly when his hand starts rubbing my back during our dance. I slowly lift my head from his shoulder and look in his stunning eyes. I see nothing there but contentment and joy radiating from him.

"Hey, Suz, I'm so proud of you. You're gonna do great in Hilton Head! You know, I'm secretly your number one fan." He whispers in my ear. His breath so close, sends chills throughout my body. Sliding my hands from around his neck to cup his face, I pull him close and whisper back.

"Thanks, Wyatt. Now, if we're finished talking about golf, I'd rather not talk at all." He looks at me with surprise. Even I am surprised that I have been that bold. Blame it on the alcohol, or the excitement of my news, or how shitty last night was. Blame it on whatever, but I can't go a minute longer without kissing this man. This man has stood by me every step of my journey and is now here with me to share my milestone. Before I can change my mind, I pull his face close and lightly brush my lips against his. At first I don't think he is going to respond, but then he leans into the kiss, and it deepens. I open my lips, and our tongues begin their exploration of each other. It is as if we have been starving for each other for so long and have finally given in to the forbidden fruit. I am so caught up in this magnificent kiss that I don't realize the music has changed. Obviously, neither does Wyatt until people start bumping into us from their gyrating moves. Pulling back to catch my breath, Wyatt looks at me with a burning desire in his eyes.

"You want to get out of here?" I ask shyly.

"Yeah. Let me go pay the bill while you tell Chloe we're leaving," he whispers in my ear, sending shock waves straight to my core. Not wanting to lose physical contact with him, I hold his hand until we have to separate, him going towards the bar to close out with our waitress and me headed back to the table to let Chloe know I am leaving. When I finally make it the booth, Chloe and Brian are still engaged in excessive smooching and giggling.

"Hey guys, I think Wyatt and I are gonna take off. Brian, are you okay to give Chloe a ride home?"

Without even looking my way, he replies, "Yep, be glad to take Miss Chloe home!" I can barely understand his words while he continues to kiss Chloe up and down her neck.

"Okay, great. Chloe I'll see you tomorrow." She only half responds with a strangled sigh, which is my cue to leave right then. They really need to get a room! I meet back up with Wyatt at the bar just as he finishes paying the bill.

"Ready?" he asks, almost hesitantly like I may have changed my mind. Trying to reassure him, I push up on my tip toes and give him another kiss.

"Yes, I'm ready." There is more meaning in that statement than just us leaving. It means I am ready to go, yes, but it also, means I am ready for more. I am ready to move on with Wyatt. I am ready to start a career as a professional golfer. I am ready to put the past behind me and stop feeling guilty, and I am ready to know once and for all if Patrick still loves me.

Chapter Seven

(Present Day)

The drive from the restaurant to Wyatt's apartment in the downtown area is short. Before I know it we are out of his car and walking up the stairs to his second story apartment. He quickly gets his keys out and unlocks the door while I wait nervously behind him. He ushers me in and closes the door behind him. Before my eyes can adjust to the dim lighting, he grabs me by my shoulders and swings me around to face him. Then he fiercely pushes his lips to mine, continuing what we started on the dance floor. My hands wrap around his neck, pulling his head forward trying to deepen the already passionate kiss. His hands are around by waist, rubbing up and down by sides. Trying to walk and kiss at the same time, we slowly make it down the hallway to his bedroom. Once inside, we come up for a breath just briefly before we start kissing again. I am totally lost in the euphoric feeling of being consumed by Wyatt. I let my hands slip under the hem of his t-shirt and start slowing lifting it up his body. Cooperating, he raises his arms and helps me take his shirt over his head and off his body. Placing my hands back on his shoulders, I rub the sculpted muscles of his arms and continue my hand movements down his hard chest and sculpted abs. Reaching the top of his pants, I start fumbling with his belt buckle. Finally getting the belt undone, I undo the top button of his button-fly jeans. With trembling fingers I manage to unbutton his jeans enough that they start to slide down his legs with the help of my hands. I soon realize that Wyatt is almost completely undressed and I am wearing entirely too many clothes. Wyatt must realize the same thing and begins to undress me. Slowly, he pulls my shirt over my head, dropping it on the floor with his pile of discarded clothing. Then, with much precision, he unbuttons my jeans and pulls the zipper down. Using his thumbs that are now hooked through my belt loops, he helps me shimmy out of my jeans in one fluid motion. Taking in my body, now only covered with my bra and panties he looks over me carefully, enjoying every inch.

"God, Suzanna. You. Are. Absolutely. Beautiful!" he says placing emphasis on each word. Seeing the longing in his eyes, I step in closer so that our bodies are touching. I can feel the anticipation between us. It is especially obvious between Wyatt's legs. He grabs me in a hurried embrace, pushing me towards his bed. When the back of my knees met the edge of the mattress, we both fall on top of the bed, Wyatt gently covering my body. Wyatt rises up on his elbows, each placed beside my face, and cups my face with his hands.

"Suz, I want this so badly. I've wanted this for a long time. But, I want you to be sure. I want you to want this, too." His lips are so close, and I can feel his breath cover my skin with each word he speaks. Pushing every rational thought out of my mind, and only concentrating on this exact moment, I am quite sure this is exactly what I want.

"I want this, Wyatt and I want it with *you*." The moment Wyatt comprehends my words, he unleashes years of lust that has been caged like a wild animal. Wyatt starts kissing me, crushing his lips to mine. He showers kisses up my jaw line, straight to an exotic place just behind my ear. Each kiss causes overall tingling, sending heat waves to all the nerve endings in my entire body. Thinking it can't get any better, Wyatt lowers his head and starts covering my neck with sweet kisses, gradually making it to my chest area. Not bothering to take off my bra, he impatiently pulls down its cup to expose my breast. Taking the already puckered nipple into his mouth, he starts sucking it with the occasional nipping of his teeth. I am beyond the pleasure point, not sure if I can last much longer. I start arching my back in hopes to alleviate the throbbing between my legs. Attentive to my need, Wyatt moves his hand to cup my sex through my underwear, rubbing ever so softly. I can feel my body respond, evident by the dampness in my panties. I am going to go crazy if I don't find my release very soon. Trying to speed up the process, I pull my hands from his hair that I have been gripping and reach down to slide my panties down my legs. Feeling just as urgent as me, Wyatt helps me relieve myself of the panties. We are both breathing heavily when Wyatt pauses for a quick moment to look me in my eyes.

"This is your last chance, Suz, to stop me. If I go any further I won't be able to stop myself." My body has my brain all discombobulated, I can't think of any good reason for either of us to stop. This is what I want, right? Do I even need to question my decision? Sure, this isn't Patrick. But Patrick has chosen someone else. Patrick hasn't been there for me in four years, whereas Wyatt has. He has been so good to me for so long, I know I can never repay him. I've always felt something for Wyatt other than just friendship, but not anything like I felt for Patrick. Pushing all thoughts of Patrick away, I concentrate on the here and now. Wyatt is here, right now and all I want is some mind blowing sex from someone who obviously cares deeply for me.

Looking into Wyatt's eyes and with sincerity in my voice, I say, "Wyatt, don't question this. I want this now. I want you now, and I'm not willing to stop it." Those are the last words that are spoken. Wyatt kisses me long and hard, pressing every inch of his body to mine. I feel his erection between my legs, and anticipation surges through me. My agony of finding my release continues as Wyatt pulls away briefly. Thinking he has changed his mind, I prop up on my elbows to see what is wrong. Wyatt reaches in his bedside table drawer and produces a foil packet. Realizing that he was searching for a condom, I immediately relax. I hear the foil rip open and watch as Wyatt places the condom on his hardness. Lowering himself back down to me, he gently rubs the head of his cock up and down my sensitive folds and begins teasing me when he circles around the entrance to my sex. Not wanting to wait another second, I arch up meeting him, allowing his entrance into my body.

"Oh my," I gasp feeling him enter me, slowly sliding in. Wyatt stills inside me.

"Are you okay, Suz?" he asks with concern written all over his beautiful face.

"Yeah, um, it's just been a while," I answer embarrassed and try to look away.

Wyatt cups my cheek and turns my head to look back into his desire-filled eyes. "Baby, I don't want to hurt you. We'll take it slow. Okay?"

It has been too long, way too long. Sure, I have had my share of hook ups during college, but never one for just casual sex I chose to remain celibate. The last time I gave it all to a man was in high school, and that was with Patrick. This is so different. Maybe it is because I am older now and so is Wyatt. But, this doesn't even compare. Although painful at first, it actually starts to feel really good. Once Wyatt waits for me to accommodate his size, as promised he slowly begins to move in and out. A building pressure ignites my core and I need more.

Thinking I can't wait any longer I break from Wyatt's lips and plead, "Wyatt, please, I need to come." Never one to deny me anything, he picks up the pace, slamming into me hard and fast. My body quivers around him, giving into the explosion within. Feeling limp and exhausted from my climax, I watch as Wyatt thrusts a few more times and finds his release. Collapsing on top of me, Wyatt and I ride out the waves of satisfaction brought on by our orgasms. Nuzzling my neck, Wyatt kisses me sweetly making his way to my mouth. The kiss is incredible, saying all he has wanted to say to me for years that words cannot communicate. When our lips finally part, he looks at me like he never has before. He has a look of a hero, who had conquered the impossible.

Smiling, he says, "I always knew it would be good, but I didn't know it could ever feel this great! I need to throw this away," referring to the now used condom, "and get cleaned up. You need anything? Want something to drink?"

Cupping his face and planting a quick kiss to his lips I ask, "Actually, do you mind if I take a quick shower? I just want to wash off the alcohol and smoke smell from the bar earlier tonight. Plus, we did manage to work up a sweat."

Laughing, Wyatt extends his hand to me and pulls me off the bed. "Come on. I'll take good care of you and get you nice and clean."

I follow Wyatt into the bathroom and watch him in all his naked glory. He starts the water and waits until the temperature is perfect before leading me into the shower. I am suddenly self conscious about my naked body on display, and try to cover up my private area by wrapping my arms around my body.

"Hey, Suz, don't be shy. You are beautiful and I could spend the remainder of this night just looking at your sexy body. But, I did promise you a cleaning so let's get started." Before my mind can register all the compliments he is throwing my way, Wyatt gently guides me under the spray of water. He then lathers up a wash cloth and begins to gingerly wash every inch of body. When he reaches between my legs to clean, he looks up at me with hooded eyes. "This is about to kill me, but I imagine you are a little sore. I'll be real easy on you." Slowly and softly he washes my privates, then, turns me around to wash the back of my body. This is better than a spa day. After an extensive lathering session, he again places me under the spray of water to rinse off. Pulling me into an embrace, he tenderly kisses me and leads me to exit the shower.

"Wait, don't you want me to return the favor? I can wash you now."

With a frustrated sigh, Wyatt shakes his head. "Suzanna, it's taking all the control I possess not to pin you up against the wall and have you again. Just go dry off and I'll meet you in the bed once I take a very, cold shower." He swats my ass and I giggle and jump out of the shower to wait for him in bed.

Feeling quite content, I pull the cover of the bed up and over my naked body and get comfortable. As I am waiting for Wyatt to return, my mind starts racing with questions I have no answers to. Why have I just slept with Wyatt? We have known each other for years and both of us have not been in serious relationships, since high school. Okay, so the sex was amazing, but why now? Did this have something to do with the engagement invitation I received the day before? Did my decision have something to do with Patrick? Surely, I wouldn't have revenge sex. Would I? Oh my gosh, what if I slept with Wyatt, subconsciously just to get back at Patrick? It's not like Patrick would ever know. Hell, he may not even care, considering he is engaged to be married. Shit! Had I just used a dear friend to make me feel better about myself?

I hear the bathroom light click off and Wyatt returns to the bed, climbing in beside me. I snuggle in close to Wyatt, letting the warmth of his body wash away all my unanswered and disturbing questions. He seems to feel my need for his closeness, and wraps me in his arms in a tight embrace. Kissing my forehead, he picks up on the tension that has made an unwelcome visit in my body.

"Hey, you okay?" he asks. Hearing the uncertainty in his voice, I have to reassure him that I have absolutely no regrets.

I pull back and look up in his eyes. "Yes, I'm great. Just a little tired, that's all."

"Well, let's get some sleep," he answers believing my small white lie. "Good night, Suz. I enjoyed tonight more than you know. More than you will ever realize." His words hit me hard, knowing that this probably means way more to him than it does to me. Guilt washes over me like the blanket on his bed. Although, I enjoyed being with Wyatt too, I mean really enjoyed it, I don't know what tomorrow will hold.

Before I wait too long to respond, giving him reason that I might doubt what happened between us, I speak quickly. "Me too, goodnight Wyatt." Silence falls and soon all I hear is the even breathing coming from Wyatt knowing he has found sleep. I don't think I will be that lucky. Questioning all I have done in the last twenty-four hours, from my breakdown over Patrick to my revenge fuck with Wyatt, I quickly despise the person I have become. And sleep doesn't like me either because, it never comes.

Chapter Eight

(Present Day)

Morning could not have come fast enough. The effects of the alcohol last night are pretty evident considering my head is about to split in two. Top the hangover off with a sleepless night and I am a wreck. School is supposed to start back today from the Easter break and the thought of having to be anywhere other than my own bed is making my headache even worse. Wyatt is still sound asleep, probably dreaming of last night when I finally surrendered my body to him. Just thinking of what I have done sends another sharp pain to my head. Ugh, how am I gonna survive the rest of this day? I make a move to try to get out of the bed without disturbing Wyatt, but my sudden movement causes him to stir. Slowly awakening, Wyatt pulls me back into the bed and begins to snuggle against my body.

"Good morning, beautiful," he whispers.

I laugh, "Obviously you're not quite awake because I assure you I am far from beautiful this morning. I'm afraid to even look in the mirror." Taking my comment to mean I may be in a joking mood, Wyatt starts trying to get frisky, planting soft kisses on my cheeks, trailing them down my neck. Memories of last night rush back to me, feeling that we may have made a mistake. I don't want to hurt Wyatt, although I already know I inadvertently hurt him by leading him to believe that we are more than friends.

Breaking away from him without seeming too cold, I say, "Wyatt, my head is splitting from the alcohol I consumed last night and I really just want to sleep away the day. You think we could go back to Sharkey's to get my car. If I can make it home soon, I might have time to make it to my class."

Wyatt doesn't seem to take the hint that I'm not in the mood for round two and continues kissing me while his hands roam all over my body. I relax a bit when my body warms to his touches. My mind and my body seemed to be in battle with each other. My mind is telling me to stop this, this isn't what I want. But my body screams at me to let go, loosen up and enjoy the pleasure this man is offering. "Um, Wyatt, I uh, really, oh..." Obviously, my mind is losing the battle since I'm not able to form a coherent sentence. My body is raging with sensations that can't be stopped. Wyatt has lowered his kisses from my face and neck and is making a beeline down my chest, lower and lower over my abdominals. Feeling every nerve ending explode with heat, I stop listening to my mind, actually shutting it completely down and give in to my victorious body. Wyatt has gone down even lower until his head is positioned between my legs. His breath is tickling that sensual spot while his hands massage my breasts. Who knew waking up with a hangover could be so enjoyable. Wyatt starts kissing my most private area using his tongue to gain access between my folds. I let out a slight moan when his finger enters me, one then another. His tongue continues at a more rapid pace, licking my swollen clit.

"Ohhhh, Wyatt," I groan, letting out any reservations I ever had about regretting our time together.

"That's it baby, just sit back and enjoy. This works so much better than aspirin." God, he is right. My hangover seems to be a thing of the past. Feeling close to an earth shattering explosion, my body starts to tremble slightly. Wyatt senses that I am close and increases his pace with his tongue and finger, taking me over the edge. My body goes limp against the mattress upon my release and I am basking in my post orgasmic bliss. Wyatt, knowing that I have been completely satisfied, raises his head from between my legs and starts the kissing process in the opposite direction back toward my face, stopping at my navel, breasts and neck before returning to my lips. I can taste myself when his tongue plunges into my mouth. Instead of being gross like

I always thought it would be, it actually fuels my raging hormones even more. Wyatt briefly pulls away, to grab another condom from the bedside drawer. Like a professional, he has the wrapper opened and the condom on in seconds. Before I can completely fully recover from my previous orgasm, Wyatt begins to enter me, slowly at first, but then building speed and finding his rhythm. Feeling another sensation building, I meet him thrust for thrust, enjoying the fast pace and roughness of it all. Wyatt and I are staring straight at each other, eyes locked in consuming passion. His intense stare tells me all I need to know. He is exactly where he wants to be, inside me, making me moan, beg, plead, and scream his name. And that's exactly what I do, when I begin to tighten around his cock, feeling the excruciating pleasure reach its boiling point before spilling over.

"Wyatt!" I scream, almost in the same moment he calls out my name in a breathy voice, reaching his climax. His body covers mine as we recover from our morning tango. Once our breathing has returned to normal, Wyatt leans up and rolls to my side gently brushing some hair from my face that is stuck there bedded in sweat from my between the sheet workout.

"Now, that's the way I like to start my day," Wyatt jokes with a chuckle in his voice. "I'm gonna go jump in the shower real quick and then I'll take you to your car. Okay?"

Leaning up to give him a quick peck on the lips, I say, "Sure, that's fine. I'll get dressed and wait for you to finish. You got any coffee here?"

"Afraid not, but I'll treat you to Starbucks on the way to get your car." Wyatt then leaves the bedroom entering the bathroom to grab a shower. When I hear the water start to run, I stretch and wince, feeling the slight pain of sore muscles that haven't been used in years. But, the aches are nothing compared to the pleasure that caused them. Smiling for the first time in what seems like days, I quickly get dressed and wait for Wyatt to reemerge. Looking back to last night and this morning, I realize I enjoyed myself completely for the first time in a long time. I let my heart make the decisions for me and not my head. Maybe this thing with Wyatt is just a fling. I mean really, I love Patrick, right? But I can at least enjoy it while it lasts. And I intend to do just that.

Chapter Nine

(Present Day)

The ride to get my car is quick, making only the one stop for coffee at the nearby Starbucks. Wyatt and I chat comfortably about matters that are unrelated to what happened between us last night. I am thankful that Wyatt doesn't feel the need for us to "talk about" last night. I am not quite sure yet where Wyatt fits into my life today. Sure, we are friends, and have been for years. But now we have definitely taken it a step further than friendship. My still throbbing head is keeping me from analyzing anything that deals with the new characteristics of our relationship. Pulling into the Sharkey's parking lot, Wyatt parks his car right next to mine. Leaving the car running, he turns to me.

"Well, here you are. You got your keys?" Wyatt is acting so casual. Almost like last night never happened. Maybe he didn't enjoy it and he thinks I am lame in bed. Oh God! Was I a terrible lay? I duck my head to look in my purse for my keys before he can see the humiliation all over my face. Finally finding them, amongst the junk that I house inside the oversized purse, I pull them out and reach for the door handle.

"Suz, can you wait a second?" I hear Wyatt ask. Turning back to face him, I can tell he wants to say more, but isn't sure how to put it in words. My worst fears are a reality. Wyatt is not interested in me, even after our amazing sex. Or what I thought was amazing; obviously he thought it not so.

Before he can continue, I quickly cut him off. "Hey, thanks for the ride." Oh my gosh! Did I really just thank Wyatt for the *ride*? He probably thinks I'm thanking him for the really great sex last night. Well, great sex for me, at least. I am so lame! My mind is in the gutter. "I mean, thanks for bringing me to my car. I really have to get going if I'm gonna make it to class in time. It was, um, fun. I'll call you later." I lean over and give him a friendly kiss on the cheek and dash out of the car before he can add anything to the conversation. I quickly unlock the car and am about to slide inside, when I hear Wyatt.

"Okay, I'll wait to hear from you later. Have a great day, Suz!" Well, it would have been a great day, if you hadn't just acted like the last twenty-four hours of your life meant nothing to you. That is what I want to say, but instead I just smile and start my car to leave, giving Wyatt a wave goodbye. Driving out of the parking lot, I head to the home that Chloe and I share. My mind is full of thoughts that are so conflicting, it is making my hangover headache even worse. I just slept with my dear friend and I am in love with an engaged man. This is like an episode of The Young and the Restless. Oh my, what had I gotten myself into?

Chloe's car is still in the driveway when I get home. So, either she stayed at Brian's last night or she has blown off class today. I am hoping the house will be empty this morning upon my arrival because I don't want to explain to Chloe all that happened since I left her at the bar. No such luck. Chloe is in the living room, curled up with a blanket, a diet coke and a pop tart. Hearing me enter the house, she doesn't look my way, just asks, "Suz, is that you?"

"Hey Chloe. Yeah, it's me. How are you this morning?"

Still not acknowledging my presence with any body motion, she says, "Ugh, tell me again why I drink tequila? I feel like someone ran me over with a semi-truck, pushing all my organs inside my head which will explode soon if I can't get any relief!"

Laughing, I reply, "Yeah, I know how you feel, just didn't need that gross picture you just painted. I think I'm gonna gag!" I move over to the other side of the couch and plop down next to Chloe. The sudden movement doesn't do much for her headache and she sends me a 'if looks could kill, you would be dead' look.

"Sorry," I say sympathizing with her just a little. I'm not feeling very chipper either. If I am going to make it to class in time, I need to shower right now. But the couch is so comfy and I just don't have the energy to get up. "Hey, are you going to class today?" I ask Chloe, thinking that she might give me some motivation.

She looks away from the television show she is pretending to watch. "Hell no, I'm not moving from this couch unless the house catches fire. Are you?"

Well, there went my motivation. "Nah, I guess I'll skip too, and we can hang and recover together. Plus, I'd be late anyway, seeing as my class starts in thirty minutes." Chloe smiles, enjoying the idea that I am feeling just as bad as she is and that we will just hang out for the rest of the day together. "So, where's Brian? Did he stay here with you last night?"

Chloe shakes her head no, which she immediately regrets from the look of pain it caused. "Ouch, that hurt. We had a cab drop me off here and he was dropped off at his place. We were both pretty hammered and just wanted to pass out. How about you? You stayed a Wyatt's, I presume."

And here it is, the question of me and Wyatt. Do I play it cool and just let Chloe think it was innocent or do I spill my guts? I try for cool. "Yeah, just slept over at his place, no big deal. He took me to get my car this morning." Sipping my now cold coffee, I can feel Chloe staring at me like I am under investigation. I only hope that her head hurts too much to question me further, because if she asks, I know I can't lie and I'm just not sure how she will react. Again, lady luck was is not in my favor as Chloe starts to interrogate me.

"Suzanna Claire Caulder, are you trying to hide something from me?" Play it cool, play it cool...that is my mantra and I'm sticking to it.

"Like what Chloe? What would I have to hide? Wyatt and I are friends. He drove, which thinking back probably wasn't such a good idea since he had been doing shots just like us, so we went to his house which was closer. No big deal, really!" Hoping the subject is closed I advert my attention to the mindless TV show. Chloe isn't buying it, though. She takes a good long look at me and then squeals, almost splitting my head in two.

"OMG, you slept with him, didn't you?" she asks. Never much of a poker player but hoping I might be able to win this hand, I reply.

"Define 'slept with'."

Chloe starts giggling, "Come on Suz. You know what I mean. Here's my definition...fucked. Did you fuck Wyatt?"

"You're grossing me out again. Why do you have to be so crude?" I could really use that subject change right about now.

Chloe stares at me long and hard before stating, "Suz, you might need professional help, beyond what I can offer you. If you slept with Wyatt last night, I hope that it was for the right reason, because you care about him more than a friend. But if you did it because of the near breakdown you had when you heard from Patrick, who is now engaged, then you might have really screwed up!"

Well there it is, in a nut shell. I never admitted anything to Chloe, yet she knows every thought that is bouncing back and forth in my head. Dropping my head in my hands and releasing a loud sigh, I confess. "Yes, I slept with, or fucked Wyatt last night and this morning. And yes, I enjoyed it! But I don't know why I did it. I don't know if Wyatt means anymore to me today than he did yesterday. I don't know if this has anything to do with Patrick, and if it does, then I'm really pathetic. I haven't a clue what I'm doing with my life at the moment."

Chloe finally moves from her reclined position on the couch to inch closer beside me. She throws her arm around my shoulder and squeezes me in tight for a sideways hug. Her support is exactly what I need when the stress of the last couple of days come crashing out in the form of tears and sobs. I cry, not really knowing why, but it feels good to release my frustrations. Chloe remains silent while I indulge in my grief. When I feel that I can control my emotions, I hold my head up and look at Chloe. "You think I'm a bad person, don't you? You think I used Wyatt to make myself feel better." I ask her, not really sure if I want to hear a truthful answer. But Chloe would never be anything but honest with me. Chloe remains silent, not wanting to rush her answer even though it is bound to hurt me.

Finally, she speaks. "Suzanna, I think you are caught living in the past, but wanting to move into the future. You love Patrick, no doubt. But is it the love that will last forever? Will it be there in years to come? You have held onto that love for so long, not living your life because you are waiting on him. Well, he isn't waiting on you, which is obvious because he is engaged. But I agree that you have to know for sure before you can go on with your life. However, I don't agree with using Wyatt, who has been there for you during this whole time, just to feel better about yourself. Sure, Wyatt loves you, as a friend, or more. I don't know what you two have as a relationship. But you have to decide if Wyatt is more, can you move on and leave Patrick in the past? Please Suzanna. Don't ruin anymore friendships because you may run out of friends."

I am stunned and speechless. Chloe has been brutally honest, pulling no punches. Another sob threatens to break through, but I push it down to ask Chloe one very important question. "Would I ever lose your friendship?"

Chloe immediately hugs me tighter. "Never! You can never push me away, Suz. I know you too well. I'll always be there for you. I just hate to see you hurt and hurting others in the process." Feeling a little relief, I hug her back tightly, as the tears start to flow again. I cry some more until I'm ready to talk again. I pull away from Chloe wiping at my eyes.

"Chloe, you're right. I don't want to live in the past. But I have to know for sure if Patrick is happy. If there's a chance he still wants me, then I need to know. Plus, I don't think Wyatt wants anymore than friendship where I'm concerned."

Chloe has a questioning look on her face. "What are you talking about? Didn't you say y'all did the nasty last night and again this morning?"

Hearing her terms for sex causes me to laugh. At least she isn't using such crude language again. "Yes, we did "do the nasty", twice. But this morning when he dropped me off at my car, he seemed very casual, like things were just as normal between us as they were last week. He didn't say anything about it and I didn't bring it up either. Maybe he just wants to forget what happened and let's just be friends like before."

Chloe thinks about what I just told her. "Well, maybe he was waiting for you to bring it up. You know guys don't like to talk serious relationship stuff."

She could have a point. But I'm in no shape or form to have that serious conversation this morning. Even this conversation with Chloe is tiring. "You might be right, but I wasn't ready to talk about it with him. I was scared he didn't like it with me last night."

Chloe chuckles, "You're funny, Suz! If he didn't like it last night, there wouldn't have been round two this morning."

Oh, I hadn't thought about it like that. A smile creeps on my face. So I hadn't been so lame. "Good point. Can we not talk about this right now? I'll try and figure out what to do about Wyatt later. I just want to veg out on this couch and cure my hangover," I say having enough psychoanalysis of Suzanna today.

"Sure, but just one more quick question. A yes or no answer will suffice," Chloe says. Oh no, what in the world does she want to know? "So, here it goes...is Wyatt good in bed? Is he a good lover?" Chloe giggles when she asks.

Rolling my eyes I respond. "That's actually two questions."

Chloe is now pleading with me. "Suzanna, just answer the questions, please. Curiosity is killing the cat."

Laughing at Chloe's dramatic plea, I answer, being very honest with myself for the first time in a long time. Not that I have much to compare it to, only ever being intimate with Patrick when we were in high school, I realize that last night was the best sex I have ever had. Well, except until this morning. With a sly smile I scream, "Yes and yes!!!"

We both burst out in giggles. Always getting in the last word, Chloe adds, "Glad the cobwebs have been cleared away. Welcome back to the land of the sexually satisfied, my friend." Hysterical laughter ensues until we are able to resume our positions as couch potatoes for the rest of the day.

Chapter Ten

(Present Day)

Feeling well rested after hours of dozing in and out of sleep, I wake from my final cat nap of the day starving. We slept through lunch and my stomach is growling in need of some greasy food to take away the remaining evidence of last night's alcohol. I also realize I have yet to take a shower. I am still dressed in my clothes from last night which smell of liquor and smoke from the bar. Making an executive decision that a shower is indeed my first priority, I jump off the couch and head towards my bedroom. Chloe is just beginning to stir from our day of relaxation.

"Hey, whatcha doing?" she asks groggily.

"I'm headed to take a shower. I stink from last night!" I giggle in response.

"Gross, Suz. Just because you got lucky last night and still smell of sex, you don't have to rub it in my face!" Chloe says with her nose pinched, trying her best to make a disgusting face while hiding a smile at the same time.

"I wasn't referring to any smell other than those caused by the bar last night, but now that you bring it up..."

Chloe immediately interrupts, "Too much information right now, I'm actually starving and I'm in need of a shower also. Let's get cleaned up and order out. And make it snappy!" Totally agreeing with her, I head into my bedroom, stripping off my clothes as I enter and walk straight into my bathroom to turn on the water. My bedroom is the master suite of the house. Chloe insisted that I get the biggest bedroom since my parents actually own the place. I didn't really argue with her on that point because I like having my own bathroom attached to the bedroom. Poor Chloe has to use the hallway bathroom that is also used by our guests whenever we entertain. Both Chloe and I are fairly clean people, but I tend to be more of slob than she is. I never worry that our guests will encounter a dirty bathroom because Chloe is much more of a neat freak.

Once the water has warmed to my liking, I step in the shower and let the hot water engulf my body. Enjoying the warmth, my mind starts drifting back to last night and Wyatt. The sex had been amazing, both times. I can't believe I went without my entire college career. That has to be some sort of world record. But the good feelings from last night are lost to the bad ones from days so long ago. I try to remain in the present, but my mind won't let me and I get lost in my memories.

Spring Break, Junior Year of High School

Patrick and I have been dating since August and openly dating, now that our friends were made privy to our relationship, since November. We spent our first Christmas together, exchanging sweet gifts between each other. We rang in the New Year together with a tender kiss as the clock struck midnight. February brought with it unexpected snow for the south, and we made our first snowman together and had our first snowball fight, kissing each time we hit each other with a snowball. Our friends were happy for us, but got sick of our mushy, gushy affection. Valentines was especially sweet when we each wrote the other per-sonalized letters, sharing our mutual affection. Our parents, who were skeptical at first of our dating, finally came around and Patrick became an instant member of our family, while I was like the daughter Patrick's mom never had. I spent more and more time at Patrick's home. His mom, Mrs. Miles, always invited me to stay for dinner. She insisted I call her Marie and quit with the formalities of calling her Mrs. Miles. Patrick's dad, although I didn't see him as often, also requested that I call him Jim. So it was not unexpected when Marie and Jim asked me to join them at their beach home during the spring break week. Since my parents wouldn't be coming to the beach until the latter part of the week to enjoy the long holiday weekend, this was my chance to spend the entire week with Patrick. I had begged my parents to let me take some girl-friends from school down for the week until they could get there. But they had said no, insisting that since we were only juniors in high school, we needed an adult chaperone. Marie had called my mom, explaining that they would love for me to join their family until my parents arrived on Thursday. Dad and Mom agreed since I would now be chaperoned the entire week. Patrick and I couldn't wait. We were going to spend the whole week together at a place we both loved and considered our homes away from home. Of course, we would be sharing separate bedrooms, which was probably best considering we were approaching nine months of dating. Patrick and I had gone through every base, all the way to third but had yet made it to home plate. We were both nervous about taking that next step. Patrick and I had talked about it and he was so sweet, never once pushing me into something I wasn't yet willing to do.

So spring break week arrived and I packed my suitcase and waited for Patrick to pick me up. We were driving down separately and meet-ing his parents there. When we arrived the sun was shining and the weather was warm enough to go for a walk on the beach, which we did immediately. Walking hand and hand with Patrick, listening to the ocean waves crashing on the shore and the smell of salt in the air, it was the most romantic thing I had ever experienced in my life. At that moment, I knew I loved Patrick and would always love him. He was my first love, and maybe the first of many things in my life. Later that week, we embarked on another first.

My parents gave me a key to the beach house asking if I would go open the house on Wednesday to turn the air on before they arrived on Thursday. Patrick and I decided that we would go open the house before we went out to dinner that night. Marie and Jim were entertain-ing some friends at their home and we wanted to make ourselves scarce for a while, trying to escape the adult chit chat. We left Patrick's beach house around six that evening and drove the less than a mile distance south before pulling into the driveway of my parent's beach home.

God, I love this house! It has been in our family for years. My grandparents owned it before I was born and I have been coming here my whole life. I have such fond memories of family vacations and summer parties. It really is like my second home. Patrick parks the car under the house and unloads the laundry baskets in the backseat that are full of bed linens. Mom just meant for me to drop the linens off at the house, not expecting me to make the beds, but I want the house to be perfect for their arrival. So as soon as we enter the dark house and turn on the lights, I begin walking from bedroom to bedroom making the beds. As I make the beds, Patrick opens the windows to let in the cool ocean breezes to rid the house of the stuffy, winterized smell since the house has not been used since last fall. I am on my last room, my bedroom, when Patrick joins me to help me finish putting the sheets on.

"Last one," I say, "and then we can go to dinner." Patrick is having a hard time getting the fitted sheet to cover the last corner of the mattress. Seeing his frustration, I offer my assistance. "Hey need some help over there?" I walk around to help him standing behind him, reaching my hands around him to grab the sheet. My chest is pushed against his strong back, while my arms are hugging him. Teasing him, I say, "Now this is how you get the sheet to fit over the corner." I pull the sheet hard to get an extra bit of fabric to make it fit over the corner. When I pull, Patrick is caught off guard and we almost fall backwards, but his quick reflexes shoot both of our bodies forward, falling on top of the mattress. I am lying on top of his back and he is face down on the bed, both of us laughing hysterically.

"Remind me never to let you teach me how to make a bed," he says between laughs. He flips me over so that our bodies are facing each other and the earlier laughter seizes. I meet his eyes staring at me with more longing than I have ever seen them hold. His hands wrap around me and begin to rub the small of my back very gently. My hands have moved from his shoulders to the sides of his face, touching his hair line.

"God, Suzanna, you are so beautiful." He whispers, his face so close to mine I can feel his breath on my lips. Heat rushes through my entire body at hearing him whisper my name. Any inhibitions I had up to this point, fly out of the windows with the ocean breezes. I crush my lips to his in a forceful kiss. He reciprocates with just as much force, bringing my body even closer to his. Pulling back to catch our breath, Patrick looks into my eyes and says the words I know I am ready to hear. "Suzanna, I love you and I want you, all of you."

I feel the exact same way. "I love you too, Patrick. I want you to make love to me," I whisper shyly, but feel bold and brave on the inside. Patrick smiles at my words and leans up to kiss me again, more softly this time. Never parting lips, he gently rolls my body beside him, and starts to pull up my shirt. Helping the process along, I shimmy until the shirt is up above my breasts. I lift my hands and Patrick pulls the shirt over my head and drops it to the floor beside the bed. Then I help him get out of his shirt. We are now skin to skin, except for my bra, and the feeling is exquisite. Patrick hugs me close and I feel his fingers slide around my back to my bra strap. With trembling fingers, he manages to unhook the bra and slowly slide it off of my body, leaving me very exposed. Feeling nervous for the first time, Patrick quickly kisses me, whispering over and over how beautiful I am. His words calm me and I relax in his arms. His lips leave mine and move to my neck. He makes a trail of kisses down my neck, to my collarbone and then he is at my chest. I hear him breathing heavily, as he gently squeezes my right breast in his hands, massaging it. Then he lightly kisses my nipple, sucking and pulling it into his warm mouth until it is hard and perky. I moan as he continues to pleasure my other breast, giving it the expert attention he had given the other. My body is on fire with new feelings I have never given into. My body involuntarily arches up into his with each lick he administers. Feeling like I will never get enough of him, I slide my hands from his back and squeeze them between our stomachs stopping at the top of the waistband of his jeans. My fingers nervously fumble with his button until it releases and I slowly unzip him. Reaching in the opened jeans, I feel him through his boxer shorts. He is very hard. At my touch, he groans which spurs me on. I reach into the boxer shorts and place him in my hand gently stoking him up and down.

"God, Suzanna, this feels so good!" he says returning his attention to my lips. His hands shift down my body, finding the waist band of my pants. He is extremely quick unbuttoning and unzipping me. His hands start to pull on my belt loops, making my pants slide down my hips, thighs, and eventually my shins. Using my feet, I push my pants completely off my body and kick them off the bed to join our shirts already on the floor. Patrick starts the entire process over, peeling my panties off. Hurriedly, I pull at his remaining clothes so that he will soon be naked beside me. When all clothing is gone, we lie side by side, skin to skin, very still and quiet.

"Suzanna, are you sure this is what you want? I don't think I will be able to stop if we continue. I just want to know that you are ready," Patrick says, breaking the silence. Just his concern for my well being at this moment makes my decision so easy.

Looking into his eyes, I kiss him softly and whisper, "I'm ready, Patrick. I've never been more ready for anything in my life. I love you." With that, Patrick flips me on my back and rolls on top of me. He reaches towards the floor and grabs his wallet from the pocket of his jeans. He plucks a foil packet containing a condom out and returns the wallet to the floor.

"How very presumptuous of you," I joke, trying to lighten the mood.

With his full dimpled grin he honestly states, "Suzanna, I've been carrying this thing around with me since we started dating. How we've gone this long without using it I will never understand. But I can't wait to restock my supply."

I laugh out loud, falling into a fit of giggles. Finally, Patrick has to kiss me to get me to shut up. When the kiss becomes heated, I know that the time is near. Breaking the kiss, I take hold of the foil packet and open it. Patrick places the condom on his erection and slowly starts to tease me with its tip. Sliding his cock up and down my folds, I immediately become wet and ready. Soon Patrick is circling my entrance, waiting for the green light. With one last kiss, I look into his beautiful blue eyes and nod. He enters me slowly, with caution. I gasp at the initial pain. Patrick's wide eyes are filled with concern. I suddenly kiss him to reassure him that I am indeed okay. The pain is soon replaced with pleasure as Patrick finds a slow, very satisfying rhythm. His concerned look from moments earlier is transformed into a look of hunger, at which point he quickens his pace. Passion fills the small bedroom. We are both lost in each other. Our eyes lock as we each find the experience heightened to an unimaginable feeling. I feel my body start to tremble with each thrust until a heightened amount of pleasure is unleashed between my legs, causing an immediate feeling of exhaustion. Almost simultaneously, Patrick's face scrunches together in a look of pleasure crossed with pain, as his thrusts come to an abrupt halt. I feel his cock quiver inside of me, as his body begins to relax and he collapses on top of me. We lie there like that for a long time, relishing in the pleasure we have found with each other. Moments later, Patrick raises his head up and places a tender kiss on my lips. Pulling away, we look at each other, the love evident between us.

"I love you, Suzanna. I love that we were each other's first."

Tears sting my eyes at his declaration. "I love you too, Patrick. I will never forget tonight as long as I live."

I did not lose my virginity that night, I gave it away. I gave it freely to Patrick and I will never regret that decision.

Chapter Eleven

(Present)

Memories of my first sexual experience with Patrick flood my mind as the water in the shower begins to run cold. How could the first time be so incredible? Tears I hadn't known were there fall down my cheeks. God, I miss him so much. I had pushed him away, for fear of hurting him, when all I was really doing was hurting myself. Patrick has moved on and is now engaged. I wonder if his fiancé has experienced his tender love making. Well, obviously she has. I mean I am probably the only college senior who didn't spread her legs the entirety of her college years. Well, not exactly the entire time. I did make it to the last month of my senior year before enjoying sex again. Wyatt suddenly enters my mind. What to do about Wyatt? I don't have time to dwell on him because Chloe is pounding at my door.

"Suz, hurry up! I'm starving!" Pulling me back to the present, I quickly dry off, get dressed and leave Patrick and Wyatt to think about another day. Now is the time for food!

A couple of hours later, Chloe and I have resumed our positions on the couch, both feeling very full. We had devoured chili cheeseburgers and fries that we picked up through the Rush's drive-thru. Rush's is a local hamburger franchise that serves the best burgers in the state. The greasy burger did the trick, and I am finally feeling back to normal now that all the symptoms of my hangover are gone. Curling up for a night of mindless television, I am startled to hear a knock at the door. "Are you expecting someone?" I ask Chloe. Chloe looks back at me shaking her head, too comfortable to actually form words. Knowing I am the one who has to remove myself to open the door, I slowly swing my feet from the couch, standing with a lazy strength. Making my way to the door, I wonder who in the world would be coming by at 6:00 p.m. on a Tuesday evening. Opening the door, I see Wyatt standing on the porch. He is dressed in black slacks that are tailored perfectly to hug his thighs and emphasize his narrow waist. He wears a white button down shirt, embroidered with the logo of the restaurant where he tends bar. The logo is positioned over his left chest muscle, clinging to the defined pectoral. His hair is still damp from what I assume was a recent shower. I can smell his manly body wash blowing in from the light breeze outside. He casts a shy smile across his handsome face, making him seem nervous about being on our front porch. I am so enthralled with the vision of the man before me I almost jump hearing him speak.

"Hi Suzanna, care to invite me in?"

Flustered, I stutter, "Oh, um, yeah sure. Come on in Wyatt." I pull the door open, stepping back so that he can enter. As he walks in, I get another whiff of his manly scent. What a divine smell! Shutting the door, I turn around to see Wyatt walking towards the living area. I get a good look at his backside, and am not at all disappointed. His back muscles ripple with each step he takes. I glance a little further down, noticing his tight ass move and flex as he continues his motion towards the couch. This man is ripped in all the right places. Why have I never noticed before now? Bringing me from my trance, I hear Wyatt's sexy voice again addressing Chloe.

"Hi Chloe, how are you this evening?" I guess Chloe decides he is worth the effort for words when I hear her respond.

"Well, well...I must say I am doing just fine, Wyatt. The big question is how are you?" Chloe teases.

Wyatt glances back my way before responding. "Well, I had a pretty spectacular night and morning, so I guess I am doing great as of now," Wyatt says, with a wink in my direction.

Chloe laughs, "I bet you are!" Making my way to the couch I feel a flush of heat rising up my neck. I know what Wyatt and Chloe are both referring to; our previous night and morning between the sheets.

Speaking for the first time since Wyatt arrived, I blurt out, "What are you doing here?" It comes out more harshly than I had intended because both Chloe and Wyatt turn and look at me. Trying to back pedal, I insert, "I mean, don't you have to work tonight?"

Wyatt relaxes a bit, but still seems on edge. "Yeah, I am heading over there now to work my shift, but thought I would come over for a quick visit."

Chloe obviously feels the need to take my embarrassment even farther. "Is that the only quick thing you came over for?"

My embarrassment is turning to full blown anger. "Chloe!"

She laughs again as she starts to make her way up off the couch to become scarce. "I'm just kidding, Suz. Good grief, can you just lighten up?" I know I am making a complete fool of myself, but don't know how to stop the train wreck that is happening in my living area. Giving up, I plop back down on the couch that Chloe has now vacated with a huge sigh. Wyatt is still standing behind the couch, smiling at Chloe's antics. Chloe takes the opportunity to leave. "I've got some studying to do in my room. Good to see you Wyatt." And with that she is gone, leaving Wyatt and me alone. Recovering and finding my manners, I motion for Wyatt to take a seat. He rounds the couch and sits down next to me, keeping a comfortable distance between us.

Breaking the ice he asks, "So, how'd you feel this morning? Bad hangover?"

Relieved to get back to a more comfortable subject I answer. "Yeah, I was feeling pretty lousy most of the day. But now I'm feeling better, back to normal. How about you?"

Wyatt smiles, "I felt great! I can handle my liquor, Suzanna."

I smile back at him, probably the first smile he has received from me since his arrival. "Well, that's just not fair, you cocky bastard!" I fake pout. "I'll have to remember that the next time we go out and you slam shots down my throat."

Wyatt is quiet for a brief second before he asks, "So, will there be a next time?" I'm not sure what he means. Does he mean a next time when we all get together for drinks, or does he mean a next time for a roll in the hay? Feeling the flush of heat rising again, I turn and break eye contact to gather my thoughts. I just can't think straight while look-ing into his big, hazel eyes.

Playing the friend card I casually say, "Of course there will be a next time. Chloe and I love hanging out with you. You are our dear friend. Plus, your connections at the Blue Marlin bar don't hurt either." I laugh hoping he will laugh with me enjoying the light spin I have put on this sticky situation. No such luck. He actually seems slightly offended.

"So, Suzanna, are you referring to me tonight as your friend? Maybe I should go into Chloe's bedroom and fuck her. She's my friend too, right?" I can feel the hurt in his voice, even though I am taken aback with his crass language. I don't mean to hurt him, I just haven't had time to think this whole thing through.

"I'm sorry, Wyatt. I don't mean it like that. I wasn't quite sure what you were referring to when you said something about 'a next time'". Okay, so I had a pretty good idea, but let him believe I am clueless. I know exactly what he is referring to now since his sudden temper tantrum.

Piercing me again with those deadly eyes, Wyatt's voice softens a bit. "Let's be honest Suzanna, after last night and this morning, I'm not sure we can refer to each other as just friends anymore. At least I can't." I remain silent not really knowing what to say. Wyatt continues on. "Look, I know what happened last night was unexpected. Hell, I was as surprised as you that we had sex. But this morning," pausing to catch a breath, "this morning was not just sex. It was more. I felt it. Didn't you?"

His question needs an answer, but I still just sit in silence, not find-ing the words. Moments go by before he speaks again. "Suzanna, I have to tell you something. I don't do casual. I'm not looking for a convenient hook up every now and then. If I was, I could have any woman that I serve a drink to at the bar."

I interrupt. "Wow, think a lot of yourself, don't you?"

He smirks, but continues with his honesty. "Well, it's true. But the point I'm trying to make here is I chose you. Finally, you. We've been walking towards this for years, and I think we could have a shot at some-thing more. Obviously, you feel something too, or else last night and this morning wouldn't have happened. You aren't any more casual than

I am." He is right. I don't mess around, or for that matter really even date. I haven't had a relationship since, well Patrick. God, why does he suddenly appear in my thoughts? Here I sit on my couch listening to a delicious looking man tell me he wants more with me and there Patrick is popping up uninvited. Shaking my head to rid it of the blonde boy who has just surfaced, I focus back to Wyatt who is waiting patiently. Choosing my words carefully, I finally join in this conversation.

"Wyatt, I'm not sure what you want from me. I'm really not sure what I want for myself. I don't regret last night or this morning. It was wonderful. And you're right. I would have never done that with just anyone. Hell, I haven't done that in years. But I'm not sure I'm ready for anything more at the moment. I have graduation and the move to the beach. Plus, I will be consumed with golf this summer, practicing for the qualifying round. I'm not sure I have much to offer in a way of a relationship and I don't think that would be fair to you."

Wyatt hangs his head, thinking of the things I have just said. Then he looks back to me and asks the question I'm not ready to hear. "Can we try?" I am stunned into silence. Wyatt scoots closer, his leg brushes against me, and a strangled gasp tries to escape. Then he grabs my hand, intertwining his fingers with mine and this time the gasp does escape followed by rapid breathing. Wyatt can tell how he affects me so he continues to touch me, this time placing his arm around the back of the couch, tracing slow circles on my shoulder with his finger. Pulling on the hand he has laced with mine, it causes my upper body to turn facing him. We are face to face, and I can feel his breath cover my face every time he exhales. Then there are those eyes again, filled with a look of lust. This man wants me and he has practically just confessed it to me. And now he is waiting for my decision, although, he isn't playing fair with his sensual touches. But those touches are doing something to me and I want more of them. Plus, I know Wyatt and I can't go back to just friends. So being selfish, just to keep him a part of my life, I agree to try.

"Alright, let's try this." Wyatt looks shocked that I have conceded.

I laugh at his expression. "What? Did you think I'd turn you away? Is that why you felt the need to torture me with your touches?"

Wyatt smiles. "So, you like my touches, huh?" My face reddens as soon as I confess to liking his hands on my body, actually everywhere on my body. But before I can take it back, Wyatt leans in and plants a sweet wet kiss on my lips. Now, this touch I really enjoy. So much so, I willingly open my mouth and let our tongues unite. Wyatt embraces me in his arms, pulling me closer as our kiss deepens. I know this could be a disaster. I mean, wasn't it just yesterday I had decided to attend Patrick's engagement party to see if he had any feelings left for me? What if he does? Then where would that leave me and Wyatt? I know I should not agree to "try" this thing between me and Wyatt. I shouldn't have been in his bed either. But there is something that has opened up in me. Something is telling me that I deserve to feel this good. I deserve to feel wanted. And oh, if this kiss is any indication, Wyatt definitely wants me. All too soon, Wyatt pulls away, leaving me breathless. If he doesn't leave soon, I'll cave under his sensuous eyes and take him right here on this couch. What has gotten into me? Bringing me back to reality, Wyatt gently caresses my cheek, quickly kissing my lips again.

"You're right, Suzanna. I don't play fair. But I know what I want and I intend to win, no matter what rules I break. Unfortunately, I would continue to torture you but I've got to get to work." I suddenly feel a stab of disappointment in the fact that he is leaving. But I need the space to figure out what has just happened and what I have agreed to. Standing with Wyatt, I walk him to the door. Looking smug and more confident than when he arrived, Wyatt turns to face me before leaving. "Suzanna, I'm glad you agreed to try. I have big plans for us."

I love the fact that he is so honest with his feelings about me, and us. "Well, you better have big plans. When I agreed to this, I was envisioning flowers, candy, awesome dates, and the works. Think you can deliver?" I ask, playing the tease.

"Oh, I plan to deliver all of that and more," Wyatt assures me by pressing a kiss on my lips. A kiss that indicates all the *more* he has planned for us. "I'll call you later, Suzanna," he says as he makes his way to his car. Watching him leave, I feel excitement over all the things he has promised to deliver. I also feel guilty knowing he might be losing a battle he doesn't even know has started.

Chapter Twelve

(Present Day)

The rest of the week seems to fly by. I settle back into my routine of attending classes each morning and playing golf in the afternoons. When I tell my teammates and coach about receiving the letter of invitation for playing in the LPGA regional qualifying round, they can't be any happier for me. We all promise to get together before graduation to celebrate my good fortune. Coach Brown even contacts a few of his colleagues at the beach to set up some practice rounds to help me prepare. He offers his assistance as well, telling me he will make weekly trips to the beach to check on my game and make sure I am practicing enough. I offer my teammates an open invitation to stay with me at the beach and play some rounds to keep me focused. I know I have to concentrate on golf all summer to play my best in the qualifying round in early August. Golf is a mind game. When playing, you need to think only about that little white ball, making sure it makes it into the hole with the flag, in as few strokes as possible. Normally, my mind is the best part of my game. Up until now, I only thought of golf. But lately, other things have taken temporary residence in my head. Two other things, or people rather, to be precise. Patrick and Wyatt.

After Wyatt and I decided to 'try', our relationship has been flourishing. He made good on his promises, giving me the full dating experience. This week alone, we have gone out to lunch together, saw a movie one night, and even went on a walk together enjoying the warm spring weather. Our time together has been easy. We talk about everything involving school, work, and golf. Wyatt and I had a nice friendship before, so talking with him has never been a problem. Surprisingly, the physical part of our relationship is just as easy between us. We hold hands, snuggle with each other on the couch and end each date with a kiss. I thought things may be awkward, but they aren't. We just seem to click. Maybe it is because we have so much history together and have known each other for so long. Or, maybe it is because I am finally seeing Wyatt as someone other than a friend. Whatever the reason, it is nice and scary all at the same time.

I have always been a creature of habit and very structured. Throwing a romantic relationship in the mix was not in my overall plan, especially since I am so close to achieving my career goal of being a professional golfer. I know what is ahead of me and I'm not sure how Wyatt is going fit into the life I have conjured up for myself. This is why every time Wyatt tries to talk about 'us', as in defining the relationship, I avoid giving him any concrete answer and will quickly change the subject. Wyatt never pushes and seems content to let me be in control. I guess he realizes that he will have to wait for me to take us to the next level. I haven't even told Chloe that Wyatt and I have agreed to try for something more. I think if I verbalize it to Chloe, it will be true and I am not ready to accept that much truth yet. So from the outside view, Wyatt and I continue to spend time together as friends. But from the inside, both he and I know it is something more.

Two weeks before graduation, my golf buddies decide it is time for that celebration. They want a night out before the craziness of exam week. Coach Brown made dinner reservations for the team and we all plan to meet up this evening. I have been so busy I didn't even inquire about where we are dining, figuring I will just get the information last minute and show up. I am placing my clubs in the back of my car after playing eighteen holes, when I hear Bridgett approach. Bridgett and I have been teammates for the past three years and developed a nice friendship. Bridgett is from Florida and will be heading home after graduation to start an internship at one of the junior golf academies there.

"Hey Bridgett, you played great out there today," I say when she walks by heading to her car. Our season ended a month prior, but some of us still meet to play in the afternoons. I am thankful for all the practice I can get, considering my hope of making this my career. "Thanks again for playing with me."

"No problem, I love playing, especially when the weather is so nice. Florida weather is going to be some kind of hot when I return," Bridgett responds.

"Well, it'll get just as hot here too, and humid!" I groan knowing the South Carolina heat accompanied with its humidity is almost unbearable at times. But I love the hot weather. I will take a one-hundred degree day over a snowy, winter day any chance I get.

"Yeah, but you'll have the nice ocean breezes to alleviate your pain," Bridgett reminds me. Just thinking about the cool ocean breezes puts a smile on my face. I can't wait to get to the beach this summer.

"Guess I shouldn't complain, huh?" I laugh letting her win this round of who will be more miserable. "By the way, where and what time are we meeting tonight for our team get together? I completely forgot to ask coach," I ask before Bridgett makes it to her car parked a few spaces down.

"The Blue Marlin, at 7:30. Meeting at the bar first, then dinner at eight."

I must have gone white, because Bridgett suddenly looks at me funny and asks, "You okay, Suzanna?"

Shaking off the nerves, I answer. "Yeah, guess the Columbia heat just got to me for a minute." Not thinking anything of it, Bridgett starts loading her gear in the trunk of her car continuing our chat.

"Well, I really need to get a move on. I want to look extra hot tonight!" I laugh at Bridgett, because she could wear a burlap sack and look hot. She is by far the prettiest girl on our team. Her skin is golden from the sun. With her long, lean legs, she is tall and tone, putting any model's body to shame. Her hair is long and wavy, an auburn color, which only accentuates her emerald green eyes.

"Really, Bridgett, you don't have to get all dressed up for me!" I tease her.

She quickly responds, "Oh, it's not for you. There's this guy I'm trying to impress."

"Coach Brown is married, silly!" I say joking with her some more. Bridgett is always going on and on about guys. She has many dates and I think frequent one night stands. She is kind of the love 'em and leave 'em type. Not that I think the guys mind. Bridgett just isn't quite the type to settle down.

"Eww, Coach Brown!" she squeals. I am almost doubled over in laughter now, just picturing Bridgett trying to seduce our elderly coach.

"Well, since it's a girls' golf team and Coach Brown is the only male, I guess I just assumed he is the one you've got your eye on." Bridgett is now also laughing at my obnoxious assumption.

"Suzanna, you are crazy. Actually, there's this guy I want to impress, and it's not Coach Brown!" she explains.

"I didn't know we were going out after dinner," I say still not understanding what guy is going to be Bridgett's latest conquest with a group full of girls.

"We're not. Mr. Oh-so-handsome will be at the restaurant. He works there." Suddenly, I stop laughing. There are plenty of people who work at The Blue Marlin, but the most handsome is definitely Wyatt. Could she be talking about my man? My man? He isn't really mine, although he could be. I just haven't been ready to announce to myself or anyone else that we are together. Are we really together, though? Maybe Wyatt wants more, but because of my indecisiveness he may entertain thoughts of being with someone else. Maybe he would like to be conquered by Bridgett. The thought of Wyatt and Bridgett together is making me physically sick. I become a little light headed and have to brace myself by leaning against my car. Bridgett notices and again asks, "You sure you're okay, Suzanna? You are starting to look pale again."

Waving her off, I stand back up without the assistance of my car, letting her know I am fine. I have to know exactly which Blue Marlin employee she is talking about. Trying my best to sound nonchalant, I ask, "So, tell me about this mystery man you want to sink your teeth into." Please don't be Wyatt, please don't be Wyatt, is all that is running through my head. I agonizingly wait while Bridgett finishes filling her trunk with the rest of her golfing equipment before she answers.

"Well, he's a bartender there. Just wait 'til you see him. He is so hot! His name is Wyatt and we've been flirting the last couple of times I've been there. I'm hoping tonight we'll do more than flirt, if you know what I mean." Silence, I am stunned into complete silence. A full minute must have gone by as I just stand there looking at Bridgett with her model beauty, thinking of her and Wyatt flirting. Jealousy is raging through my entire body, causing my fist to clench by sides. Bridgett just stands there looking at me, like maybe there is something wrong. "Suzanna, let me go get you some water, you're starting to scare me." She doesn't know that there isn't anything physically wrong with me. There is something emotionally wrong and all because of her latest revelation. How the hell am I going to get through this team dinner knowing my teammate and friend has the hots for Wyatt? Who is also my friend? Right? If he is just my friend why can't I be happy that a beautiful girl is interested in him? Realization suddenly dawns on me and I know then that I don't want Wyatt to be my friend. I want Wyatt to be more. I want him to be mine. But how fair is that knowing that I have plans this summer to seduce my ex-boyfriend who is now engaged to be married? Who am I and when did I become the lead character of a bad soap opera? I don't even realize Bridgett has left and returned until I feel her shove a cold bottle of water in my hand, suddenly stopping the thoughts consuming my brain.

"Here, drink this. I think you may be dehydrated. You're acting awfully strange," she says standing next to me, fearing I may faint from the heat. Thank God it is, indeed, hotter today than it has been because I need to blame my reactions on something other than the truth.

The weather seems to work because Bridgett buys into my next statement. "Yeah, guess I'm not quite used to the heat yet. Thanks for the water." I smile after taking a good long sip.

"You think you're okay to drive? I'll be glad to give you a ride home. But we need to get going, like now. I've got someone to impress!"

Walking to the driver's side door of my car, trying to hide my face so that Bridgett can't see the anger caused by her last words, I quickly shout over my shoulder. "No, I think I'll be fine. I'll just see you later at the restaurant." I jump in my car and immediately shut the door.

Fumbling with my keys, I finally get the car started and speed out of the parking lot, leaving Bridgett standing there. I know I am being rude, but I can't escape fast enough. Tears are starting to burn my eyes and I have to push them back before the road becomes a blur and I wreck. Where these feelings have come from, I don't know. I have only felt these once before, actually four years ago to be exact. But those feelings were because I loved and lost Patrick. Certainly, I don't love Wyatt. Not this soon. We only began our little relationship two weeks prior. I honestly don't think it is possible to love someone in two weeks. Really, what the fuck is wrong with me? Before I know it I have pulled into my driveway. I fly out of the car, run into the house and slam the door. Chloe watches in horror, as I make my way into the kitchen and pull out a bottle of tequila, slamming a shot down my throat before even acknowledging her. I take another shot, letting the alcohol warm my body and hoping it will take away all these feelings I am having that I can't explain. Chloe just watches as I proceed to fill the glass with the third shot before she lunges at me and takes the bottle and the shot glass away.

"Suzanna, what are you doing? Are you trying to get drunk? I'm all for a good party but, it's only 5:30! What the hell happened?" I don't know if it is the alcohol or Chloe yelling at me, but for some reason I give up the anger and sink onto the kitchen chair filled with despair. With a heavy sigh, I lay my head on the kitchen table and weep. Chloe doesn't push for immediate answers. She just sits beside me and lets me cry. I have cried more in the last two weeks than in the last two years. When did I become such a cry baby? Once my tears subside, I slowly peel my head from the table and look at Chloe. "You ready to talk about this?" She asks in such a calm reassuring voice that I am so grateful she is my friend.

"I don't even know where to begin," I answer.

"Maybe you should start with what you did to the Suzanna I used to know, and who is this new girl sitting before me suddenly showing all kinds of emotions. You have gone from one end of the emotional spectrum to the other faster than Jimmy Johnson at Daytona." I laugh at Chloe's auto racing analogy, especially since she used Jimmy Johnson, NASCAR's bad boy and her secret crush. Yep, that's when you know you're in the south when you crush on auto racers. At least she has lightened the mood somewhat. "Okay, Suzanna, spill it. What's gotten into you these last couple of weeks?"

I know I am starting to freak Chloe out with my all over the map emotions, knowing I owe her an explanation. I just hope that I can give her one that doesn't make me sound flat out crazy. "Well, I'm not really sure what's going on with me, Chloe. Up until two weeks ago, I was fine. Just living my life like any normal college senior getting ready to graduate. But then, I got that invitation from Patrick announcing his engagement and I fell apart."

Chloe interrupts, "Yeah, I already know that part. Remember, I was there to pick you up off the floor."

Nodding, letting her know I did remember, I go on. "Yeah, but that's just the beginning. Then, I went and slept with Wyatt."

Chloe just can't seem to keep her mouth shut. "Yeah, know that too. So, what does that have to do with you taking tequila shots early in the afternoon?"

"Well, if you'd be quiet, I'll try to explain," I say with frustration.

Chloe makes a hand gesture pretending she is zipping her lips and throwing away the key. Then she signals with the other hand for me to continue.

"So, what you don't know is that Wyatt and I talked about our indiscretion and he confessed that he has feelings for me that he wants to explore."

Chloe breaks her promise of silence with a big surprised "Oh!" But that's as far as she gets before I look at her with narrowed eyes, silencing her so that I can continue to get this off my chest.

"I told Wyatt that I would 'try' the whole dating thing, but that we would have to keep it on the down low. I guess I wasn't ready to admit that I could want more with him, or any other man. I haven't had these types of feelings since Patrick and it's really scary. Plus, as we discussed and you urged me, I decided to attend that stupid engagement party to see Patrick and find out for myself if I am ready to let him go. And also see if I can still affect him. I realize that it's not very fair to Wyatt to start something with him when I am secretly pining after my ex, who just so happens to be engaged. Gosh, doesn't this sound like a bad chick flick?"

Chloe waits to respond, seeking my permission to talk again. I smile, letting her know that, yes, it is her turn to add to this dysfunctional conversation. "I don't get it Suzanna. Then why are you so upset? You are the one making the decision to keep Wyatt at arm's length because of Patrick. So has something changed your mind?"

Ugh, more like someone. "Yes, Bridgett!" I yell. Chloe looks puzzled as her brows pinch together. "See, no one knows the extent of my and Wyatt's relationship, if that's what you can even call it. I mean, even you didn't know that we have been spending more time together, alone. He has even taken me on sweet, little lunch dates and for ice cream and all that other mushy, gushy stuff people do when dating. We haven't been physical since that first night, other than holding hands, and the occasional kiss, but it feels very intimate. I'm so confused about my feelings for him, but I don't want to hurt him."

Chloe asks, "So what does this have to do with Bridgett?"

I am starting to get a headache trying to analyze and explain my feelings all at the same time. "Bridgett informed me today of her hopes to seduce Wyatt tonight during our end of the season golf dinner at The Blue Marlin. Evidently, they have been flirting the last couple of times she has been to the restaurant." Chloe bursts out laughing. "What, you think that's funny?" I ask stunned that she can be so cruel as I sit here pouring my heart out to her.

Finally catching her breath to speak she says, "No, I think it's funny because you're jealous!" Her laughing fit starts again and it is really pissing me off.

"I don't think this is very funny," I bark out, which only makes Chloe laugh harder. I try to snatch the bottle of tequila back because I need more alcohol now that my dearest friend thinks I am a freaking joke. But Chloe holds the bottle back behind her so that it is out of my reach.

"Sorry Suzanna, I'm not laughing at you. Well, maybe I am. But it's so damn funny!"

My anger is returning fast. "What's so damn funny?" I shout.

"You Suzanna!" Chloe says as a matter of fact. "You're quite funny when you're in love." Love, did she just say love? Now who's the crazy person at the table? Chloe continues her nonsense. "It's so obvious you are in love with Wyatt McCain. Why else would you be so pissed that Bridgett has a thing for him?"

I let Chloe's words sink in. I'm not quite sure it is love, but I know it comes somewhere close enough. "What do I do, Chloe? Everything is moving too fast. Why did it take my entire college career to find someone I care enough about to have a romantic relationship with? In two weeks, I will graduate and then I'll be gone. What then? I can't imagine Wyatt wanting anything long distance. Plus, what about Patrick? Where does he fit into all of this?" I am blabbering on like a toddler who has just learned to talk. All the questions start tumbling out and I can't seem to stop them.

"Whoa!" Chloe stops me before I can spit out another question. "Suzanna, you are always overanalyzing everything. Just live in the moment and let the chips fall where they may."

I wish it was that simple. "I did that once, a long time ago, Chloe. And you saw what happened then. I barely made it out alive, and my heart is still broken and hasn't fully healed. I don't think I'm ready to just throw caution to the wind and risk being hurt again."

"But you're willing to hurt all over again by going to see Patrick and his fiancé at the party? Really, Suz, there is a big chance that Patrick is extremely happy now and will go through with his wedding. It has been over four years! You're holding onto something that was gone a long time ago."

Chloe's words hit me hard. "Well, you were the one that encouraged me to go to that stupid party," I remind her with frustration.

"Yes, I did because you need closure. You never got it the way things ended with Patrick and this might be just what you need to get on with your life. Maybe that chapter will close, and another one will open. Actually, it might be opening right now with Wyatt if you would just unseal that hard head of yours and see what could be. This could be really good Suz, and I'd hate for you to miss out on a wonderful man." I know in my heart that Chloe is right, but my head keeps telling me that

I will get hurt. Chloe seems to read my mind. "Listen to your heart this time, not your head. Take a risk. Who knows, you could be happy."

I think about what she said for a few moments. I don't want to admit that I have wasted the last four years of my life loving someone who doesn't love me back. But that is exactly what I have done, shutting myself off from any possibility of love. I never let anyone get close enough, until Wyatt. That had been a moment of weakness for me. I had been reeling from the news of Patrick's engagement and his invitation to his party. I let my despair over Patrick weaken my defensive walls and somehow, Wyatt sneaked through the cracks. That night with Wyatt, I let my heart take over and pushed everything out of my mind. It felt good, until I started thinking again, questioning what happened. Maybe Chloe is on to something with this heart and mind thing. I need to live my life and let my heart be the guide, not my head. I am going to start tonight. Looking at Chloe with a shy smile I finally respond to her very wise words.

"You're right, again. I'm going to start letting my heart make the decisions for me. Maybe Wyatt and I will work out. Maybe not. But I'll never know if I don't give it a try."

Chloe smiles back, "I knew you'd make the right decision. Now, don't you have somewhere to be?"

Oh shit! What time is it anyway? I spent the last hour sobbing in my kitchen with a tequila bottle, while I'm sure Bridgett is getting all dolled up. I don't have a chance to outshine her beauty, even with hours of preparation. But now, I only have half an hour before I need to leave to be at the restaurant on time.

Chloe senses my panic and takes control of the situation. "Go, get in the shower. I'll get you something to wear and help you with your hair. We can get it done in time, but you have to get started now. Go!"

With that I jump out my chair and race down the hall to my bedroom to change and shower quickly. "Thanks Chloe, you are truly my dearest, bestest friend in the whole wide world!" I yell in my haste. I hear her sarcastic "Ahhhh" before jumping into the steaming hot water.

Chapter Thirteen

(Present Day)

Minutes later, I'm out of the shower and eyeing the outfit Chloe has picked out for me. She has paired my skinny black pants with a hot pink silk halter top that ties around my neck and drapes my chest, showing a little bit of cleavage. It is sexy, with not showing too much. Instead of my typical Tory Burch black flats, Chloe chooses my peep toe black heels, giving the outfit a more sophisticated look. Topping the ensemble off, I add some sparkly chandelier earrings and some silver bangle bracelets. Spring has arrived, but the nights are still a little cool, so I wrap my shoulders with a black pashmina and walk out into the living area. Chloe whistles when she sees her finished product. She helped me dry and straighten my hair, which I wear down letting in hang over my shoulders and down my back.

"Suz, you look amazing," she gushes.

I giggle back to her. "Well, I couldn't have pulled this off without my personal stylist."

"I am truly talented, aren't I?" Chloe says with no shame. I roll my eyes at her, inwardly wishing I had half of her confidence.

"I wish you could go with me. I just know once I get there I'm going to get scared and totally mess this up."

Chloe is very reassuring. "You'll be fine, Suzanna. Just be yourself. Wyatt already likes you for you. You don't have to do anything special. Plus, he's going to bust a gut when he sees you in that outfit. Beats your dumb golf shirt and skirts any day!" I laugh realizing that I really need to update my wardrobe. I basically wear golf attire all the time. No wonder I haven't had a romantic relationship in over four years. Pulling me from my thoughts I hear Chloe reach for her keys.

"Come on Suzanna, we better get a move on or you're going to be late. Wouldn't want Bridgett to beat you there," she teases. For a moment I'm confused. Has Chloe reconsidered being my side kick tonight? I have practically begged her to go accompany me for moral support. Making my way to the door Chloe explains. "I'm your DD tonight. I don't think you should drive after the tequila shots." Oh yeah, at least someone is thinking straight.

"I still wish you were going with me." I plead trying my impersonation of her perfect, pouty face.

"I'll give you a pep talk in the car. You'll be fine. Plus, I have plans tonight with Brian. Maybe we'll meet you later for drinks after dinner." I'll take whatever she is willing to offer. I'll probably need her more after dinner anyway. That is when I am sure Bridgett will make her move for Wyatt.

"That would be great Chloe. Please, please come!"

"We'll think about it. But let's get a move on." And with that Chloe rushes me out of the door.

I make my way into the busy restaurant. The Blue Marlin is a hip bar/restaurant that caters to the young professionals and college students. The bar is always busy, especially during hour happy. Making my way through the crowd at the front of the restaurant, I see that tonight is no exception. The place is packed, all the bar stools being occupied. There is also a row of people standing around behind those that are seated waiting patiently to be served. I finally spot some of my teammates at the very end of the bar, along with Coach Brown. Walking over, I still haven't seen Wyatt. I'm not even sure if he is working tonight or not. Bridgett is going to be extremely upset if he isn't on the schedule. I guess I will be too. Speaking of Bridgett, where is she? Coach Brown spots me just as I am getting close and starts clapping like a fool. My other teammates join in, whooping and hollering. The entire bar seems to notice, causing me to turn as pink as my shirt.

"There she is, our own soon to be golf professional," Coach Brown announces to the crowd. I am bombarded with hugs and kisses from my teammates and even some strangers nearby send congrats my way. I'm not used to all the attention and just want to crawl in a hole.

"Oh, please stop!" I beg. "This isn't about me. Tonight we celebrate our great season. Not another word about me and qualifying. I'm nervous enough as it is." Golf is actually the last thing I am nervous about tonight. I am nervous about seeing Wyatt. But no one has to know that. I really need a drink.

"What will you have Suzanna?" I hear Coach Brown ask. Needing some more liquid courage to get through this evening, I ask for a margarita. Hey, the tequila seemed to work earlier. Why not stick with it? Coach Brown maneuvers himself up to the bar to place my order. Looking at my teammates, I notice everyone is accounted for except Bridgett.

"Guess we're waiting for Bridgett to arrive before being seated," I state to no one in particular. Anna and Beth start giggling. Coach Brown returns from the bar with my drink.

"Bridgett's already here," I hear Beth say. "We're just waiting for her to come join us. Seems she got sidetracked by that hot bartender she's had her eye on." I start casing the entire restaurant looking for Bridgett.

"I don't think she's inside. The bartender went on break and Bridgett followed him out back. There's no telling what those two are doing right now," Anna informs me bursting out in another fit of giggles. I am finding it hard to swallow. What the hell? What are they doing outside, together? I down my drink in one gulp.

"Whoa, Suzanna. You better pace yourself. We want you to make through dinner."

I can't even think straight I am so mad. Wyatt has some explaining to do. First, flirting with Bridgett, now taking her out back during his break. I know we aren't exclusive, but really? It was he that had wanted to 'try' for more. I push my way back up to the bar to order another drink. I was going to get another margarita, but change my order when

I see Bridgett and Wyatt appear through the service entrance. They are laughing and talking like old friends. Bridgett is practically swooning over him and it makes me disgusted.

"What can I get you, miss?" I hear another bartender say.

"I'll have a tequila shot. Better make it a double," I say never taking my eyes off Wyatt and Bridgett. When they get close to the bar, Bridgett makes her way towards our party while Wyatt walks behind the bar to help some customers at the other end. He still hasn't noticed I am at the restaurant. The other bartender puts the shot in front of me while I pull out some cash. Just when I finish paying, Wyatt turns to head my way. He stops abruptly when he sees me and our eyes lock. That's when Bridgett comes up next to me, placing her arm around my shoulder.

"Hey Suzanna, you made it," she says while squeezing me into a girl hug. I am still watching Wyatt and his expression is classic. Busted!

"Hi Bridgett, is that the hot bartender you told me all about earlier? The one you have been flirting with for weeks?" I ask her loud enough for Wyatt to hear me.

"Yep, that's him. Isn't he dreamy?" I pick up my shot of tequila and down it in one gulp, licking my lips to catch any excess alcohol that tries to escape.

"Looks like my worst nightmare." Then I walk off towards our table, leaving Wyatt with a jaw dropping expression.

Dinner is excruciating. I have to hear Bridgett go on and on about Wyatt this and Wyatt that. The other girls giggle and laugh. Coach Brown tries to ignore the girl talk. He talks to me about this summer and my plans for practice getting ready for qualifying. I keep my answers short and sweet, wishing this dinner will end fast. Coach Brown gives a toast to our winning season and a special toast for me and my future golf success. Our meals arrive and I barely eat, just push my food around on my plate. Finally the bills are paid and everyone is making plans for the night. Bridgett grabs my hand.

"Want to come hang with me at the bar? I want to be here when they close so that maybe Wyatt and I can go somewhere later." I was going to tell her no, but then I see Chloe and Brian walk in. She waves to me from the bar and motions me over. Okay, this could be fun. I can torture Wyatt some more, now that he is obviously busted. Then Chloe and Brian can take me home while I lick my wounds. I am already well on my way to being drunk since I have consumed much alcohol and little food.

"Why the hell not?" I tell Bridgett. She looks stunned at my blunt reply but then starts sashaying over to the bar. I tell everyone else good-bye and goodnight and head to the bar area to join Chloe and Brian, as well as bitch Bridgett. Chloe has the most puzzled look on her face as both Bridgett and I sit down at the bar to join them.

"Chloe, you remember Bridgett, my golf teammate?" I try really hard to hide the hatred dripping from my voice. Chloe reaches out to shake Bridgett's hand.

"Hi Bridgett, good to see you again?" Her reply is more a question than a greeting.

"Oh, hi Chloe. And who's this handsome fellow with you?" Bridgett asks eyeing Brian head to toe. Does this girl have no couth? Chloe snakes her hand through Brian's arm before making the introduction, showing Bridgett that Brian is her possession and to not even think about it. Brian hesitantly says hello, sensing drama ahead and bows out of any more conversation with Bridgett.

As luck would have it, all the other bartenders are busy, so Wyatt is left to take our orders. Slowly approaching us, Wyatt asks, "Hello, girls, what can I get you?"

Before Bridgett can answer, I immediately place my order. "I think I'd like to *try* a tequila shot. Would anyone else like to *try* a tequila shot with me?" Sarcasm is dripping from each of my words, especially the word try. I want to emphasize that particular word to see what kind of reaction I will get from Wyatt.

"Oh, tequila sounds yummy. Wyatt, honey, I think I'll have what Suzanna's having," Bridgett says as she flutters her eyelashes at Wyatt in a seductive manner.

I hear Chloe say under her breath, "I bet you will have what Suzanna already had!"

I burst out laughing not caring that people around us think I am loud and drunk. Wyatt rolls his eyes at me and Chloe and goes to fix our drinks.

"So Bridgett, what do you have planned for the rest of the night?" Chloe asks fishing for information.

"Well, I'm hoping to hook up with Wyatt, our bartender. Isn't he sooooo hot?" Bridgett exclaims, not at all embarrassed with herself for acting like such a whore. Wyatt has returned with our drinks so I start back in with my torture.

"You sure you want to *try* to hook up with a bartender? Don't you think you're setting the bar a little low, no pun intended?" Chloe gasps at my bitchy comment. She grabs and squeezes my leg up under the bar letting me know I have gone too far. What Chloe doesn't know about is Wyatt and Bridgett's outdoor escape earlier. I'm not about to forget that and I will go as far as I want with the hurtful conversation. Looking Wyatt straight in the eye, I say, "Maybe we should ask the bartender, Wyatt, isn't it?" acting like I have never met him. "Wyatt you want to *try* and get laid tonight? Although, Bridgett here is a pretty sure thing, so I don't think there will be much *trying* on your part. Some of us I guess just have to *try* a little harder for what we want." Ouch, that is downright mean. I can't believe the venom I am spewing. But I am furious, and that gives me courage, as well as the alcohol. I have stunned everyone around me into complete silence, giving me the opportunity to continue with my rant. I notice other people around the bar have stopped their conversations to listen in on my drama. "You know, I just may *try* to get laid tonight too," I say as I stand up on the lower ring of the barstool to raise myself up. "Hmmmm, I wonder if there is anybody out there who would be willing to *try* that with me tonight." Before I can continue my little performance, Wyatt rushes around the bar and grabs my arm.

"That's enough, Suzanna. Outside now!" he barks, dragging me towards the service entrance.

"Oh goody, this must be where you take all your special customers." I glance back at Bridgett to find her dumbfounded. When the doors shut behind us, Wyatt swings me around to face him. He is so angry I can envision steam shooting out of his ears.

"What the fuck was that?"

I scream back. "What? I was just getting you an in with Bridgett, you know, my teammate. The one you've been flirting with for weeks now. The one you brought out here earlier."

Wyatt stands his ground actually inching closer to me than he already is. "And what do you think I did with your teammate, Bridgett, when she followed me *uninvited* out here earlier during my break?"

"Well, I don't know for sure because I didn't ask, but obviously something happened because you are all she has talked about all night. Not to mention, she is in there now waiting for you to get off work so she can jump your bones!" I answer with a raised voice. Wyatt starts smiling that sexy, delicious smile. I mean really, how can he smile during a time like this? "What's so funny?" I spit out.

"You're jealous!" he snorts.

"Am not!" I state like a bratty child.

"Oh Suzanna, yes you are, and I love it!" He is still grinning which only makes me angrier.

"Let go of me, I need to go *try* to get laid!" Now that wipes the cocky smile completely off of his face.

He comes closer so that we are now face to face, his hot breath brushing against my skin. His eyes darken, giving him that lust filled look. He leans in and whispers against my ear. "Oh, you'll get laid tonight and it'll be by me, and only me!" His sexy voice sends a warm tingling feeling throughout my body causing my nerve endings to all come to life at once. Wyatt then starts kissing my neck, right below my ear and I can't contain the moan that escapes my lips. I am still angry and have lots of questions that need answers, mainly questions about Bridgett, but all I am consumed with at the moment is Wyatt's lips and how they dance across my neck and jaw line. He slowly makes his way to my mouth and crushes his lips to mine. Giving in to my desires, I open my mouth for him to enter and he deepens the kiss with his tongue. My arms have involuntarily wrapped around his neck pulling him closer, if that is even possible. I am pressed up against the outside wall of the patio area of the restaurant. I can feel the hard, cold brick against my back through the thin silk material of my shirt. But it doesn't bother me because Wyatt's touch is the only thing my body cares about at this instance.

Suddenly, we are interrupted as the service entrance door swings open. Bridgett is standing at the door, mouth opened in surprise to see me and Wyatt engaged in a dirty lip lock. "So, I guess you two know each other, huh?" I detect a little hurt in her voice and I quickly remember all the mean stuff I said earlier. But before I can apologize, Bridgett starts asking Wyatt a question. "So, is Suzanna the girl you kept telling me about? Is she the one who owns your heart?"

Wyatt looks at me with a sly grin. "Yep, she's the one and only." Now I feel really, really bad.

Bridgett walks over slowly. "Suzanna, why didn't you tell me that you knew Wyatt and that y'all are seeing each other? Gosh, I feel just horrible admitting that I have been flirting with your man for weeks now. I can't imagine what you were thinking all night as I went on and on about trying to take him home. Damn, I'm so embarrassed." Here Bridgett is apologizing to me when I have essentially called her a whore in front of the entire restaurant.

"Bridgett, don't apologize to me. You didn't know. I should be apologizing to you. I am soooo sorry for all the mean stuff I said earlier. Wyatt and I, well it's complicated." Bridgett seems to understand that I am being sincere and shrugs it off.

"Hey, don't worry about it Suzanna. I would have done the same thing if some woman was hitting on my man. I'm curious though, why didn't you just tell me? I would never have pursued him had I known." I sigh because I really don't know what to say to truthfully answer her question. But I know I have to be honest with her and Wyatt since he is standing there listening to this entire conversation.

"Wyatt and I are old friends. We've known each other since high school. He was my savior during a very difficult period in my life. Things just started to transition from friendship to more just a few weeks ago. I asked Wyatt to keep our relationship simple and secret. I think I was just scared." Now I am really talking to Wyatt more than Bridgett. This is for his benefit, so I look him straight in the eyes and continue. "I am scared of being hurt again, I am scared of losing a friend should we not work out, but most of all, I am scared of the feelings I am having about Wyatt, feelings I haven't had for anyone in a very, very long time. But today, I decided I was going to stop being scared. I am going to let my heart make decisions for me, rather than my head. I'm sorry for being scared, Wyatt. You are the best thing to happen to me in the last few years. I just hope I haven't royally screwed things up tonight." I finish with a loud exhale, relieved to get all that off my chest and out in the open.

Wyatt gently pushes my hair from my face and wipes a stray tear from my cheek that escaped during my speech. He seems to understand how hard it is for me to love again, knowing all the dirty secret details of my break up with Patrick. He plants a sweet tender kiss on my lips and whispers, "You never have to be scared again, Suzanna. I'll keep you safe and I will never hurt you." That sends the water works into over drive and I cry in his arms, tears of joy. We have completely forgotten that Bridgett is still standing a few feet away until she clears her throat.

"Well, aren't y'all just the sweetest, cutest couple. I'm just gonna head back inside and grab a cab home. I'll see you around Suzanna." She turns to make her way back into the restaurant. Before she enters, I rush over and give her a big hug.

"You're a beautiful, sweet girl, Bridgett. I hope you are as lucky as me and find a great man like Wyatt. You deserve it!" Looking over at Wyatt one last time, she sends a sad smile my way. Bridgett walks back inside the restaurant leaving me alone again with Wyatt.

"So, I guess I completely acted like a fool tonight, huh?" I say as I walk his way to get back into his warm, strong arms.

He chuckles, "Yeah, you did. But I like seeing that side of you."

"Really, you like seeing the crazy bitch Suzanna come out?"

"Not so much the crazy and bitchy part. But I did like the jealous part. Jealousy looks sexy on you! Seriously though, you just showed me tonight how much you care."

I hug Wyatt with all my might, resting my head on his chest. "It scares me how much I actually do care," I whisper so only my ears can hear my fear.

Chapter Fourteen

(Present Day)

Since the night at the restaurant, Wyatt and I have been spending all our spare time with each other. When I'm not in class or on the golf course, I am with Wyatt. I will even sometimes visit Wyatt at the restaurant on the nights he is working. I am constantly teased by the other bartenders who witnessed my little jealousy outburst. At first I had been horrified, but I now I am learning to take it in stride. I guess it helps that Wyatt comes to give me a reassuring kiss every time I get teased by one of his colleagues, so I actually enjoy it. By far, my most favorite time I spend with Wyatt is at night, either at his place or mine. It is so nice falling asleep in his arms and waking up with him every morning. Okay, so the sleeping isn't the greatest part. It is the sex. We have the most incredible sex I have ever experienced. Granted, I only have my few high school experiences to compare it to and that was with only one other person. However, I feel that Wyatt and I connect on a different level between the sheets. He is such a passionate lover, paying attention to every inch of my body. Just thinking about being close to him makes me throb with longing between my thighs. The night of the infamous restaurant fiasco, Wyatt took me back to his place and we made love the entire night. I mean the entire night, no falling asleep until the sun came up the next morning. We explored each other's bodies like they were hidden treasures. I find I can never be satisfied when it comes to Wyatt in the bedroom, always wanting more. He seems to feel the same and we can barely keep our hands off of each other.

Wyatt explained the whole Bridgett thing to me. Just as Bridgett had confessed, he told me how she would come in the bar frequently to flirt. Obviously, many women come into the bar to flirt with Wyatt because he is so damn good looking. And, he's a charmer to boot. Wyatt confessed that he has flirted back with Bridgett and many of the other women, but with no intentions of carrying it any further, other than a big, fat, cash tip. At first, just the thought of Wyatt flirting with other women made me see green, but as I watch Wyatt in action at work, he seems oblivious to his charming ways and probably doesn't even know how flirtatious he is actually being. He is very innocent and I realize that he would never seek out a woman from the bar, especially now that we are together. Anyway, Wyatt said that Bridgett is actually more aggressive than the average woman and continued her assault up until that specific night. Wyatt had just gone on break, when Bridgett followed him out back. She made her intentions clear right up to the point when she had Wyatt backed up against the brick wall (yeah, that same wall) and was about to lay it on him. He said that was when he started telling her about me. Not revealing my name, but telling her that he was involved with a girl. A beautiful, smart, talented girl that he cared for deeply. He told her, kindly but boldly, that she didn't stand a chance and to give up immediately, because this girl owned his heart. It had Bridgett back down for the moment and that's when they went inside. I asked Wyatt why he looked so 'busted' once he saw me at the bar. He told me that his look had been one of appreciation. He had been blown away to see me there at all, but to see me looking so beautiful, I completely took his breath away. I wondered why Bridgett continued to pursue Wyatt even though he had turned down her advances. I figured she would have been embarrassed to admit to all us girls and Coach Brown that she had struck out with Wyatt. I guess she just continued the charade to make herself feel better.

Wyatt couldn't believe that I would think he would ever be interested in Bridgett anyway. I questioned Wyatt's eye sight. Had he not seen the girl? She was beyond beautiful. Wyatt said he only had eyes for me, his blond haired, blue eyed, petite little dynamite. After those cheesy, yet effective words, we never really talked about Bridgett again.

Wyatt did ask had he not stopped me, would I have continued to search for some man to get laid that night. I laughed in his face and told him, no. I would probably have continued to shoot tequila until I passed out or hugged the porcelain gods, whichever came first.

The week of finals is here and between work and studying, Wyatt and I have barely seen each other. He has his last final tomorrow. I am wrapping things up today. So Chloe and I agreed to make tonight a girls night only. Since I have spent so much time with Wyatt, Chloe and I barely get any alone time together. So tonight we are going to catch up. I make it home first, so I start cooking a pot of spaghetti. I have the sauce on the stove and am getting ready to boil the noodles when I hear Chloe come through the front door. She's been at rehearsals all day. Part of her theatre final assignment is performing in the end of the school year production that the university puts on every year. Even though Chloe is just a junior, she nabbed the leading actress role. That role historically has always been given to a senior student. Chloe is just that talented and her peers know it. They sometimes treat Chloe meanly, only because they are jealous. But it still hurts her, even though she tries to hide behind her tough as nails exterior. Chloe storms into the kitchen throwing her books and purse on the top of the table in obvious frustration.

"Hey Chloe, something wrong?" I ask while tending to the pots on the stove.

"Ugh, I hate Tinsley Bratton! I just hate her! Do you know she had the nerve to critique my entire performance today, which by the way was flawless, and then goes to tell Brian that I don't deserve the lead role and it is obvious that the only reason I got it is because I am sleeping with him! Can you believe her nerve?" Brian was chosen to direct the performance, so he had some say when it came to casting. However, the professors of the drama department have the final decision making power and they are the ones who chose Chloe as the lead.

"Well, you know that's a bunch of bull. Brian didn't have the final say, so what does it really matter what Tinsley Bratton thinks?"

"Well, it wouldn't matter if she didn't have a thing for Brian. I honestly think she would do just about anything to see me fail. Then she would blame the failure of the entire production on me, causing Brian to hate me. Of course that is when she would make her move, tearing me and Brian apart and putting her flabby ass in my place, right between his sheets."

I laugh, "That's a well thought out plan, much too smart for Tinsley Bratton to come up with."

"Hey, you're right", Chloe agrees. "Tinsley's brain is about as big as my pinky toe. How she has managed to make it through all her classes and be considered a senior is beyond me." We both laugh because we know exactly how Tinsley has passed all her prior courses...she has slept with most of the male professors in the drama department. Rumor has it, she might have even slept with some of the female professors for a passing grade. Not judging but so not my thing!

"Yummy, the spaghetti smells delicious. I'm starved!" Chloe says changing the subject.

"It's almost ready, just waiting for the noodles to boil. Why don't you open that bottle of red wine and let's drink."

"You read my mind, Suzanna! I really need a drink!" Chloe opens the wine and pours us each a glass.

"So, you and Brian, you're not letting this whole production assignment get between you two, are you?" Chloe and Brian have been seeing each other since right after Easter break. I don't know exactly how serious they are because Chloe never lets on to her true feelings. Chloe is very much a free spirit. She will date a guy and be extremely happy, then just all of a sudden it will be over. Once Chloe tires of someone, she doesn't look back. She just ends it and moves on. I don't know exactly where Brian fits into the laundry list of Chloe's relationships, but she seems to enjoy his company and they spend oodles of time together. Maybe that is because they share the same major.

"Brian and I are fine. He is actually a great director and is doing a fantastic job with the production. We try to be very professional during rehearsals. I still don't know how Tinsley found out we are sleeping together."

"Well, where do you see this thing with Brian going?" I ask, still not sure how serious things are between them.

"I don't exactly know, yet," Chloe answers. "Brian is a great guy and we have lots of fun together. I guess time will tell. Oh, by the way, I wanted to let you know I talked with James and Landon. They were actually thrilled that you agreed to attend the engagement party, mind you a little shocked as well." I was a little shocked that they were thrilled about me attending, but oh well. "Anyway," Chloe continues, "they are up for us all going to the party together, but they have already lined up dates. I was thinking I would ask Brian to go with me. Okay, if we both stay at your beach house? James and Landon might need to crash there, also." Um, dates, I hadn't even thought of bringing a date to the engagement party. Wonder what Patrick would think if I showed up with a date. Probably, nothing you stupid idiot. He is the one that's engaged!

"Sure, Chloe, you and Brian, as well as the boys and their dates are all welcome to stay at the beach house. It should be lots of fun. And I'll have plenty of extra room since Mom and Dad won't be there that week-end." Chloe finishes off her first glass of wine and goes to check on the bread that she placed in the oven a few minutes ago. I walk over to the stove to stir the sauce and drain the noodles. Everything is just about ready to eat. "Hey, how about filling me up again when you replenish your glass, would you?" I ask Chloe as she grabs the wine bottle.

"I didn't realize your parents weren't going to the party. Weren't they invited?" Chloe asks.

"Yeah, but Dad has some out of town conference and Mom wants to go with him rather than show up stag to the party. Can't say I blame her."

"Well, speaking of going stag, you planning to go alone or bring Wyatt?" Oh my gosh. I can't possibly bring Wyatt to my ex-boyfriends engagement party. Patrick had already drawn his own conclusions about me and Wyatt years ago. This would be adding fuel to an already burning fire.

"Hell no, I'm not asking Wyatt!" I exclaim. Chloe narrows her beautiful brown eyes my way leading up to what I am sure is a lecture.

"And exactly how will you manage wiggling out of that one, huh? Does Wyatt even know that you're going to the party?" I don't answer which tells Chloe all she needs to know. "Suzanna, you have got to be kidding me! You and Wyatt haven't even talked about Patrick and the fact that he is engaged and that you're attending his party. Why?"

"Well, things have been so great between us, I just really forgot to bring it up."

"Bullshit!" she calls. "You're avoiding bringing it up because you might have to admit some ugly truths." Does Chloe have to be right all the time?

Sighing, I say, "I haven't told Wyatt yet because I know he'll want to come and I'm just not sure I want to take him there. It's already awkward with the way things went down years ago, not just between Patrick and Wyatt, but with the rest of the crew. I'm not ready to introduce anymore friction to an already electric situation." Chloe knows I have a right to worry about how people would accept the fact that Wyatt and I are seeing each other. When I left during senior year, the rumor mill went into overdrive, insinuating that Wyatt and I had been carrying on a secret love affair behind Patrick's back. Wyatt was just a friend to me during that sad time, and only a friend. Although, he never denied the rumors, because then people would seek out the truth. He, unselfishly, took the abuse of Patrick and his friends, plus their hoity-toity parents at the club for my benefit. We hadn't even begun our romance until years later, but still I managed to cause him hurt and pain. Seems to be what I do to all the men in my life. I need a change of subject fast so I concentrate on finishing the preparations of our dinner. The faster I can get food in Chloe's mouth, the faster she will shut up about anything to do with Wyatt or Patrick.

"Let's eat, dinner is ready and I'm hungry," I command. Chloe shrugs it off for now, but I know she isn't letting it go. We settle at the table stuffing ourselves with spaghetti and bread, skimping on the salad. Both Chloe and I have been in overdrive trying to finish this semester and we are loading up on carbohydrates tonight.

"I just can't believe in a few short weeks, you'll not live here anymore." Chloe says suddenly sounding sad.

"Well, you know you can always come live with me at the beach this summer and keep me company."

"Suzanna, you know good and well you will be too busy playing all 100,000 holes of golf the beach has to offer. You won't need the company. Plus, I think I may pick up some classes this summer to lighten my load during my senior year." Chloe is right, yet again. Although I am looking forward to spending the summer at the beach, this isn't going to be any type of vacation. I plan to play as much golf this summer in preparation for the qualifying round of the LPGA in early August. Coach Brown has already penciled me in to play the first three weeks with colleagues of his that live at the beach. Plus, Dad has contacted the coach at Coastal Carolina University and he is willing to coach me the rest of the summer. I don't even want to know what that is setting my parents back. I am thankful that I have something to fill my time, especially since Wyatt is spending the summer in Columbia. I am already apprehensive about dealing with a long distance relationship. Those usually never work out and it scares me to think of myself without Wyatt. And that thought scares me even more. I have never pictured myself as the girl who can't function without her man. But the distance between Columbia and Myrtle Beach seems like the distance between the east and west coasts. That's how much I hate being away from him. I haven't realized how much I have let him get under my skin in the short amount of time we have been dating. It just happened. I followed the advice of Chloe and lived in the moment, but that moment is fading fast and is about to change.

Sensing my uneasy thoughts, Chloe asks, "Are you okay, Suz? You suddenly seem sad."

I try a convincing smile, but it doesn't reach my eyes, giving me away. "I am sad. Everything is going to change soon. My college career is almost over, we won't be roommates anymore, and I'm leaving Wyatt. I'm not sure how to carry on a long distance relationship. I'm not even sure Wyatt wants one."

Chloe reaches over and grabs my hand. "You should be happy Suz. You graduated with honors and on time. You have a great career ahead of you, maybe even as a professional golfer, doing what you have always loved. Sure, we won't be roommates anymore, but we will always be the best of friends and I promise to come see you every chance I get. That is, only if you promise some beach time away from the course and a couple of girls nights out."

I laugh, "If you promise to come visit, I guess I can find the time to lounge on thc beach with you and get drunk at night!"

"You better! And sweetie, don't worry about Wyatt. He is head over heels, crazy for you. I don't think he will mind the distance as long as you two are back together after the summer." I know Wyatt's feelings for me run deep. He is always reassuring me about how much I mean to him. We haven't yet said anything about loving the other, but I think that is where we are headed. I just hope our feelings for each other will get us through the summer.

"I know I'm being paranoid with everything happening at once. I just wish we could all move to the beach together and have a hell of a house party all summer long!"

"That sounds divine, girlfriend, but your parents would never go for it!" We both burst into laughter thinking about my mom and dad busting up to a house full of drunken college kids.

Chloe and I finish dinner in a fit of giggles, remembering fun times together in our home as college students. We clean the dishes from dinner and open our second bottle of wine, making our way to lounge on the couch.

"Hey, did James and Landon happen to say who they are bringing to the party as their dates?" I ask Chloe.

"James is bringing Lisa. Remember her? She went to the private school in Florence. She's our age I think. Anyway, they reconnected in college and have been dating for a few months." I remember Lisa. She was a cute girl in high school. She and James had gone out briefly during our senior year. I remember liking her a lot. She was easy going, unlike James and his high strung self and they seemed to balance each other out. James could always be a little uptight.

"What about Landon?" Chloe doesn't respond at first, playing with the remote as a distraction. I feel like she is trying to avoid answering the question. "Chloe, answer me. Who is Landon bringing to the party?"

Chloe lets out the breath she has been holding and blurts out her answer. "Landon is bringing Leslie." Was that supposed to mean something to me? I didn't know any Leslie other than the high school whore that screwed anything that moved. It couldn't be the same Leslie. Landon hated her in high school because she was such a slut.

"Who's Leslie?" I ask.

"Leslie Townsend, from high school," Chloe answers as my mouth almost hits the floor.

"You have got to be joking! Landon and Leslie? I thought Landon hated her. When did this happen? And does she have any diseases or children?" Chloe doubles over in fits of laughter.

"You are so mean, Suz. I love it!"

"Well, we are talking about the same Leslie, right? It's a valid question."

When Chloe can finally speak so that I can understand her she explains. "Yep, same girl. Supposedly, when Leslie went off to college she changed her ways, got very religious or something. Come to find out, Landon and Leslie hooked up at some sorority fraternity mixer. They talked and seemed to hit it off. Actually, they have been dating on and off for over a year now."

"Wow!" Funny how this world works. I remember Landon being the only one out of the Fab Five never to accept the fact that Patrick and I were dating. He always said derogatory things about our relationship, never giving it much substance. He belittled it as just a fling. He was also the one who refused to speak to me after Patrick and I were over. I wouldn't be surprised to find out that he actually started the rumor about me and Wyatt, though I have no concrete proof. Karma's a bitch!

"Well, good for them. Takes one to know one I guess."

Chloe shrugs, "Don't be too hard on Landon. He handled things the wrong way when you left, but I think other than Patrick, he missed you the most." I can't believe what I have just heard out of Chloe's mouth.

"Come on Chloe, even I know that Landon never liked that Patrick and I dated. Plus, he hated me when things ended. I'm surprised that he even agreed to this absurd idea of us all showing up together to Patrick's engagement party. I was kind of under the impression that we wouldn't even like being in the same room together."

Chloe is shaking her head in total disagreement. "Look, Landon is thrilled that he is going to get to see you. I think he has let go of a lot of pent up anger he was holding onto during high school. Give him a chance, I think he has changed." I will just have to see it to believe because Chloe isn't selling it.

"Yeah, yeah whatever you say. Should be interesting, though." I am actually starting to get nervous about the whole thing. It has been about a month since Chloe talked me into going. I can't blame the entire decision on her, though. I know in my heart that I have to see Patrick again. Just to see if he is happy. All I have ever wanted is his happiness. At one point, I thought we would be happy together. But that was taken away from us. So, I guess if he is really happy with someone else, I'll be okay with it. Will I be okay with it? Here come the questions that keep popping through my head clouding it with doubt and despair. Am I wrong to hope that maybe Patrick will see me and remember all that we shared? Yes, I am. Especially since I now have someone in my life that cares about me. If Wyatt had any idea I was entertaining ideas about Patrick, he would leave me and never look back. The thought makes my chest hurt.

"So, James will be with Lisa, Landon with Leslie and me with Brian. That leaves you, Suzanna. Who's your date to this affair?" Here we go again. I knew Chloe would not let this go.

"Maybe I'll hire a male escort to be my date. Will that shut you up?" I say in hopes that she won't push the issue.

"Be serious, Suzanna. I'm not letting this go." Okay, so that was a failed attempt.

"Chloe, I can't take Wyatt. I just can't. Don't ask me why because I can't really give you a good explanation. All I know is that Wyatt can't be there, not yet anyway." Chloe is still persistent.

"Look, I kind of understand to some extent. I'm not crazy about this hair brained idea of yours that maybe something still lurks on the surface between you and Patrick and you need to investigate. However, I was the one to push you for closure, which I'm hoping you'll find and can move on with Wyatt. But if Wyatt finds out about this party, he's going to wonder why you didn't invite him. Will you have the answers for him that you don't have for me now?" Probably not, I think. I can't even come up with a good answer for myself other than just a gut feeling. Wyatt won't buy into my gut feelings and neither will Chloe.

"Maybe it won't come to that. Maybe I'll just tell Wyatt we all attended the party at the last minute. He'd be proud that I was strong enough to go show my congratulations to my ex-boyfriend and send him off to a life of marital bliss." Chloe makes a 'humph' sound, like any good southern housemaid from the movie The Help. Having seen the movie, I know that 'humph' sound is the equivalent to calling bullshit. She doesn't believe that will work anymore than me. "Look, Chloe, I know you're concerned. So am I. But let me figure this out. I just need some time. Maybe in the next two weeks I'll change my mind and ask Wyatt as my date. But if not, then don't bring it up again, okay. A very wise woman once told me to let the chips fall where they may. Well, I'm taking her advice and I'll deal with the consequences." Chloe smiles, remembering that she is the referred to very wise woman giving me advice just a few weeks back.

"Fine, I'll let it go and pinky promise to not bring it up again, but I still have the right to say 'I told you so' when this goes to hell in a hand-bag." Finally, I think, she has conceded.

"Sure, you have my permission to tell me 'I told you so' as long as you pick me up and put me back together should this blow up in my face." I have a bad feeling it may come to that.

Chapter Fifteen

(Present Day)

The next day, Wyatt breezes into the house, with his drop dead gorgeous self and a smile plastered across his beautiful face. "Hey sweetie," he says right before planting a kiss on my lips. Yummy, he tastes so good, I want another bite.

"Well, hello to you too! What's got you in such a fine mood?"

Pulling me down on the couch and kissing me more, I really don't care what has made him so happy, as long as he keeps kissing me. "I have news, very good news!" he says between kisses. That piques my interest enough to pull away waiting to hear what could make him so happy.

"Well, are you going to tell me or do I have to guess?" Wyatt pulls away briefly to get a letter out of the backpack he carried in and dropped on the floor at his feet.

"First, I just aced my final exam for macro economics and I am done with this semester." Fabulous, but not very exciting, though. I already know Wyatt is a top notch student, always excelling in all his classes.

"That's great honey, but is that all?" I ask not wanting to rain on his parade but anxious to hear more.

"No silly, that's not all. Here's the most exciting part. Remember I told you that I have been applying for all these internships in international business?" Wyatt has been consumed the last month filling out applications for internships. His graduate degree will be complete at the end of the summer, once he completes an internship and writes a dissertation coinciding with the internship in his field of study during that time. I know he has his favorites, most of which are in New York, but he felt like they were long shots so I never really worried about him being accepted. He has already been invited to intern at three prestigious brokerage firms in the Columbia area and I assume he will accept one of those offers to stay in the state. Selfishly, I want him to stay close to me but I never voiced that to him because I know he has dreams of making it big. Feeling uneasy all of sudden, I don't want to know what is in the envelope. But he looks so damn happy I have to be happy for him, no matter what the news.

"Yeah, I remember. So go on...don't keep me waiting."

Wyatt teases, "But you're so cute when you're waiting." Kissing me again, I almost forget that he is getting ready to tell me something big. Very big.

"Okay, Wyatt, spill it. What's got you so frisky?"

"Well, I just received word that I got accepted to participate in an internship at Galloway and Meads brokerage firm."

I haven't a clue what Galloway and Meads brokerage firm is, but I figure it is big since he is so excited. "And, are you going to accept?" I ask knowing what his answer will be.

"Hell yeah! Baby this is huge. They only award five internships each summer to international business graduates throughout the entire country. I was one of their five. I'd be a complete idiot to turn it down. I don't know if anyone has ever turned them down."

Wow, that is impressive. "Wyatt, I'm so proud of you. When do you start?" His excitement is contagious and I am so happy I'm with him to share this important moment.

"I start May 15th, which means I'll move the week prior," he says still grinning like a Cheshire cat. Wait, did I hear him right? Move? Move where? His grin slowly fades as he watches my excitement change to full blown terror. "Baby, what's wrong? Aren't you happy for me? This is a huge deal. This could do wonders for our future."

Our future? Whoa, when did it become ours? I don't even know where he is moving. "Um, I'm really happy for you, but you mentioned moving and I'm not exactly sure where that is," I say trying to hide the shakiness in my voice.

"Oh, yeah well, this firm is big, Suz. It's located in New York."

Holy crap, New York. I was thinking Charlotte or Atlanta. At least those places are only a state away and within driving distance. He is moving to New York. Panic kicks in and I'm finding it hard to breathe. My hands start trembling and I can't make them stop. Wyatt is leaving me. All this time I was worried about moving a mere two hours away to the beach. Now he is moving up the east coast and is ecstatic about it. I feel tears sting my eyes. I don't want to take away from his happiness. I want to be joyful and celebrate with him, but my mind isn't having it. I bolt from the couch as fast as I can and run to the restroom to hide. I am hiding from my boyfriend. I don't want him to see me cry and fall apart. I only want him to be as happy as he was when he walked in the front door. Oh my, I'm a terrible girlfriend!

I hear a soft knock on the bathroom door. I don't answer at first still consumed by my misery. "Suzanna, please let me in. We need to talk," Wyatt says in a calm voice. How can I talk to him without turning into a blubbering mess? Quickly looking in the mirror, I see my eyes have become red and swollen and my face is streaked with tears. There is no chance he is going to buy a lie about a sudden tummy ache. I slowly open the door to find Wyatt sitting on my bed, with his head hung low. Oh no, what have I done? Where did the happy, smiling Wyatt go? I have destroyed him and brought despair filled Wyatt to the surface. I seem to suck the happiness right out of him. I run from the bathroom door and collapse in his arms, hugging him tightly.

"I'm so sorry Wyatt. I really am happy for you. And proud, too. You deserve this so much. You have worked so hard." I don't even try to hide the tears I am shedding now. Wyatt pulls back and looks at my crying face.

"Suzanna, you have a funny way of showing your happiness about this." Ouch, that stings. Why can't he see that I am happy for him, but sad that he will be moving? Use your words, Suzanna. Tell him exactly how you feel. Make him understand that this will be so hard for you to let him go. Tell him how much you'll miss him. All of it sounds so easy in my head. I just can't get my mouth to move. So, I just sit there and stare at him like he is an exotic animal on display at the local zoo.

Moments go by that feel like hours. We are just sitting there atop my bed staring at each other in silence. Well, not complete silence. I hear a sob escape from my throat, indicating my crying spell is yet to be over. Finally, Wyatt's hands cup both sides of my face and he slowly starts wiping the tears away with his thumbs.

"You're scared again, aren't you Suz?" he says in a sad voice. I nod, still not using my words. "I thought you decided not to be scared anymore when it came to you and me. Remember, that night at the restaurant. You told me you had stopped being scared to live Suz. That's when everything changed for us. Please, don't be scared now. This is only the beginning." Then why does it feel like the end? Let him know Suzanna, let him know how you feel. Tell him you love him, not to make him stay, but to make him go and do wonderful things to build for the future you're going to have together. Finally, I find my voice. But what comes out next isn't what I have been practicing in my head.

"Don't go. I'm scared. Please don't go," I beg. Wyatt just looks wounded. Like someone has actually caused him physical pain.

"I'm sorry Suzanna, but I have to go." And before I know what is happening, he has walked out of my bedroom, down the hall and out the front door. I collapse on my bed in a heaping pile of sobs, crying until there aren't any tears left. Exhaustion takes over and I slip into sleep.

It is dark. There are only a few lights still on at this hour. Most of the wait staff has left for the night. I'm alone, leaving my friends waiting for me in the parking lot. I left my coat in the bar area when we came to grab some beers to hide in the cooler while we partied on the golf course earlier tonight. When I arrive at the bar, it is empty. I find my jacket exactly where I left it on the back of the chair at the corner table. I walk over to get it, trying not to trip since I can't see really well. I reach my hand out to grab the coat, but someone pulls my arm away. Pain slices through my arm and shoulder due to the sheer force of someone grabbing me. It isn't long before I am pushed up against the back wall of the country club bar. I try to scream, but a hand is placed over my mouth preventing me to call for help. The assailant's other hand releases my arm to feel my female body parts in a harsh manner. I know what is going to happen, and I can't even call for help. I hear the ripping of clothing and that is when my dress begins to slide over my shoulder. My breasts are hurting now, caused by the force of this man's hands when he grabs them and pushes them up and outside of my bra. I am pinned against the wall with his knee between my legs. Oh God, this can't be happening. He is planting wet forced kisses down my neck and over my chest, constantly saying all types of disgusting things in my ear. I have to shake my head back and forth to keep him from entering my mouth. He smells of alcohol and cigarette smoke, making me want to puke. "No, stop!" I cry when his hand slips from my mouth. He forcefully slaps me across the face to shut me up. He is trying to unbuckle his pants to finish his intrusion of my body. Tears are streaming down my face. I just want him to stop. "Please, no! Don't! Please stop!" I am trembling with fear. With all the strength my voice can muster I scream. "Wyatt!"

"Suzanna, wake up. Wake up Suz, it's me Chloe." My eyes shoot open taking in my surroundings. I'm in my bed in the home that I share with Chloe. It is dark outside, but my bedside lamp is on. "Oh dear Suz, I think you were having a nightmare. You okay?" Chloe is sitting on the edge of my bed, pushing the wet hair from my eyes. I have been sweating profusely during my dream. My body is still shaking with fear from what I have just relived in my sleep. Taking slow deep breaths, I try to calm myself down.

"I'm so scared," is all can voice at the moment. Chloe wraps her arms around me in a big hug.

"Shhh, everything's all right now Suz. I'm right here." Her words are like silk, draping over my fragile body, finally stopping the violent tremors. Feeling that I have calmed enough to talk about it, Chloe releases me to look at her.

"What were you dreaming about doll?" she asks. I lean back against my headboard and stare at the ceiling.

"That night at the club," I answer. Chloe doesn't need more details. She knows what happened four and a half years ago. She won't make me elaborate on the horrid details of my dream. I've had nightmares about that night before. Chloe and I never speak about that night and I haven't thought of what happened for a long time now. I'm not sure what brought the dream on tonight.

"Did I say anything while I was dreaming?" I ask Chloe hoping I can come up with an explanation about why this would be resurfacing.

"Just the usual, 'please stop, don't, no' stuff that you have said before while dreaming." Hmm, strange because that is always what I say when I have that dream. Just like it played out that night. "You did scream for Wyatt right before I woke you up," Chloe adds.

Oh my gosh, Wyatt. Where is he? Taking a few moments to collect my thoughts, I remember the horrible afternoon when Wyatt had been beaming with pride telling me about the New York City internship he was offered. Then, I remember my awful reaction, crying like a baby and begging him not to go. That's when he walked out. Fresh tears appear just thinking of Wyatt leaving me this afternoon. Chloe hugs me again and lets me cry on her shoulder. When I can finally speak so she can understand me, I tell her everything that happened earlier this afternoon all the way to the moment Wyatt left. I conclude that I cried myself to sleep after that and hours later Chloe finds me having the nightmare.

"I'm so sorry Suzanna. I think all that talk last night about Patrick and the engagement party may have triggered your subconscious memories causing the nightmare," Chloe says. Could be, I think. "Maybe all this stress is just getting to you. Plus, now the added stress of Wyatt moving away, no wonder you had restless sleep." I nod in agreement to her. My heart hurts every time I think of Wyatt living in New York so far away from me. Actually, I am the one moving away first. I will be gone right after graduation, at the beginning of next week to spend the summer at the beach. Wyatt isn't leaving until the week after that. Suddenly, I feel like we need to spend every moment we have left together. But will Wyatt want to see me after my selfish reaction to his awesome accomplishment? I bolt out the bed, ready to go find out. It has taken me over four, long years to let someone into my heart again. I'm not about to give it up so easily. Sure, long distance will be hard. But Wyatt has made it clear that he is doing this for our future. He sees me in his future. I hold onto that thought as I make my way into my bathroom to freshen up.

"What are you doing Suzanna?" Chloe asks surprised that my mood has suddenly changed.

"I've got to go see Wyatt, Chloe. I need him to know how proud I am of him and that I will support him no matter where his career takes him. Chloe, I think I love him. I have to let him know that and it has to be tonight."

Chloe responds with an "ahhhh". "Why tonight though, you sure you're up for this after the nightmare?" Chloe ask with concern.

"The nightmare is exactly why I need to tell him. I screamed for him Chloe. I need him, he keeps me safe. I can't imagine going through the rest of my life without him by my side. Sure, it's going to be hard. But anything worth fighting for is worth having, right?"

Chloe smiles. "Right! Now finish getting ready and I'll drive you over. You make me a nervous wreck with all these emotions you've got going on. I'll feel better if I get you there safely."

"Oh Chloe, thank you. What would I do without you?"

Chloe goes to get her keys. "You'll never have to find out, doll!"

Chapter Sixteen

(Present Day)

The drive to Wyatt's is short, but anxious. I am still determined to tell him how I feel. I'm just not sure what his response will be. I haven't had long to plan out an eloquent speech. Realization has just dawned on me that I do, indeed, love Wyatt McCain. I guess I will just have to wing it.

Chloe drops me off at Wyatt's apartment complex. I see his car in the parking lot so I know he is at home instead of working tonight. Blowing a kiss to Chloe, I watch her drive away. Well, here I go. I make the walk to his second story apartment taking two steps at a time. Once I reach his door, I pause to take a deep breath. I have never laid out my feelings to another man other than Patrick. I feel raw. What if Wyatt doesn't reciprocate? I will be heartbroken, but at least I will have tried, which is more than I have been willing to do in a very long time. I raise my hand to begin knocking on the door. But before my hand makes contact with the hard wood, the door immediately opens. Wyatt, with keys in hand, almost walks straight into me before realizing that I am standing in front of him on his door step.

Startled, he says, "Damn, Suz, you almost scared me to death! What are you doing here?"

Oh no, that didn't sound good. Maybe he is still pissed about earlier today. I imagined that the minute he saw me, he would be so overjoyed that he would wrap me up in his welcoming arms and shower me in kisses. Never did I imagine this welcome. "Uh, I'm sorry. Guess this is a bad time. I can go," I reply being the coward I am.

"No, don't go!" he commands. "I didn't mean it like that. I just wasn't expecting you. Please, come in." Okay, so maybe I caught him off guard a bit. I accept his invitation and walk slowly through the door. When we are both inside his apartment, Wyatt closes the door and turns to face me. "Can I get you something to drink?" he asks. It is like I am just any other random guest and he is forced to use all his social manners. I hate the rift that seems to be between us now.

"No, thank you, I'm fine," I answer. We stand there for at least a minute just looking at each other. I see something in his eyes that I have never seen before. There is sadness. I have caused his overwhelming excitement from earlier to turn into sadness. My heart breaks at how selfish I acted earlier. Suddenly, I have to make him see that he can be happy again, that *we* can be happy again.

Without any lead in, I suddenly blurt out, "I love you, Wyatt!" There, I said it. He continues to just stand there looking at me. I wait and wait for him to respond, but he still looks at me without speaking. The silence between us is making me nervous. I can't take it anymore, so I start filling the silence as a blabber on. "I love you, and I'm sorry. I don't know how long I've loved you, because it just dawned on me today. The thought of you leaving made me realize I don't want to live without you. But, I would never keep you from fulfilling your dreams. I am so proud of you for getting that highly sought for internship. You have worked so hard to get to where you are today and you deserve it. I want you to go and knock their socks off up in New York. I, also, want you to know that I will miss you terribly and love you every single day you are gone. But I have faith in this, you and me. You are building our future together, just like you said. I'll be doing the same this summer with my golf game. It will be hard, not seeing each other. But I'm willing to try and make it work. I'm sorry I wasn't supportive earlier. But I'm here now and I'll be here when you come back. Or I'll go to you, that is, if you still want me. I love you." The words fly out of my mouth like a speeding train. Wyatt still stands just looking at me. We are back to that unbearable silence. I am starting to suspect that I have been a little too late baring my feelings to him. That dark cloud of rejection is hanging in the air. If he doesn't say something, anything, really soon, I will crumple. I have waited long enough.

"Well, I just wanted to let you know how I feel." I turn and start to walk to the door to leave, with my tail between my legs. Tears sting my eyes, but I will not let him see me cry. If you love someone, you let them go. He needs to follow his dreams and take the opportunity that he has been given. I won't let him feel guilty for leaving me behind. It will hurt like hell, but I will walk away for Wyatt to walk towards the start of a successful career. I make it to the door and I am getting ready to turn the handle to leave when I feel Wyatt close in behind me. He places both his hands against the door, trapping me against it so that I can't get it open. I feel his hard, strong body pressed against my back. He is so close his warm breath flies across the back of my neck sending shivers throughout my entire body. He leans over my right shoulder and starts placing light, tender kisses up my neck toward my ear. Then he whispers, "Say it again." My mind is clouded with only thoughts of Wyatt at the moment and how he is making my body feel. He continues kissing my neck. I am weak in the knees and will collapse soon if he continues the pleasurable torture.

"Say it again, Suzanna, I need to hear you say it," he whispers again.

My shaky voice manages to croak out, "I love you, Wyatt...I love you." Upon hearing those words, his hands wrap around my waist reaching for the bottom hem of my shirt. Before I know what has happened, my shirt is up over my head and tossed onto the floor beside us. Wyatt then caresses my stomach with both hands, sliding them down to the button of my jeans. With nimble fingers, he unbuttons my jeans and quickly pushes them, along with my panties, down my thighs, knees, and calves until they are a puddle at my feet. I manage to get untangled from the leg of my jeans, just as Wyatt's hands make their way back up my body, cupping my ass on the way up my back to unhook my bra strap. His kisses continue up my back and over my shoulders. I feel physical pain when his hands leave me briefly to get himself undressed. I am still facing the door and Wyatt is now naked behind me. I am relieved when I feel Wyatt's touch soon again. His hands come around my waist and travel down toward the throbbing between my legs. His fingers dance over my wet folds, making me moan in anticipation. I can feel his body's reaction which is evident by his hard length now pressed against my backside. I pushed my hips backwards to feel him and get closer. Now my hands are pressed against the door trying to sturdy myself and keep from falling into a puddle on the floor. We are urgent to find each other after my revelation of love. Wyatt's hands brace my hips, pulling me backwards towards him. He leans over me, his chest lying across my back and his lips near my ear.

His breathing is heavy when he says, "Oh Suzanna, I love you, too. So much." Then he enters me from behind with a hard thrust, filling me with his love. He glides in and out of me until we both simultaneously find our release. If Wyatt didn't have both his arms wrapped securely around my waist, I would have collapsed right there on the floor. Pulling out of my body, Wyatt turns me around to face him and gives me the most delicious kiss I have ever received. We are both desperate to hang onto this moment and the few more we will share before being separated by thousands of miles. I can't bring myself to think about that right now. I am completely happy to be just where I am, wrapped up in the arms of the man I love.

A couple of hours later, we are lying together tangled in the sheets of Wyatt's bed. He made sweet, tender love to me again, after the animalistic sex at the front door. Both have left me satisfied, but exhausted. I am, also, very hungry. I have not eaten a bite since lunch and it is now approaching ten o'clock at night. Wyatt is flat on his back and I am lying beside him with my head resting on his chest. When I hear his stomach growl, I know he is hungry too.

"Hey, where were you going when I surprised you at the door?" I ask.

"Actually, I was going out to get a bite to eat. But you sidetracked me and satisfied my hunger," Wyatt teases happily.

"Well, I may have satisfied your sexual hunger, but your stomach is screaming to be fed." Wyatt laughs knowing I have heard his stomach growling.

"Come to think of it I am starving, for food."

"Me, too. Want to order a pizza? I don't feel like getting dressed and going out to get anything," I say.

Wyatt pulls me on top of him, our naked bodies pressing together again. "I wasn't about to let you get dressed and leave my apartment anytime soon! So, going out is completely out of the question." He kisses me firmly on the lips. "I'll get my phone and a menu and order something for us right now. Be back in a second!" Wyatt kisses me again before he leaves the bed.

I snuggle back under the covers and watch Wyatt as he walks around the front of the bed in all his naked glory. Man, he is gorgeous. His lean, toned muscles ripple with each step he takes. I ogle every inch of his defined chest and work my eyes down to his flat abs that narrow at the hips. Sneaking a glance even further down, I appreciate his long cock, which is semi aroused. The man is never completely satisfied when I am in his close proximity. That brings a smile to my face that I am solely responsible for making his body react that way. I immediately bring my eyes back to his face when I hear Wyatt chuckle.

"You like the view? If you don't quit looking at me like that, we may never get that pizza ordered." My face flushes with embarrassment. I wave Wyatt out the room before I can eye fuck him anymore. Thirty minutes later our pizza has been delivered. I throw on one of Wyatt's t-shirts and walk out into the kitchen.

"Hey, I think there are a few beers in the fridge. How about grab two for us and I'll get the plates," Wyatt says. Wyatt places the pizza box on the coffee table in front of the couch so I assume we are eating there. I grab the beers and head over to the couch. I am famished and can't wait to eat. Wyatt joins me with the plates and we immediately dig in. After a few slices, I am stuffed. I watch Wyatt continue to eat. How can he make eating pizza look so damn sexy?

"So," Wyatt says after swallowing his last bite, "not that I'm complaining, but what brought you to the realization that you are in love with me?"

"A nightmare," I blurt out. The look on Wyatt's face is priceless. I can't hold back the smirk that is breaking across my face.

"What? A nightmare?" Wyatt questions.

"It's not what you think. After you left this afternoon, I cried myself to sleep. Next thing I know, Chloe wakes me up from my bad dream. I dreamt about that night." Wyatt's expression although still puzzled also shows signs of concern. He knows exactly what night I dreamt about.

"Chloe said that I was talking in my dream, the usual words like 'stop, no, don't'. But then, she told me the last word I screamed before she woke me was your name." Wyatt wipes his greasy pizza hands with his napkin before cupping them around my face.

"Oh baby, I'm so sorry, I should have been there with you."

Needing to explain further, I go on. "No, you see that's just it. You were there for me that night. You were my savior. I haven't had a bad dream about that night in a long time. I guess you have always been in my life since that night in some capacity. We were just friends up until recently. But when you walked out the door today, I thought I had lost you forever. My dream helped me realize that no matter where you are, I will always scream your name. I need you Wyatt. And I love you." Wyatt is quiet for a moment, deep in his own thoughts.

Then he whispers something I almost don't hear. "I don't have to go, Suzanna."

Shaking my head fervently, I say, "No, you're going to New York. Don't you even think about giving that up," I demand. "Look, it's going to be so hard not having you nearby, but I would never ask you to give up something this important for me. I don't want you to look back on our relationship with what ifs and resent me later in life. Sure, I'm going to miss you like crazy, but we can make this work."

Wyatt hugs me fiercely. "Oh Suz, I'm going to miss you, too. Leaving you will be the hardest thing I'll ever have to do. But I was serious when I told you I am doing this for our future. You are my future, Suzanna. I've waited years to make you mine, and now that you are, I'm not going to let anything get in the way of us, I promise." And then he seals that promise with a kiss.

"Wait a minute, you waited years? For me? What does that mean?" I ask Wyatt.

He shrugs, "I've wanted you since that night, or maybe even before, but especially since that night. I saw how hurt you were and I just wanted to help you heal. But then you were gone, and I didn't want to make things worse than they already were. Plus, I knew you were having a hard time with the Patrick breakup. So I hung in there and continued to be your friend, hoping that one day you could see it as more. Lucky for me, you finally did. It just sucks that it happened when you might be traveling the country on the professional tour and I'll be in New York. What the hell took you so long woman?"

Wow, I had no idea Wyatt had feelings for me other than friend-ship until just recently. He is obviously a very patient man. "Well, good things come to those who wait, right?" I tease. Wyatt's eyes turn from playful to lustful. He pushes me flat on my back against the cushions of the couch and presses his body over mine.

"You are most certainly a very good thing and worth every minute of the wait." And with that, we satisfy our other hunger, again.

Chapter Seventeen

(Present Day)

I spend almost every night with Wyatt before graduation. When he is working, I keep myself busy at home packing my things to move to the beach for the summer. Luckily, I need just need my clothes and golf equipment. The beach house is fully furnished and I am leaving my furniture in Columbia so if Chloe decides to get a new roommate, she or he can just move in. Thursday night Wyatt and I go to watch Chloe bring the house down in her leading role of the drama department's end of the semester production. She is fabulous! I know it won't be long before some talent scout snatches her up and she makes a name for herself. Brian does an excellent job as producer and director of the play. He also receives a standing ovation and high praises from his professors. We all meet up for drinks at The Blue Marlin. The bar is busy tonight, so we decide to get a table in the dining area instead. I feel bad that we chose The Blue Marlin since tonight is Wyatt's night off. He spends so much time here already. But he doesn't mind, plus he says our bill will be discounted since he is an employee. Chloe and Brian ramble on and on about the production and its success. I know they both have put in a lot of hard work and they are relieved that it is finally over. I'm a little nervous that Brian will mention being Chloe's date to Patrick's engagement party. I have yet to tell Wyatt about the invitation and that I will be attending. There never seems to be a good time to bring it up and I haven't wanted to spoil the little time we have left to spend together before the summer. Brian and Chloe spot some friends from the drama school over at the bar and leave our table to join them.

"Hey, you ready to get out of here?" I ask Wyatt with a wicked smile on my lips. I am so ready to jump in bed with this man.

"More than you know!" he replies kissing my neck sending shivers of anticipation of what is to come later tonight. "Let's go up to the bar to pay the bill. It'll be faster that way." He grabs my hand and pulls me up out of my seat to follow him.

When we get to the bar, I am surprised to see Bridgett there. I still feel badly about the mean things I said about her during our last visit here, even though I apologized profusely and she accepted. She is talking to a co-worker of Wyatt's and they seem pretty chummy. Well good, at least she won't be flirting with Wyatt if she has set her sights on someone else. I walk up to Bridgett to say hello.

"Hi Bridgett, how are you tonight?" Bridgett turns and looks at me with a guilty expression. Seeming to compose herself she embraces me in a quick hug.

"Oh hi, Suzanna. Good to see you. Are you here to see Wyatt?"

"Well, actually I'm here with Wyatt. We just went to watch Chloe in her performance and came by to grab some dinner before heading home. Are you here with anyone?"

The bartender that Bridgett has been talking to overhears us and throws his comment our way. "Bridgett's always here, she's a regular." Huh, that's odd. Wyatt hasn't mentioned running into Bridgett again after her failed attempts to seduce him. Guess he finds her pathetic still hanging around after being rejected. Maybe she just likes the bar scene and especially likes bartenders. Wyatt comes over to where we are standing and Bridgett looks like a child on Christmas morning. Whoa, does she still have the hots for him even after he chose me over her slutty self? My bitchy side is back. Bridgett just seems to bring out that side of me. Feeling the need be extra aggressive, I reach up to press a big, wet kiss on Wyatt's lips.

"Bridgett, you remember Wyatt, right? My boyfriend."

Bridgett barely glances back at me, focusing solely on Wyatt. "Hi Wyatt, so good to see you again. I'm surprised you're not working tonight," Bridgett says flashing him a big bright smile.

"Good to see you Bridgett. I'm off tonight, spending some quality time with my sweetie." Ahh, I love this man.

"Well, I just thought you were on the schedule tonight. I must have been mistaken." Okay, so this is stalker territory. Is she calling the restaurant and planning her 'regular' visits around Wyatt's schedule? Unbelievable! I hear someone calling Wyatt's name from the end of the bar. I glance that way to see one of the other bartenders waving Wyatt's credit card and receipt at him.

"Wyatt your check's ready, just need your signature, man." I watch as Wyatt leans over the bar to get his credit card and sign the receipt, admiring his backside. I catch Bridgett admiring him as well, and that just pisses me off. But what really gets my anger boiling is what I hear, next. Wyatt is speaking to the bartender who is cashing us out.

"Man, thanks again for covering for me tonight. Let me know if you need me to work a shift for you before I leave."

"No problem, Wyatt. I needed the extra tips anyway." Wyatt has just confirmed that he was on the schedule tonight and Bridgett knew he was supposed to be here tonight as an employee.

"Ready, Suz?" Wyatt asks as he wraps his arm around my waist to walk me to the door. I tense at his touch. I shouldn't be mad at him, but something isn't adding up. If Bridgett has been stalking him, then she probably is here each night he has worked and he hasn't mentioned a word to me. This is all too strange. My mood continues to go down the tubes when I hear Bridgett's voice.

"Well, goodnight Suzanna. Good luck this summer with golf." Then her voice takes on a sugary, syrupy quality. "Night Wyatt, guess I'll see you around." I don't even respond, just turn and walk out of the door leaving Wyatt to follow.

"Whoa, wait up Suz. You in a hurry?" I hear Wyatt ask as I reach the car.

"Let's just go!" I spit out through gritted teeth. Instead of walking to the driver's side, Wyatt walks over to me and leans me against the car door.

"Hey, what's wrong?" he asks.

"Bridgett! That's what's wrong." I can't hold it in any longer. "How often does she come up and hang out at the bar?" Wyatt looks dumbfounded.

"I don't know, maybe a couple of time a week. Why?" Is he blind? Doesn't he see what she is up too?

"Well, she was surprised to learn that you weren't working tonight, which I learned you were in fact on the schedule, but had switched with someone else. I think she only comes to the bar when you're on the clock. I think she may be stalking you."

Wyatt lets out a whooping laugh. I really don't think any of this is funny. "Suzanna, I don't think she is stalking me. I wouldn't know because I barely speak to her when she comes in. I and the other bartenders are usually so busy we don't really have much time for chit chat. Besides, I'm in such a hurry to finish work I can't concentrate on anything other than getting home to you. You are all I think about." Okay, so maybe I have overreacted, but Bridgett still pisses me off. I trust Wyatt and I know he loves me. He wouldn't jeopardize what we have for someone as meaningless as Bridgett. My body seems to relax at his words of reassurance. Maybe my insecurities are getting the best of me since we have so few days left to spend together before the move.

Wrapping my arms around Wyatt's neck I say, "I'm sorry, but girls like Bridgett just get under my skin. They're only out for one thing. I don't want to spend anymore of my time worrying about Bridgett." I kiss Wyatt hard letting him know he is mine, and no one else can have him. "Let's go home, Wyatt. I want you to make love to me." I have never seen Wyatt move so fast. Before I know it, he shoves me in the passenger seat, runs around and jumps in the driver's seat, and pulls out on the street, barreling through downtown. We make it to his place in record time. Then, he shows me that the only woman that exists for him is me.

Chapter Eighteen

(Present Day)

I wake up the day of graduation wrapped up in Wyatt's arms. He worked last night, and although I tried to stay awake for him to come join me in my bed, I had been exhausted from packing and guess I just fell asleep. I can tell he is still sleeping, his breathing steady and even. I wish I could stay like this forever. It feels wonderful waking up with him right beside me, protecting me and loving me. We have not been cohabiting for very long. We don't even live together. But we usually end up at his place or mine every night. We are trying to make the most of the few days we have left together before the distance up the east coast separates us. I am really going to miss this when I move to the beach and he moves to New York. Pushing my sadness aside, I'm not going to dwell on unhappy thoughts today. This is my graduation day after all. I am going to enjoy it. I have spent the last four years studying and playing golf and that really is the extent of all my activities. I haven't had the typical college experience of frat parties and mindless hook ups. I didn't even date anyone more than once or twice. No, I really have just cut myself off from the socialized world to concentrate on studying and golf. How ironic, now that I am leaving my college years behind that I would find love. The door on my college experience is closing but the door on a romantic relationship is opening. I guess that old saying is true, you know, when one door closes another one opens.

I am startled from my thoughts when I feel Wyatt's strong warm hands began to move up and down my body caressing my bare skin. I hope this door never closes.

"Good morning, sunshine," Wyatt says while his breath on the back of my neck ignites all my nerve endings. I turned over so that we are now face to face.

"Good morning. I'm sorry I wasn't awake when you got home last night," I say in between giving him kisses all over his face.

"That's okay. I got off later than usual. It was a busy night with all the out of town guests in for graduation. Speaking of graduation, you excited?" Getting as close as our bodies will allow, I pull him in tight.

"I'm more excited about waking up with you in my bed this morning." Wyatt's smile turns devious as his hands explore more of me under the sheets. He pushes his hips towards me and chuckles.

"As you can feel, you're not the only one excited this morning!" I giggle at his comment.

"Well, we'll have to do something about all this excitement." Wyatt pushes me on my back and kisses me passionately. All thoughts of graduation and moving escape me. The only thing on my mind is Wyatt and how incredible he makes me feel. He makes me feel completely wanted, something I haven't felt in over four years.

After a mind blowing love making session, Wyatt and I are still snuggling together in the sheets. I am lying beside him grinning like an idiot. I hope Chloe didn't hear us during the last thirty minutes. Wyatt always seems to make my inhibitions and shyness fly out of the window. Thinking back, I was a little vocal. Oh God, Chloe probably did hear us and I will never hear the end of it. Glancing over at the clock I realize what time it is.

"Oh shit, Wyatt you have to go!" I shout.

"Is that any way to treat me after all the things I just did to you?" Wyatt teases still embracing me in his arms.

"Wyatt, my parents. They'll be here any minute. Plus, I really need to shower. I can't concentrate on graduation with your smell all over me."

Wyatt laughs. "I like putting my smell all over you. Actually, I'd like to do it again." I am trying really hard to keep a straight face while pushing away from him. Truthfully, I'd really like him to do everything with me again, but there just isn't time.

"Really, Wyatt. I have to get ready and you have to go. How the hell would I explain you to my parents, especially when they find you in my bed?" I say starting to get a little nervous.

"You haven't told them about us yet?" Wyatt asks and I can hear the disappointment in his voice.

"No, I am going to tell them today. I haven't really talked to them all that much." Wyatt smiles, but it doesn't reach his eyes. I know he is thinking I haven't said anything to my parents because I may be ashamed of us. Wyatt isn't a part of my family's elite circle of friends. His parents are hard working middle class people. Wyatt worked all during high school and college to support himself. His parents helped when they could, but Wyatt wasn't one hundred percent financially supported like me and Chloe and the rest of our crew. The social class system is still a part of every small southern town, ours included. Everyone knows whose parents are whose and what they do for a living. I don't really care, but I can't say the same for my parents. I have never dated outside our circle of friends so I'm not sure what they will think. Besides, I don't see Wyatt as any less than me. Wyatt holds the strongest work ethic of anyone I have ever known. He excels in his studies and is getting ready to graduate with a master's degree in international business from one of the top programs in the country. Plus, the internship he has nabbed is coveted by all graduates in his field and he earned it all by himself. Wyatt is managing to make a splash in this world and jump a few levels on the social class structure. But all that is beside the point because regardless of what Wyatt does for a living, I love the man he is on the inside.

Needing to reassure him I say, "Wyatt, I love you and my parents will love you, too. I just haven't had time to tell them because I have been spending all my minutes with you. I'll tell them today, I promise. And then we can all have dinner after graduation." Wyatt seems to accept my answer pulling me in for another kiss. Before I can let this go any further, I push him away. "Don't make this hard for me, but I really need to kick you out of here now."

"Okay, okay I got it." Wyatt says releasing me from his possessive grip. I immediately feel the lost of his warm touch. I roll out of the bed and throw Wyatt his clothes so he can get dressed. I much prefer him in his birthday suit, but I don't need him streaking down my hallway and out my front door. What would the neighbors say?

"Hey Suz, what time will dinner be over?" Wyatt asks while pulling his shirt over his head.

"Looking forward to the end of dinner with my parents already are you? They're not that bad!" I exclaim.

"No, I just have a graduation gift for you and I would like to give it to you in private," Wyatt says fully dressed now.

"I thought you just gave me my graduation gift," referring to our intimate moment earlier this morning.

Wyatt snickers. "Oh honey, what I just gave you wasn't a graduation gift. That was a daily gift that I will keep on giving you as long as you'll have me."

Walking over to Wyatt, I wrap my hands around his neck and kiss him softly on his perfect lips. "Don't make me promises you can't keep, because I will never tire of your gifts," I tell him seriously.

Pulling me in closer for one last kiss, Wyatt says, "Good, because I don't plan to give anyone but you that gift for the rest of my life." We'll never leave my bedroom if he keeps talking to me like this. One last kiss and I push him out the door.

"We should be done by 9:00 and, hopefully, my parents will hit the road shortly after, so let's have my graduation party right here," motioning back towards my bed, "just you and me are invited."

"Suz, I can't wait. I'll bring the presents!"

Blowing him a kiss as I walk into the bathroom to start showering, I call out, "Bye Wyatt, love you."

"You too, have fun at graduation. I'll miss you! Can't wait for tonight!"

I jump in the shower as I hear the front door close. My heart breaks a little just from Wyatt's absence. But I am filled with anticipation of our night together and all of his gifts. I actually smile and let the shower take me away.

My parents arrive just as I finish getting dressed. I have chosen a simple black linen sheath dress. I will be a complete wrinkled mess by the time we get to dinner, but I don't care. Linen is a cool fabric and I can only imagine how hot the temperatures in the coliseum will be with the thousands of graduates and spectators crammed inside. Plus, I'll be covered by my graduation robe and cap. I hate that I have to wear that stupid graduation cap. I hear Chloe answer the door and let my parents inside. "Mr. and Mrs. Caulder, so good to see you. Y'all come on in." I hear my mom fussing over Chloe like she is her own daughter.

"My, Chloe, you get prettier every time we see you," my mom gushes. I can see Chloe now, eating up the compliments that are being thrown her way.

"Where's the girl of honor?" Dad asks looking around the house.

"She's still getting ready. She had a busy morning," Chloe says then laughs like it is an inside joke. I come barreling down the hall with narrowed eyes that are pointing daggers at Chloe. She smiles very innocently, but I know she knows exactly how busy I was this morning. Like I said earlier, I'll never hear the end of this from her. Right now, I just need to shut her up before she gives out any more information to my parents.

"Mom, Dad," I shout as I make my way over to them. I give each of them big hugs. I love my parents dearly and haven't seen them since Easter weekend.

"Oh honey, you look lovely. We are so proud of you!" Mom says pulling me back from my hug to take a once over of my appearance. Appearances are a big deal to both of them. Guess that's why both me and Flynn have always looked like the all American kids, dressed in LL bean and Polo clothing. Thinking of Flynn I suddenly notice he isn't with my parents.

"Where's Flynn?" I ask.

"Now Suzanna, Flynn is so busy finishing exams and doing all that extra soccer conditioning for this summer overseas, he just couldn't get away. He feels terrible about it, but he said he'd be sure to call you later," Dad answers. I'm a little disappointed that my only brother won't be here to see me graduate from college. But I understand. I mean, who really wants to sit through hours of hearing random names called just to see one person walk across the stage to receive a piece of paper. That's exactly why I told Wyatt not to bother coming to the ceremony. He has too much to do before leaving for New York anyway, and he could take the three plus hours to get them done and we'd celebrate together afterwards, in private. A smile creeps across my face just thinking of Wyatt.

"My Suzanna, I thought you would take the news about Flynn a little harder," Mom says when she notices my uncontrollable smile.

"Oh, I'm sad he's not here, but I'm happy about his soccer success and the fact that he is so dedicated. Plus, we'll catch up at the beach before he leaves for Europe." I am totally lying knowing Wyatt put that smile on my face, not Flynn's dedication to soccer.

"That's my girl, always thinking positive," Dad exclaims. Chloe looks more disappointed at Flynn's absence than me and I laugh at her. She pouts, but then recovers quickly. We chat a bit more before I have to leave. I need to arrive an hour early to get in line with the graduates. Chloe has offered to drive my parents to the ceremony and we'll meet up afterwards for dinner.

Thinking of dinner, "Mom, since Flynn's not here for dinner and we have reservations for five people, would you mind if I invited someone to join us?" Mom and Dad both look at me like I have grown an extra head. They are not used to me inviting people to join our close knit group. I have always been surrounded by my family and close friends and that has been enough for me the last few years. Mom speaks with a surprised tone in her voice.

"Well, sure Suzanna, we'd love for one of your friends to join us." I want to say this unexpected guest is definitely more than a friend but I'll leave that conversation for later.

"Great!" is all I say.

"Mind telling us who will be joining us for dinner?" Mom asks intrigued. Guess I can't wait until after the ceremony to fill them in.

"Do you remember Wyatt McCain? He's from Florence originally." Mom and Dad look lost in thought like they are racking their brains trying to place Wyatt.

Dad finally responds. "Isn't he the guy who used to bartend in the lounge at the country club?"

"Yes, that's him. I'd like to ask him to join us for dinner." Mom and Dad still look thoroughly confused. Chloe joins the conversation sensing I need some help.

"Wyatt lives here in Columbia and we have all remained close friends." Mom exhales a breath that she has been holding.

"Well, we'd love for him to join us." I feel like I should say more but I really need to leave. Grabbing my keys, I give Mom and Dad another swift hug.

"Next time I see you guys, I'll be a college graduate." I squeal. Mom and Dad are not accustomed to me squealing and being so chipper. Chloe hugs me before I can slip out of the door.

"Hey, thanks for the save earlier about Wyatt," I whisper.

"Yeah, no problem. I can't wait for dinner tonight, should be very entertaining. By the way, your parents seem to have noticed the changes in you. Don't think you'll go unscathed tonight." Sighing, I know the inevitable is looming. I'll have to confess that my relationship with Wyatt is more than platonic.

"I know, but try to keep your mouth shut, please." Chloe swats me on the back and pushes me to leave. "Will do. And Suz, I'm proud of you, too!"

The ceremony is long and boring. My few seconds of fame happen in the blink of the eye. I walk across the stage, shake the university president's hand as they call my name. I receive my diploma and it is over. Too bad I have to sit for another hour while the rest of the graduates do the exact same thing. After the ceremony, I am met with hugs and kisses from my parents and Chloe. Most grads might be ashamed that only three people came to watch them graduate. I just don't care. I am done with college and ready to start the rest of my life. I should be terrified. I don't have a job waiting for me, like some of the graduates. Nor am I enrolled in a master's program to accumulate more higher learning degrees. I am planning to play golf all summer and live at the beach. It probably sounds more like a vacation to some, but I know I will be working my tail off to win that qualifying round and make it on the professional golf circuit. I am also excited about finally having someone other than my family and Chloe to share things with. I have Wyatt in my life now and he is everything. Just the thought of him sends shivers running up and down my spine. I can't wait to see him soon for the family dinner.

Just I as am about to send him a text telling him I am on my way to pick him up, I see him out of the corner of my eye. He is standing off to the side looking dashing in dress pants and a sports coat. Even though I told him not to come, he somehow managed to see the ceremony and is here to congratulate me. He is across the lawn of the coliseum and is walking towards us, in a slow sexy way. It's like my body is magnetically pulled towards him because I completely turn away from my parents and Chloe who are in a full blown conversation and start walking towards him. My walking turns to running when I decide that I can't wait any longer to be in his arms. I finally reach him and throw my arms and legs around him in a very un-lady like fashion. But I don't care. I am so glad he is here. He doesn't have time to even say anything before my mouth covers his in a full on kiss. The kiss is a tad inappropriate to have in public. Realizing that we are being stared at, my parents included, I finally pull away.

"You're here," I say breathless looking at Wyatt face to face.

"Of course, Suz. I had to see my girl graduate, even though you begged me not to come." I feel guilty for telling not to come and share in this moment, but I was trying to help him manage his time. Looking back, I probably should have just insisted he be here.

"I'm so glad you're here. It didn't seem right that you weren't. I'm sorry I told you not to come." I am standing in front of him now, but our arms are still around each other.

"I wouldn't have missed it for the world!"

Mom, Dad and Chloe are walking over to join us. I guess the cat is out of the bag by now. Dad makes a low cough in his throat when they get close, letting us in on their arrival. I unwrap myself from Wyatt and turn to face my parents.

"Mom, Dad, this is Wyatt McCain. He will be joining us for dinner." As if that is all the explanation they deserve. Do they really need more after that public display of affection? Chloe starts to giggle, but quickly shuts it off when she sees the looks on my parents' faces. Stunned disbelief may be a good way to describe them. We stand in silence for a few seconds before Wyatt finally takes the initiative.

"Mr. and Mrs. Caulder, it's so good to see you again. It has been years," Wyatt says and extends his hand towards my father. My father shakes Wyatt's hand, but still doesn't find his words.

Mom recovers more quickly. "Well, Wyatt, it's nice to see you, too. I didn't realize you and my daughter were, um, so close." Wyatt glances over at me with a smile.

"Suzanna and I have been friends for a long time. We just decided to take our relationship to the next level." I am just as stunned as my parents now. I didn't realize Wyatt would be so honest and forthcoming in the first conversation he had with my parents. Not that he had any choice considering our embrace and kiss they just witnessed. It should have been me to explain to my parents that Wyatt and I are a couple, but I am a coward. I chickened out earlier at the house before the ceremony. I hope Wyatt doesn't hold that against me. He was already shocked when I revealed earlier to him that my parents had no idea I was in a relationship. I need to save this moment, and fast.

"I told my parents at the house that you would be joining us for the celebratory graduation dinner. Is everyone ready to go?" I blurt out, wanting to escape the coliseum parking lot and this whole conversation.

"Yes, I'm ready and I'm starving. Come on, Mr. and Mrs. Caulder. I'll drive you to the restaurant and Wyatt and Suz can meet us there," Chloe states, coming to my rescue again. I mouth a silent 'thank you' her way and she smiles. Mom and Dad, finally, are able to come out of their temporary coma and follow Chloe to the car. I watch as they walk across the street, drilling Chloe with questions I should be answering. Sighing, I glance back up at Wyatt who is just looking at me.

"You ready for this?" I ask, more for myself than for him.

"Yes, come on. Let's go get this over with so we can get to our private party." Oh yes, that celebration I am definitely looking forward to. I can suffer through dinner with my parents for hours, knowing Wyatt and I will be alone together tonight.

Chapter Nineteen

(Present Day)

Dinner actually goes really well. I don't know what Chloe told Mom and Dad during their car ride over to the restaurant but they don't seem so shocked to see me with Wyatt as something other than friends. Wyatt is pleasant and kind to my parents, answering all of their questions. Of course, they ask about his family surely wanting to make some type of connection to his Florence roots. But they don't know his parents on a social or professional level. They ask him about school, and Wyatt just answers that he is working on his master's degree. Wyatt doesn't feel the need to brag about his latest achievements. He wants my parents to like him for him, not because he is being recruited by one of the top brokerage firms on the east coast. I love that about Wyatt. He doesn't use jobs and talent to try to score with other people. As far as I am concerned, he doesn't need to. If anyone can see Wyatt the way I see him, then they too would fall in love with him. Once dinner is over, and Wyatt finally concedes to let my dad pick up the check, we exit from the restaurant.

"Wyatt, it was a pleasure to get to know you. You seem to be a nice, young man," Mom says. Dad just shakes his hand and nods in agreement. Chloe comes to the rescue once again today and ushers my parents to the car, giving Wyatt and me a minute alone.

"Hey, thanks for coming today, to the ceremony and dinner. It means a lot to me."

Wyatt hugs me and kisses my cheek. "Don't you know yet that I want to be anywhere you are, Suz." I lay my head on his chest and we just stand there on the sidewalk outside the restaurant in a close embrace. The emotions of the day have finally caught up to me and I can't hold back the tears that escape my eyes. Wyatt pulls back and places his finger under my chin so that I can meet him eye to eye.

"Oh baby, what's wrong?" he asks suddenly concerned. I try to smile as he wipes my tears away.

"I know exactly how you feel because I feel the exact same way. I guess I am just thinking about our upcoming summer and how devastating it is going to be being away from you," I say through a now uncontrollable sob. Wyatt continues to hug me tightly.

"I don't like it any more than you, but we can do this. Plus, I think I might be able to put a smile on your face when I give you that graduation gift I promised."

Thinking that he is referring to sex, I snort. "You always put a smile on my face when we are intimate."

He laughs, "Not that gift silly. The one you haven't opened yet!" Oh, he really does have a gift for me.

Finally able to compose myself, I look at Wyatt, "I can't wait, but first I have to get rid of my parents. I'm going to owe Chloe big time." Wyatt laughs knowing I am so right about Chloe.

"Why don't you ride with them to get your car and text me once they leave? Okay?" Knowing it won't take too long, I agree to Wyatt's plan, although it is hard to tear myself away from his warm, strong embrace. He places a kiss on the top of my head. "I'll see you later Suzanna." Then he turns and walks in the opposite direction. I walk back to Chloe's car with a silly grin plastered across my face, just thinking about receiving all of Wyatt's gifts.

Once we are back at the house the inquisition begins. My parents are relentless with their questions about Wyatt. "Suz, I didn't even know you were dating anyone. Last time we were together was Easter, and you were single. How long has this been going on?" Mom asks.

"Wyatt and I have been friends since high school, Mom. It's not like we just met! We decided to take things beyond friendship about a month ago." I can see Mom calculating the weeks in her head since Easter. She would kill me if I had been dating Wyatt then and kept it from her.

"So, how serious is this thing with Wyatt?" Dad asks. I hate him calling my relationship with Wyatt 'this thing'.

"It's a relationship Dad, and it's pretty darn serious," I say a little more loudly than I intended.

"I don't really think it's a good idea to start a serious relationship right now. You have to concentrate all your energy on golf this summer. I don't want that boy getting in the way of your goal, Suzanna." Dad is using his stern voice now.

"Wyatt would never get in the way of anything, Dad. He totally supports me in my choice to pursue a professional golf career," I almost yell.

"Well, what does he plan to do while you are golfing every day? Don't tell me he wants to be your caddy. Will he be working on his tan?"

"Dad! Do you hear yourself? You sound like a stuck up snob!" This, I do yell. I don't think I have ever yelled at my dad before. It is kind of exhilarating and terrifying at the same time.

Mom interrupts before things get out of control. "Suzanna, your dad has your best interests at heart, even though he is doing a terrible job showing it." She pushes Dad aside and comes to sit by me on the couch. "Honey, it was just such a shock to us both seeing you and Wyatt together, romantically. We haven't seen you with anyone like that since, um, Patrick." I know this is hard for Mom. She never really understood why Patrick and I stopped seeing each other. I couldn't tell her the truth, so I kept it as vague as possible, just telling her that Patrick and I were taking a break to finish high school. I told her we decided to remain friends, although we never hung out again. I know my mother wasn't naïve enough to believe that something didn't happen that caused the break up, but she never pushed for more concrete answers. "We're just worried about you. You were so hurt last time," looking back at my father, both of them remembering how depressed their daughter had been after things went down with Patrick. "We just don't want to see you go through something like that again."

I understand that they are scared. I am actually still a little afraid, but I know Wyatt is worth the risk. Seeing the concern in both my parents' eyes, I surged on. "Mom and Dad, I know you worry about me, but honestly I haven't felt this happy in a very long time. Wyatt makes me happy. He came into my life and opened my heart when it had been closed for so long. I didn't want to let him in, but he managed to change my mind. I know that love involves the risk of being hurt, but I am willing_"

Before I can finish my sentence, Dad erupts. "Did you say love? Oh dear God, Carol what has gotten into our daughter?" Mom looks just as stunned as Dad. I guess my last statement was a little too much information.

"Suzanna, don't you think this relationship has moved a tad bit too fast for you to be throwing around the "L" word?" She won't even say love, like it is a bad word. Come to think of it, how many people really fall in love in a month's time? I don't know the answer to that question, but I am one of those people who fall into that category.

"I can't help it that I love him. I know it all seems so fast, but we feel the exact same way about each other. He loves me, too. Besides, don't you want me to find love, like you and Dad have?" I ask.

"Oh honey, of course we do. We just want you to be careful." I realize telling them that my love relationship is going long distance very soon is probably not a good idea at this precise moment. Wonder if that would bring them some contentment, knowing Wyatt will be states away from me? Or will it cause them to worry more about me getting hurt? There is only one way to find out.

"Dad, you asked what Wyatt is going to do this summer. He is, actually, moving to New York next week. He got one of the five coveted spots to intern at Galloway and Meads brokerage firm. He leaves next Tuesday." Mom and Dad are quiet for a moment. I figure Dad is trying to decide whether to congratulate me or console me. Mom just has a look of concern on her face.

"Well, that's quite an achievement for Wyatt. How do you feel about it, though?" Dad asks in a softer voice.

"I'm okay. I will miss him terribly, but he is doing this for our future. Plus, I will be able to practice all the golf I need for the qualifying round. See, Dad, I had it all worked out before you went on this tirade." I am teasing him now, but he remains stoic.

"Suz, are you sure that you and Wyatt can withstand a long distance relationship? Not being able to see each other can be hard," Mom inquires.

"We've talked about it and we think we can make it. I know it will be hard. But honestly, outside of golf, I haven't cared about anything more than making this work with Wyatt. I just want you two to be happy for me." Mom and Dad seem to realize that I am indeed happy, in a large part due to Wyatt. They haven't seen me open up in so long and it probably tickles them pink to know I still care about something other than golf.

"Well, you're a big girl now, Suz. A college grad, in fact. I guess we need to trust you to make your own decisions." Even though Dad is still not giving his entire blessing where Wyatt is concerned, he is letting me know he won't interfere.

Mom hugs me and says, "Suzanna, all we care about is your happiness. And I guess if Wyatt makes you this happy, then we will support you both. Plus, you are beautiful when you're this happy. I could tell the minute I walked through that door and saw you. I knew something was different, and whatever it was, I liked it." I smile at both my parents. They really do love me and want what is best. After the Wyatt conversation ends, we talk about the summer. I tell them of my plans to head down to the beach later this week, probably on Wednesday to get settled in. Dad has arranged for me to meet with my coach for the summer on Thursday and play a few rounds. I tell them I will be back in Columbia on Sunday to spend some time with Wyatt before taking him to the airport Tuesday morning.

Mom looks cautious before asking, "Will Wyatt be joining you for Patrick's engagement party?"

"No. He has some loose ends to tie up here, plus he is working all weekend. He has to train the new guy who will be replacing him," I inform her. However, I don't let her know that I have intentionally not asked Wyatt to be my date to the party. I still don't know why I haven't even said anything to him, but for some reason I deeply believe it is the best decision to keep quiet. Mom seems to accept my answer about Wyatt working all weekend and lets it go.

Minutes later, Mom and Dad say their goodbyes, giving hugs to both Chloe and myself. Mom is a little misty eyed when she leaves. I don't know if it is because her daughter has crossed a major milestone today by graduating college, or could she be crying over the information that I have, finally, given myself the ability to enjoy a romantic relationship again. I don't know for certain, but I bet it is both. When they finally pull out of the driveway headed for I-20 east to Florence, relief floods me. I hadn't anticipated their reaction to my relationship with Wyatt to cause so much distress. I need to call in more frequently from here on out and settle my mom's nerves about my love life. Collapsing on the couch, I am grateful when Chloe joins me with two glasses of wine.

"I'd like to make a toast to the newest University of South Carolina graduate and my best friend. Here's to you, Suz!" We clink our glasses together and take a sip.

"I should be toasting you. You saved my ass more than once today with my parents. Thank you!" I say.

"Don't mention it. How did your parents take the information about you and Wyatt? Don't think there was any mistaking you two as friends after what happened at the graduation." I blush just thinking about our PDA outside the coliseum.

"They were shocked, to say the least, but I think they enjoy seeing me happy after years of being alone. I think they will come to love Wyatt." I hope that will be the case anyway.

"Well, I think once the shock wears off, they'll come around," Chloe says giving me her vote of confidence.

"I'm surprised I got to wait until after the ceremony to tell them about Wyatt. I thought your comment this morning was going to give me away."

Chloe starts giggling. "Well, I'm surprised you still had the voice capacity to talk at all after your performance this morning. Didn't know you were so vocal, Suz!" My face is blood red with embarrassment. I knew Chloe had probably heard us this morning, but was I really that loud? Chloe's giggles have turned into a full blown doubling over laugh.

"This is so not funny, Chloe," I say trying to hide my smile.

"Oh yes it is, you should see how red your face is now."

"Ugh, you're never gonna let me live this down, are you?"

"Not in this lifetime!" Chloe says through snorts of laughter.

Letting my confidence win out over my embarrassment, I surprise the hell of out Chloe. "Well, you better get used to the noise because Wyatt is coming over soon for our private graduation celebration." Taking a sip of my wine, I look at Chloe who has stopped laughing and is stunned into silence. Now it is my turn to laugh. "I never thought I would see Chloe Ryder speechless!" Chloe laughs again with me as we finish our glasses of wine. I text Wyatt to let him know the coast is clear and wait for him to come over. Chloe graciously decides to join Brian and some of his friends at an on campus grad party giving Wyatt and me a little bit of privacy. I tell her she doesn't have to leave, but she assures me she has heard enough of my moans and groans for one day.

Chapter Twenty

(Present Day)

Feeling frisky and bold, I surprise Wyatt at the door wearing nothing, and I mean nothing, but my cap and gown. He stands there looking hotter than ever holding a dozen red roses, a bottle of wine and a gift wrapped in white paper. For the third time today, I have rendered someone speechless. First my parents, then Chloe and now Wyatt. I am on a roll. As Wyatt continues to just stand there with his jaw open, I lean against the door jam mustering all my inner sexy.

"Ready to get this party started?" Wyatt is suddenly brought back to his senses as he lunges forward dropping the flowers, wine and gift. He grabs me in his arms, my feet leaving the floor. Walking us inside, he closes the door with his foot and we make our way towards the couch. At least I think that is the direction we are heading, but I can't see because my face is buried in Wyatt's neck, kissing him along his jaw line. Finally at the couch, Wyatt sits down and pulls me on his lap. I am straddling him, my legs on either side of his hips. My lips leave his jaw line and find his mouth. He kisses me deeply opening my lips as our tongues dance with each other. My hips push forward against him sending warmth that spreads between my legs and to my core. I gasp each time my body brushes against his jeans and what is beginning to bulge inside of them. Wyatt's hands travel up to the inside of my gown and begin rubbing the small of my back. The gown only has a few clasps toward the top, so he has easy access to anything below my waist. Pulling one side of the gown all the way from the other side, Wyatt finds my breasts and massages them in his hands. Then, he pulls his mouth away from mine and begins making his way south. Soon his mouth has engulfed my nipple making me moan. His tongue circles the warm pink center around my nipple. He sucks and tickles my breast with his tongue and I am about to lose control. Flipping me over to my back, Wyatt continues to massage my breasts with his hands as his lips continue their southern decent. He kisses a circle around my navel, dipping his tongue inside. The fire inside me is raging. When his hands leave my breasts and wrap around my hips, I let out a louder moan. When his fingers find my wetness, I almost cry. He moves them up and down my sensitive folds until he finds my entrance and slips them inside of me.

"Oh, Wyatt...please." I am beyond caring that I am begging.

"Baby, I want to make you feel everything," Wyatt whispers against my skin. When his warm, wet lips find my sensitive area I scream his name. My hands are tangled in his thick, brown hair. My hips arch with each flick of his tongue. His fingers are still inside me, sliding in and out. Once he wraps his lips around my swollen clit, I lose all control and find my release. My body trembles as it bucks with every explosion. Before I completely come down from my ecstasy, Wyatt undresses from the waist down and lies atop of me. Needing his release, he wastes no time plunging into me.

"Oh God, Wyatt!" The words escape before he covers my mouth with his. Plunging deep in my mouth and between my legs, my body is rising again towards another mind-blowing orgasm. I feel Wyatt getting closer the minute his breathing becomes rushed and ragged. His thrusts become frantic and fast, pushing me, once again, over the edge. With one last deep thrust Wyatt screams my name as he fills me. Both breathless, we just lay there, our limbs tangled together in complete bliss. Once able to make a coherent sentence, I whisper to Wyatt.

"I love you." I can feel his lips curl into a smile against my skin.

"I love you, too Suzanna."

Later that night, we move the party into my bedroom. Thank goodness Chloe made herself scarce this evening. She would cringe at the noises I made earlier, and the fact that we made it only to the couch, before giving into our primal needs. Only Wyatt can make me feel this way and do these things. Sitting in bed, completely naked drinking the wine Wyatt brought (luckily it didn't break when he dropped it to get to me) we chat about the future. Wyatt is really excited about starting his new job in New York. I can't help but be excited for him. His excitement is contagious. But thinking about being away from each other the entire summer breaks my heart a little. Sensing that my good mood is being altered, Wyatt gently places his wine glass aside and exits the bedroom.

"Hey, where are you going?" Before he can answer, he is back holding my gift in his hands.

"Seems that I forgot to give you my gift earlier when I arrived."

Laughing, I tease. "Oh, you gave me your gift when you arrived. Actually, I remember receiving multiple gifts!" Wyatt snickers and makes his way back in the bed by my side.

"That's not the gift I'm referring to. Settle down you insatiable woman!" He places the wrapped gift box on the bed between our bodies. I look at the box and can't possibly imagine what is inside. Normally, boyfriends give girlfriends jewelry on special occasions. But this box is too large to contain a small piece of jewelry. The box is too small to contain any type of golf equipment which would be the only other thing I would want. I don't think a new club could fit into a medium sized rectangular box. Staring at the box, I have no clue what to expect when I open it. I don't make a move to even touch it because I am suddenly nervous. Wyatt watches me with amusement.

"You're trying to figure out what is in this, right?" I smile giving away that that is exactly what I am thinking. "I know you're having a hard time with the idea of us being away from each other this summer. I am too, more than you know. God, I'm going to miss you, Suzanna. Not being able to hold you, kiss you, and make you scream my name every day. It almost makes me want to give it all up and stay wherever you are. But I'm doing this for us. If I can insure a financial future for us, then you can go follow your dream of becoming a pro golfer without any worries or help from your family. I want to be the one to support you later. And this internship can guarantee that." I completely understand everything he is telling me. I am overwhelmed with emotions knowing that he wants to support me and give me my dreams. I will have to remember every word he just spoke to make it through the summer without his touch.

"Anyway, this gift can't change the fact that we can't see each other every day but I hope it will help us not wait until the end the summer to reunite. Here, go ahead and open it."

With shaky hands, I start tearing the paper from the box. When I open the lid, I see an envelope with the US Airways logo. Ripping the envelope open, I spot two roundtrip airline tickets in my name.

"I hope you like your gift and I really hope you use them. The dates are open so you can use them anytime this summer. I was hoping you could fly up during July fourth because I think I'll have some time off. I'll take you to see the city." Tears are running down my face as I hear Wyatt's words. He has purchased me the best present in the world. A chance to see him in New York not just once, but twice.

"Oh Wyatt, I love my gift! I can't wait to hop on a plane to come see you. God, I miss you already and you're not even gone." I place a soft tender kiss on his lips in appreciation of the gift. "You are so thoughtful and a very good man. I don't think I deserve you."

Wyatt is shaking his head back and forth in disagreement. Pressing his finger to my lips he whispers. "Shhh, that's nonsense. You deserve more than me. You deserve unlimited mulligans, not that you need them. You deserve a hole in one at The US Open. You deserve a gallery of fans screaming your name as you finish the 18th hole with a commanding lead. And you deserve a man who you are just as proud of as he is of you. I'm becoming that man. I'll work every day until my last breath being that man, because Suzanna, you deserve that."

Tears sting my eyes as each of Wyatt's tender words soak over my body. A sudden pang of guilt starts gnawing at my core. Here he is baring his soul to me, letting me know that I am the reason for his drive to succeed. He has become everything to me, but I continue to hide the fact that I am still seeking closure with Patrick. I need to come clean about the engagement party. I need to let Wyatt know that even though I am ninety-nine percent ready to give my everything to him, I have to close that chapter in my life that I have left open for over four years. But before I can confess, Wyatt pulls me into his arms. The security and safety of those arms keep all thoughts of Patrick away and I become consumed by my wanting and desire of the best man in my life.

"I love you Wyatt," I whisper between kisses. "You're all I will ever need, whether I deserve you or not." Wyatt shows me his love for hours that night until we finally fall asleep in each other's arms.

Chapter Twenty-One

(Present Day)

W aking the next morning, I feel like I have nothing to do. No classes to attend, since I am now a college graduate. No more packing, except for the toiletries and some personal items that can wait until the last minute. I have already packed my car with the heavier suitcases and my golf equipment earlier in the week. Wyatt is still sleeping soundly, so I take this opportunity to crawl out of bed and into the shower. As the water washes over me, an uncontrollable smile presents itself on my face. I am thinking back to last night and the emotions that Wyatt and I shared with each other. He really does love me. Strange that two people could feel so strongly about each other in such a short amount of time. I realize that Wyatt has probably felt something for me since high school, but never acted on his feelings because of Patrick. Even after years of friendship, Wyatt patiently waited until he knew I was ready to move things further. I wish I had realized what was right under my nose this whole time. I was too stubborn to see what a wonderful man Wyatt is until just recently and now our time together is ending soon. I will leave for the beach in a couple of days and Wyatt flies to New York the following Tuesday. Our month long romance will come to an abrupt halt. But our love will get us through and that is what will sustain me. Drying off my wet body with a towel, I hear Wyatt stir from the bedroom. Peeking my head around the bathroom door, I watch as Wyatt stretches his glorious muscles and yawns from a peaceful night of sleep.

"Good morning, good looking!" Wyatt tilts his head toward the bathroom and gives me his panty dropping grin.

"Well, good morning to you, too." Wyatt reaches for his boxers and lazily puts them on. I just stand there, wrapped in my towel enjoying the view. Wyatt walks over to me planting a kiss on my lips. The damp, cool feeling from the shower immediately evaporates and my body begins to heat from his touch. "Got any plans today?" Wyatt asks as his eyes roam down my body covered by just a towel.

"I was just thinking that I don't really have anything to do. How about you?" I ask.

"I've got some things to take care of before the move and a conference call with the brokerage firm to get final details before my arrival. I'll work again tonight, training the new guy, but that won't be until later. Looks like we can spend the majority of the day together," Wyatt says in a naughty voice, doing all sorts of things to my already revved up body.

"What time is the conference call?" I ask hoping we might get a little play time between the sheets in the very near future.

Wyatt glances at the clock and about loses it when he sees how late we slept. "Oh shit, I didn't realize how late it is. I should receive the call in about ten minutes." Pushing me aside so that he can enter the bathroom, Wyatt quickly turns the water on and jumps in. "I guess I'll take a quick shower and take the call here, if that's okay."

Laughing at his nervousness I reply, "Sure, that's fine. I'll get dressed and hang out in the living room to give you some privacy for the call. Just come get me when you're done."

I leave Wyatt to hurriedly finish showering and get dressed. I walk out and shut my bedroom door. Chloe is already up in the kitchen drinking her coffee. "Hi Chloe, did you have fun last night? Thanks, again, for the alone time you gave me and Wyatt."

Chloe nods and smiles. "Yeah, it was fun. And no problem. I can see from the look on that happy, pretty face that you took advantage of the alone time and thoroughly enjoyed it". My smile becomes bigger and I am about to burst with happiness.

"Oh, Chloe, I am head over heels in love with Wyatt. I just wish we hadn't waited so long to find each other. I'm going to miss him terribly.

But, he did give me two round trip tickets to come visit this summer as my grad present."

"Aww, how sweet was that. Guess he feels the same way. Don't worry, Suz. If y'all feel this deeply about each other, you can make it through the summer with no problem. And just think about when you reunite!" Chloe laughs at her own dirty thoughts that she has conjured in her head. I blush thinking those same thoughts. "Where is Wyatt anyway?" Chloe asks.

"Oh, he is going to take a conference call from the firm in NYC to finalize details before his departure. I'm giving him some privacy." Chloe and I talk and drink our coffee for the next hour or so waiting for Wyatt to emerge from my bedroom. Chloe informs me that she plans to join me Thursday at the beach house. I don't ask how long she is planning to stay. I wish she would stay all summer and keep me company, but she is throwing around the idea of taking a few classes during summer term. Maybe the beauty of the beach will change her mind. After our coffee, Chloe retreats back to her room to get ready. She is leaving today to go spend some time with her family before joining me at that beach. I am finishing the dishes when I hear my bedroom door open. Wyatt walks into the kitchen with a strange look on his face. Terrible thoughts run through my head. Did something happen with the internship? Selfishly, if it did I could keep Wyatt with me the entire summer, and the rest of my life. God, I am horrible. No, Wyatt needs to go for him and for us.

"Hey, is something wrong with the internship?" I ask.

"Um, no. Everything is set and ready for me to leave on Tuesday," Wyatt answers in clipped tones. Hmm, this isn't his usual demeanor. What in the world could be bothering him?

"Well, you had me worried. You don't seem like yourself." Wyatt watches me carefully with the same odd expression he arrived with just a few minutes earlier.

"Suzanna, what's this?" Wyatt asks as he pulls a piece of paper into view from behind his back and places it on the kitchen table. Looking down I see those pair of beautiful blue eyes that have haunted me since high school staring up at me. It is the picture of Patrick on the engagement invitation.

"Where did you find that?" I ask in an accusatory tone.

"During my conversation with the firm, I needed something to jot down some notes. I looked all around your room for something in plain sight but didn't see anything. I opened the drawer of the nightstand hoping to find a notepad, but instead I found this. Are you mad that I found it? Or are you mad you got caught?" It is hard not to notice the anger and hurt in Wyatt's voice.

Taking a deep breath, I reply. "I was gonna tell you about it. I just haven't had a chance to bring it up."

Wyatt looks at me with an arched brow. "Didn't have a chance? Really, because we have been spending a lot of time together and I think you've had plenty of chances." Okay, so he has a point. I just haven't really wanted to bring it up.

"Wyatt, I didn't tell you because it's not really important. Patrick is getting married. I love you. End of story." Wyatt still doesn't seem satisfied with my answer.

"Are you going? Looks like you got a special invite." Wyatt says this with a stone cold face pushing the invitation across the kitchen table and pointing to Patrick's handwriting.

Almost in a whisper, I answer. "Yes, I'm going."

Wyatt doesn't say anything for a long time. I hate that I have kept this from him. But what was I supposed to say? I couldn't explain my need for closure. Any other normal person would have moved on years ago. But, not me. I have clung to the hope of someday Patrick and I finding our way back to each other. Now, it doesn't really mean much since Wyatt and I have established our relationship. How can I make Wyatt understand without making him feel like he is second choice because Patrick is moving on? Bravely, I walk over to Wyatt and stand right in front of him invading any personal space between us. I look him straight in the eyes.

"I need to go. I have to go, for me and for us." Once I let those words sink in, I hesitantly grab Wyatt's hand. He receives my embrace and we lace our fingers together. I pull his hand leading him to sit with me on the couch in the living room. I am scared to explain further, but I need to be honest with Wyatt and I need to be honest with myself. Sighing, I break the silence that is present since taking our places on the couch.

"When I left in high school, I just left. No explanations to anyone, other than my parents, and even they didn't know the whole truth. Just you, Chloe and I know the real reason I ran away from everything. Since then, I have been closed off emotionally from people and haven't tried to forge any lasting relationships. Until now, until you." I glance at Wyatt and he seems to have relaxed a bit, giving me a hint of a smile. "I treasure what we have found with each other and I curse myself every day that I let myself stew for so long before finding love again. But, until I can completely commit one hundred percent of myself, I have to have some closure. Patrick's engagement announcement should be enough, but I just have to see for myself. I feel guilty for leaving the way I did all those years ago and I have to see if he is happy." I watch Wyatt carefully to see how he is taking the news. I hope he understands what I need to do for myself and for our relationship.

"Are you sure you want to go and see *him*?" Wyatt asks. At first I think he means Patrick, but the look of concern tells me different. He is referring to someone else and I know he isn't happy about me being in such close proximity with that other man.

"I'll be fine. Chloe, Landon and James will be there. I don't look forward to that part of going to the party, but I'll have reinforcements." Wyatt still looks concerned, but then disappointment and hurt flash across his face.

"Suz, I could be with you, I could protect you. You just have to say the word." I knew he'd want to go, but I can't allow it. This is something I have to do by myself, for myself.

"Wyatt, it's time I grew up and handled this myself. I know you'd be there to support and protect me. You have already saved me twice now, once in high school and now, just recently. You saved my body then, and now you have saved my heart. Had it not been for you, breaking through my armor, I would have spent the rest of my days with a hardened heart. But I can't let you go with me to this party. I'm protecting you, too. You know the rumors that circulated after I left in high school. I remember Chloe telling me how mean the club members were to you, the looks and comments you received about me. You took all of them, even though you were innocent in the entire situation. You don't deserve to go through that again. I'm sure a lot of the same club members will be in attendance at this party. Please, don't be hurt. I could never hurt you." I am pleading for his understanding and now his forgiveness for hiding the fact that I would be attending the party, and attending it without him. I wait for Wyatt to say something, anything. But he seems to consider my every word. After what feels like forever, Wyatt finally speaks.

"Honestly, I don't like this. But if you feel like you have to go, then I won't stop you. I want all of you, and if there is a tiny piece that's keeping you from me, and if going to this party will alleviate that, then I guess you need to go. I wish you would reconsider taking me though. I promise I won't make a scene, even if I have to see *him*." Relief floods me as the words come out of his mouth. For the most part, he understands. I lock my hands around his neck, pulling him close.

"Thank you. A lesser man would not be as understanding as you are. And I promise, from now on, I'll keep no more secrets from you." Wyatt wraps his arms around my waist then and we kiss.

"I trust you Suz, and I think you trust me. It's other people I don't trust." I lay my head on his shoulder and just let him hold me.

"I trust you too, Wyatt. And I love you. I can't wait for this stupid party Saturday night to be over with. I plan to be back in your arms Sunday morning." My plan is to leave first thing Sunday morning and drive back to Columbia to stay with Wyatt that night, before taking him to the airport Tuesday. It will be the last few nights we will spend together before he leaves for four months.

"I'll be waiting for you," Wyatt says and we confirm our plans with another kiss.

Chapter Twenty-Two

(Present Day)

Time continues to tick by and the next few days end more quickly than I would prefer. Wyatt and I spend as much time together as possible before I leave on Wednesday for the beach. I notice that our time in bed is desperate on both of our parts. Wyatt seems to drive into me like he is driving in the fact that I am his and he is mine. That no one, not even Patrick is going to get in our way for a future together. Days earlier he said he had understood my need to see Patrick, but our time together has given me a hint that maybe he is concerned about my devotion towards him. I am, also, more needy than usual in bed. Each time he is inside of me, I hold onto him tightly, bringing him deeper like we can never be separated. I relish the feeling of our two bodies being one. We each are dealing with our own insecurities using our bodies instead of our words.

Unfortunately, time never slows and Wednesday morning arrives. Wyatt helps me get the few things left into my car. Since Chloe left earlier in the week, I am running around the house getting it ready for the period it will be unoccupied. I turn the air up a few degrees, so the house will stay comfortable, but not as cool as if we were living in it. I make sure all windows and doors are locked. I turn the timer on that controls the lamps and lights to make it look like the house is occupied and not empty in case of burglars. Once I have completed my list, I walk into the living room where Wyatt is waiting.

"It's weird leaving today. I may never live here again." Wyatt walks over and gives me a hug. I think he secretly knows that this is harder for me than I had thought it would be.

"Everything finished, you ready to go?" he asks. Taking a final look around the house I have lived in for the past few years, I finally look back at Wyatt.

"Yes, I'm ready." We walk out the front door and lock up the house. When we get to my car, Wyatt pulls me into a bear hug making it hard for me to breathe.

"God, I'm gonna miss you," he whispers in my hair.

"I'm gonna miss you, too," I reply as my voice cracks. We stand by my car in the driveway for a long time just holding each other. It isn't the last time we will have to endure a goodbye.

"Hey, let's just focus on Sunday when we'll see each other again," Wyatt says trying to stop the tears that are now falling down my face. I know he doesn't want to send me on my way trying to drive through tears. That would be too dangerous. I smile at his concern for me.

"It's a date!" I say and make myself slide my body into the driver's seat. I smile up at Wyatt reassuring him that I will be okay until Sunday. "I'll call you and let you know when I get there safely. You call me tonight after work, no matter how late it is, okay?" He nods, but doesn't say anything. I can tell he is a little choked up about me leaving. I place my hands and both sides of his face and pull him close. I kiss those lips long and hard, since I won't be able to kiss them again until Sunday. Finally pulling away, Wyatt winks and gives me his megawatt smile.

"I love you, Suz. See you Sunday." And then, he closes my door and walks away. I am able, but just barely, to pull it together and drive safely towards I-20 and the start of summer.

The ride to the beach is easy. There is very little traffic since it is the middle of the week. I think of Wyatt every second of the drive and reminisce about the short time it has taken us to fall completely in love. With Wyatt, everything just seems to be perfect and easy. Before I know it, I smell the salt air that is seeping through my air conditioning vents. I immediately roll down my windows letting it fill my car. Driving over the bridge on Atlantic Avenue, I am overcome with memories of growing up at the beach. It has become my safe haven, the place where I escape when life gets complicated. At the stop light, I glance over to see Sam's Corner, the famous hot dog joint that has been serving up hotdogs and hamburgers to locals and tourists for thirty-seven years. The Garden City pier is directly across the street. People are already up and down the pier, fishing for the many species that swim in the ocean. I turn right once the light changes to green and travel south. I can tell you the house and street names from memory. When I pass Patrick's family beach home, I try to make myself not look to see if it has been occupied yet. But I fail, and take a glance anyway. There are no cars in the driveway or parked under the house. I figure his family won't arrive until the latter part of the week, closer to the party. I pass the Jones' house next and see some party trucks parked out front. Mrs. Jones is already preparing her home for the engagement party. The Joneses will probably spare no expense on the party. They love entertaining and have a beautiful home in which to do so. After a few moments, I am slowing down and pulling into my beach house driveway. I pull all the way in and parked under the raised beach house. Grabbing my purse and a small bag, I jump out of the car and take in a huge breath of the salt air. Just filling my lungs with it brings both a sense of peace and happiness to me. I am so glad to be here. I bounce up the white painted stairs that lead to the front porch. The porch is covered with a row of mismatched rocking chairs. I used to spend countless hours sitting on the front porch rocking as I watched the cars pass by and listened to the ocean. Unlocking the front door, I walk in going straight to the thermostat which I adjust to make the house more comfortable. I place my things in my bedroom and flip on some lights. It is still the middle of the day, but the sun will soon be fading and I don't want to get caught in the dark, especially since I will be here alone tonight before Chloe arrives tomorrow. I gather the rest of my things from the car, which takes a couple of trips. Once everything is out of the car and unpacked, I look to see what is in the fridge and pantry. I don't want to make a trip to the store tonight unless absolutely necessary. There are a couple of bottled waters and some diet cokes in the fridge along with some beer. Those are all staples at the Caulder beach house so I know we will never run out of beverages. The pantry is somewhat barer, with just a few bags of chips and a loaf of bread that has started to mold. I throw the bread away and start to make a list. I will order a salad from Gulf Stream Café later and complete my grocery list tonight. I plan to do the majority of the shopping tomorrow. Grabbing a cold beer from the fridge, and my list and pen in hand, I head to my favorite place of this house. The back porch is outfitted with a table and chairs and some other patio furniture for relaxing. The view of the inlet is perfect this time of day. Some people would rather have an ocean front house. Not me and my clan. We prefer the second row home because of our inlet access. Who cares if we have to walk across the street to sink our toes in the sand, as long as we can walk across our back yard to hop in a boat for a ride around Murrells Inlet? The marshes are gorgeous, the fishing is good, but the sunsets are spectacular. I love sitting and watching the wildlife to which the inlet is home.

Plopping down on a chaise lounge, I pull out my phone and call Wyatt. He picks up on the second ring. "Hey, you made it down okay?" I can tell he has been a little worried about my drive.

"Yes, I'm here enjoying the inlet view and missing you all at the same time."

"Good, I miss you too, but I'm glad you made it safely." We chat for the next ten minutes until he needs to go get ready for work.

"Call me after work. I love you," I say.

"Will do, love you too. Bye Suzanna."

In a weepy voice I say "Bye," but he has already ended the call. Just as well, I don't want him to hear any sadness in my voice. If he had any idea how sad I am without him, he'd drop everything and drive down. I can't have him blowing off his last few nights of work because he is worried about my emotional well being. I complete my grocery list and head back inside to call Gulf Stream for my dinner for one.

The next morning I wake up early, trying to adjust my eyes to the rising sun coming from the east. The sun just seems to shine brighter at the beach. I notice that it is only 6:30, but there is no way I am going back to sleep. I pray there is coffee in the house. I failed to check last night and will need to put it on my list if there isn't any. I pad into the kitchen and feel like I hit the jackpot when I find not only coffee, but also some creamer with an expiration date just a few days away. Still good for now. While the coffee brews, I check my schedule for the day. I will meet up with Mr. Dale Moore at 11:00 for a round of golf. He will be my golf coach this summer to help me prepare for the qualifying round. Today, he just wants to see me play so we can identify areas of my game we need to improve this summer. Chloe texted last night, letting me know she will arrive later this afternoon. I need to check in with my parents and let them know I am all settled in. But coffee first, all else can wait until I have my coffee. I fix my first cup of the day and go out the back door to my favorite place again. I think about Wyatt this morning. This is the first morning in a long time that I woke up and he wasn't by my side. I wonder how he slept. I can't call him this early, since he worked last night. I quickly decide I will send him a text.

Me - Good morning. I missed going to sleep with you last night and waking up next to you this morning. Guess that's why I'm awake so early. Didn't want to call and wake you up after working. Call me later, Don't start golf until 11. Love you, Suz

I press send and go back to drinking my coffee, almost spilling it all over myself when my phone beeps alerting me of an incoming text. Grabbing my phone, my face lights up when I read the text reply from Wyatt.

Wyatt - My bed is cold without you here and I couldn't sleep worth a shit! Needless to say, I'm awake so call me. Love you, Wyatt

Fumbling with the key pad, I immediately dial his number. Before the first ring finishes, I hear Wyatt's voice.

"Morning babe. I don't know how I'll get any work done in New York without you sharing my bed."

I laugh. "Well, don't go finding my replacement. We'll get you some sleeping medication, if necessary."

He laughs with me. "You can't be replaced, ever!"

"How was work last night? I hate that you are awake so early knowing how late you got home." Wyatt had called me after work around midnight.

"It was fine. I think I finally got the new guy trained enough that he won't screw everything up once I'm gone. The other bartenders are trying to have me a bon voyage party Saturday, so that should be fun." Oh good, I think. Just what Wyatt needs to keep his mind occupied while he knows I'll be at the engagement party.

"That's sounds fabulous. I'm sure it will be fun. Wish I could be there."

Wyatt chuckles. "Well you can, you know. Just drop everything else and come. I'd love to have you on my arm as I say my farewells."

Sighing, I know just how much I want to be on his arm, but I have made a commitment and I need to keep it. "Wyatt, you know I can't. But I'll make it up to you Sunday morning," I say teasing and hoping to change the subject.

"Oh yeah, Sunday. I think that's when we have our hot date," Wyatt says. Great, subject changed.

"Yep, really hot date. I don't think you'll even want to sleep Sunday night," I say in anticipation of a long night of just me, Wyatt and his bed.

"Promises, promises...I'll hold you to them you know."

"I'll never break a promise to you, my love." I tell him about what the rest of my day holds and he tells me about his. After about ten minutes, I realize I'd better get a move on if I want to fit in some exercise before taking off to grocery shop. Wyatt and I end our phone call with 'I love yous' and I finish my coffee. Fully awake now, I change into some gym shorts and a sports bra. I lace up my running shoes and head out the front door. I had a gym membership in Columbia that I used mostly during the winter months. But I love exercising outdoors, at the beach especially. I can't recall how many miles I have walked and ran up and down the beach and Waccamaw Drive, the street address of our beach home. After I stretch, I take off in a northern direction towards the pier. The tide is still high, so I stick to the sidewalks. I love passing by homes that I have seen all my life to see the recent improvements that some homeowners have done during the off season. Some of the homes will be rented this summer, with a new family coming in each week. Some homes are occupied by full time residents. And the rest are like mine, those who don't rent and just use their homes as weekend get-a-ways.

I am fast approaching the Jones' home, which will entertain hundreds of guests for the party Saturday night. The trucks are no longer in the drive, but the tents have been put up in the back. I assume more trucks will arrive today and tomorrow with tables and chairs and probably a dance floor. I streak past the next few houses and my adrenaline spikes. I am closing in on Patrick's house. I don't think anyone has arrived since yesterday when I passed by in my car. But I can't be sure. When I get close enough, sure enough there is a car in the driveway. I'm not sure who the car belongs to, but I'm not going to slow down and find out. I stare straight ahead and keep on running, praying the tide will go out quickly and I can run the beach back home. I make it all the way to Sam's Corner before turning around and going back. I weave in and out of some side streets before Waccamaw Drive is the only passage home. I checked the beach earlier and the tide has gone out some, but it left the sand too wet to jog so I remain on the sidewalk. I think I, actually, pick up some speed when I have to pass Patrick's house yet again. I'm not sure why I am so nervous. It isn't like anyone would recognize me or even want to talk to me. I think I am in the clear until I hear the sweetest voice yell from behind me.

"Suzanna Claire Caulder, is that you?" I slow down from a jog to a walk trying to catch my breath, before I turn around. Standing before me is the spitting image of Patrick's mother, her sister Betty.

"Aunt Betty?" I question knowing exactly who she is. Now, she starts running towards me, arms held out for an immediate hug. I can't stop her momentum when she approaches and pulls me in tight. I try not to hug her back, keeping my arms loose around her shoulders. I am a sweaty mess from my run and she is as clean as a whistle, before the hug. She unclasps her arms and anchors them on my shoulders getting a good look at me.

"Well, I'll be. I didn't think you could get any prettier, but you have proved me wrong." I look at her with skepticism because I am anything but pretty right now.

"Um, thank you. But I'm a hot, sweaty mess and I think you're exaggerating," I say giving her a smile. She waves me off with her hand, like that is just nonsense.

"So, what have you been doing with yourself the last few years?" she asks. I tell her about college and graduation. I fill her in on my golfing career at the university and how I am trying to make it on the pro tour. I inform her that I will be living at the beach this summer to practice.

"Oh good, we'll have so much time to get together and catch up," she replies. "Looks like you could use a drink of water. Come on to the house and I'll get you one," she says as she turns and waits for me to follow. I don't take a step in her direction, just stand frozen in place. When she notices that I'm not moving, she turns back to me giving me a knowing look. "Suzanna, no one is here, but me. Now don't be silly, just come join me for a drink. I've missed you girl." Reluctantly, I follow her from the sidewalk towards the house. Memories flood me as soon as I step over the threshold. The beach house décor hasn't changed since I last saw it, with the exception of a few added decorations and the updated technology. The old box television has been replaced with a flat screen that hangs on the wall. Several of the picture frames have been updated with more recent pictures of family members. But there are still some of Patrick as a child, and more which documents his life into adulthood. I smile as I view the pictures of the precious blue eyed, towheaded boy. Aunt Betty catches me smiling at the picture and smiles back at me even knowing how it may cause me pain. Walking up to me, she hands me my drink of water.

"Thanks, Aunt Betty." I drink the water fast, not because I am that thirsty, but because I am ready to get out of here.

"Oh, you must have been thirsty. Want me to fix you some more?" Aunt Betty asks when I drain the glass empty.

"Thanks, but no. I really have to go now." I reply not looking her in the eyes.

"Suzanna, please don't feel uncomfortable around me. I love you like a daughter and I've missed you. Marie would have felt the same way if she was here. Gosh, she'd be so proud of the wonderful, talented woman you have become." The mention of Marie's name does me in, and I begin to weep. Aunt Betty's consoling arms fly around me and hold me in an embrace until I manage to pull myself together.

"I'm so sorry. I didn't mean to get so upset. You and Marie look so much alike and just the mention of her name…I really miss her, too." Aunt Betty smiles at me, but her eyes are a little misty now. I still remember that night we found out Mrs. Marie was no longer with us…

Chapter Twenty-Three

(Summer Before Senior Year of High School)

The pool had just closed, and like always we are the last to leave. All five of us trudge across the driving range, making our way back to the clubhouse. We stored our golf equipment and clothes there earlier after a round of golf before taking off to the pool.

"Y'all want to go hang out on the course tonight and drink a few beers? I think Wyatt is working and he can hook us up!" Landon exclaims getting excited about our impromptu party.

"Sounds good to me. I want to stay as far away from home tonight as possible. Ashley and Mom have been at each other's throats since she decided to transfer schools just to follow her loser boyfriend," Chloe huffs. "God, she's so stupid!" We all laugh at Chloe and her stupid sister. Patrick and I are holding hands following the others, Chloe, Landon and James, across the parking lot.

He leans in and whispers, "You wanna join the rest of these clowns or do you want some alone time? My parents are at the beach and won't be back until later tonight." As a high school student, it is rare that you and your boyfriend have any alone time in the privacy of his bedroom. So yeah, I am sold on the idea as soon as the words leave his mouth.

"I vote for alone time. But, you have to come up with an excuse," I say.

"Done!" he replies. Patrick convinces the rest of the Fab Five that we have to meet his parents for dinner and can't join them for drinks on the course. Somehow, they seem to buy his lame excuse and we all say our goodbyes for the night. I ride with Patrick, leaving my car in the club parking lot. We grab some burgers from McDonalds and head to his house. Patrick texts his parents to find out exactly what time they will be home and they reply that they are just leaving the beach.

"Excellent, we have at least an hour and a half, Suz. How ever will we spend the time?" I laugh at him knowing exactly how we will spend the time...kissing, cuddling, and making love. I grab his hand and we make our way back to his bedroom. Patrick is always so patient with me as we explore each other's bodies, both virtual sexual amateurs. We have been having sex since the spring and every time it gets better. After an hour, I start to get nervous that Marie and Jim could arrive at any minute. The thought of us being caught between the sheets sends my feet flying to the floor reaching for my clothes.

"What's the hurry, Suz? We've got at least another thirty minutes," Patrick all but begs.

"Can't take that chance. Plus, it's not really a good idea for them to arrive home to find their son and his girlfriend who have been all alone. They're not idiots and I think they'll get the picture, plain and clear."

Patrick laughs. "Yeah, especially if you keep blushing like that. You're a dead giveaway." I throw his clothes in his direction.

"Get dressed, you dork. Let's go meet the guys and Chloe on the course." Ten minutes later, we are back at the club walking through the dark towards our favorite party hole. It is the seventeenth green, which is within walking distance from the club, but far enough from people's houses that we won't be a disturbance. I hear Chloe's laughter as we are getting close. She and Landon are giving James hell for asking out Kennedy Smith. She is dating the captain of the football team and James will sure hear from him or his fist whenever he finds out that James propositioned his girl.

"Hey, guys we're back," Patrick says as we approach.

"Well, that was a short dinner," Chloe chirps.

"Yeah," Landon says, "What was on the menu, hotdogs?" They all start busting out laughing while I turn blood red with embarrassment. Patrick throws a stick at Landon for his rude comment, but smiles when he tells him to shut up. We grab some beers and join the party. An hour later, we are still joking around when Patrick's cell phone buzzes.

"I guess the parents are home. Better check in," he says and kisses my lips before walking up a ways to take the call. Landon is filling us in on his brother's newest honor of becoming president of his fraternity. He will be a senior this year at Clemson University and is doing really well. Our conversation comes to an abrupt halt when we hear Patrick's panicked voice. "Dad, how's mom? No, she can't, Dad..." I jump up knowing something is wrong and run over to him right before he collapses to his knees.

"Patrick, what's wrong? Baby, what is it?" Patrick is holding his head in his hands, openly sobbing. He is such an emotional wreck he can't even tell me what has happened. I barely hear the voice of Patrick's dad on the cell phone, calling his son's name. I pick up the phone from where Patrick dropped it on the ground and hold it to my ear.

"Um, Mr. Miles, this is Suzanna. What's happened?"

Mr. Miles speaks between heavy breaths, like he himself is trying to talk through some type of emotional pain. "Suzanna, are you with Patrick?"

"Yes, sir, I'm here as well as Chloe, James and Landon."

Mr. Miles sighs. "Good, stay with him. I'll be home when I can."

"Of course, but can you tell me what's wrong? Patrick is a wreck and can't talk." I know I don't want to hear his answer, but I need to in order to help Patrick.

"It's Marie. She's gone. She was killed in a car accident on our way home." The air rushes out my lungs and I feel like I can't breathe. Patrick's mother is dead.

All four of us leave and take Patrick home. We each call our families to deliver the bad news. They all give us permission to stay as long as we need, even the entire night, to be with Patrick and help console him. Our families are devastated and immediately start cooking. That's what people in the south do. When someone dies, they deliver food like eating a meal will make things all better. I am sure the kitchen will be overflowing with hams and casseroles by lunchtime tomorrow.

We set up Patrick's bedroom like we are having a slumber party, except the mood is quite somber. Jim arrives at the house a couple of hours later, with a cut to his forehead that has required at least a dozen stitches. Other than that, he was spared any other physical trauma from the car crash. But the emotional pains will be with him forever. Family members arrive throughout the night, including Aunt Betty, Marie's twin sister. Jim looks in on Patrick, but doesn't offer much comfort seeing as how he is consumed by his own grief. I lay by Patrick in his bed. The bed we had been intimate in just hours earlier. Now, I just hold him tightly, rubbing his arms and back, trying my best to send him into sleep to escape reality. He cries until the wee hours of the morning. I cry too, not just for the loss of Marie, but for what it is doing to Patrick. I whisper multiple times in Patrick's ear that I love him, not that my love can take away any of his pain, but to just let him know I am there for him. Finally, his breathing holds steady and he falls asleep. The next few days are a blur. Family members and friends are in and out of the house showing their respects. The day of the funeral is a bright sunny, beautiful day. I bet a thousand people try to cram into the First Presbyterian Church to witness the ceremony for Marie Miles, and to celebrate her life. The burial is especially hard, watching Marie's body find its final resting place. I feel some comfort knowing that her soul is in heaven, for Marie Miles was a holy woman. Patrick seems to barely function, walking around in a daze most of the time. I make sure to be there when he needs me and to give him space when I feel my presence may be too much. Mom and Dad are very lenient with my curfew and even let me stay overnight once more to help take care of Patrick.

It takes weeks following the funeral before Patrick finally seems like himself again. School has started back and between classes, Patrick hands me a note.

Meet me after school, my house, Love P.

I haven't been to his house in over a week. Jim has been overcome with grief and isn't doing as well as Patrick. He has taken to drowning his sorrows with the bottle. The last time I was with Patrick, Jim came home completely drunk off his ass, slurring and stumbling his way into the house. He eyed me and Patrick sitting on the couch.

"Dad, are you okay?" Patrick asks as he makes his way over to help his dad walk before he falls down and makes more of an idiot of himself.

"No, son. I don't think I'll ever be okay again," Jim slurs.

"Dad, she's gone. She's not coming back. Drinking yourself into a stupor isn't helping anyone, especially you," Patrick says with wisdom beyond his years.

"Well, maybe if I had a hot, little, young thing like you," glaring at me now, "I could forget about your mom too." Patrick tenses, his fists clenched together making his knuckles turn white.

"Dad, you're drunk. Just go to bed. And don't ever talk about Suzanna like that again!" Patrick says trying to control his temper. Jim stumbles away towards his bedroom leaving us alone. I feel uncomfortable after witnessing such a moment between father and son. I grab my books and start to leave. "Suz, I'm so sorry about him, about that," Patrick says, almost embarrassed. "Please, forgive him. He doesn't even know what he's saying." I make my way to the door, really wanting to get the hell out of that house and just go home.

"No problem, Patrick. I'll see you at school tomorrow." I open the door to make my escape.

"Wait!" Patrick begs grabbing my elbow before I make a clean get-away. "Suz, I love you. I don't think of you like that, you know that. I miss my mother every second, every minute of every day. But having you by my side, makes each day easier. Please, don't let my dad get between us. I'm going to get him some help, I promise." My heart breaks for Patrick. First losing his mother, now losing his dad to alcohol. He needs me, someone constant in his life.

I pull him in close. "Hey, I'm not going anywhere, expect home for the night. I'll see you at school tomorrow. Why don't you plan to come to my house for dinner tomorrow and take a break from your dad for the night?" Patrick nods, our lips brushing together ever so slightly. "And Patrick, I love you, too." He kisses me then, long and hard and passionate, causing us to pull up for air. We say our goodbyes that night and he becomes a constant figure around our dinner table almost every night after that.

I read the note excited about seeing Patrick, but feel uneasy about meeting at his home. I don't know if Jim will be there and I really don't want another run in like last time. When I arrive at Patrick's home, his car is the only one in the driveway. I walk in through the back door and find Patrick going over some notes from history class. "Hey babe," I say as I enter the door. Patrick gives me one of his grins that melts my heart and pats the seat next to him. I rush over just to be near him.

"Hi Suz, I'm so glad you came." Wrapping me in his arms, he kisses my lips. I open my mouth and let him invade it with his tongue, sending shockwaves throughout my body. But before things get too heated, Patrick pulls away. I can tell he is nervous about something and I start to panic. Did he invite me here to break up with me? Surely not after that kiss.

"Suzanna, I would like to give you something." Oh, he has a gift for me. Then, why all the nerves? He grabs my hand and leads me down the hallway into the guest bedroom. The room looks like it has caught the remnants from all the closets in the house if they had exploded. There are old books and clothing everywhere along with some decorative items that don't go together at all. Patrick walks over to the other side of the bed, stepping over boxes and trash bags. I follow him careful not to fall. "We're cleaning out some of my mother's things. As you can see, she had a lot of things," he says with a hint of a smile at his mother's expense. "My mother thought the world of you, Suz, as do I. I know she would want you to have something of hers now that she is gone." My throat is starting to close up just thinking about Marie. I don't need anything tangible to help me remember her. She will always have a special place in my heart. "Mom wasn't much of an athlete, but she managed to try every sport at least once. Anyway, I found this." Patrick pulls out a golf bag that looks like it has been purchased just today from the local sporting goods store. "She only used it once or twice, so it didn't have much value to her. But, I'd like you to have and use it, if you want. That way she can be your lucky angel on the course."

Tears sting my eyes as I picture Marie as my guardian 'golf angel'. "I love it, Patrick. And I plan to use it every day from now until I retire. With her as my angel, I'm bound to go pro!" Patrick laughs, the first real laugh he has had associated with something about his mother. I smile, thinking Patrick is going to be just fine. Sure the pain will remain, but Marie has raised a strong, kind son who will thrive even though she isn't on Earth to see it. But she'll be watching us both from her home in Heaven.

Chapter Twenty-Four

(Present Day)

Aunt Betty is looking at me as I daydream about my lucky golf bag. "You know, I'm still using Marie's golf bag. Even during university play, when they provided us with matching team bags, I refused to use any other bag except hers. She brought me good luck over the last four years." Aunt Betty's smile couldn't have been wider. We had just gone from a sad moment to one of joy, all because of the fabulous woman we were both so fortunate to know.

"Oh, Suzanna, she's smiling at us now. Come on and have another drink of water and tell me about yourself." Feeling more comfortable than I did a few minutes ago, I accept another drink and we go out to the porch to chat. "So, you're a college grad now, planning to hit it big on the pro circuit." I nod. "And what else?"

"Well, that's really about it. The last four years I have concentrated on school and golf, with little else. Oh, I did live with Chloe the last two years, so that was interesting."

Aunt Betty laughs. "I bet, how is that girl?"

"Chloe is, well, Chloe. Just as dramatic as ever. She's my best friend," I reply with a silly grin. Thinking of Chloe just brings a smile to my face.

"I'd love to see her and catch up. I bet she's got a million stories."

"That she does and you'll get your chance to hear each and every one of them Saturday night at the engagement party. She will be there," I say. Aunt Betty gets a more serious look in her eyes, though never letting her smile fade.

"And will you be at the party as well?" she asks.

"Um, yeah, I plan to attend." Aunt Betty looks a little shocked and relieved all at the same time, if that is even possible. "Patrick specifically asked that we all show, me, Chloe, Landon and James. Kind of like a Fab Five reunion I guess. The least I can do is show up and help him celebrate this happy moment in his life," I say hoping she doesn't see through my explanation.

"Well, I'll be. All five of you rug rats together again. Should be interesting!" I don't comment on the fact that my attendance at my ex's engagement party will definitely be interesting. Aunt Betty doesn't either. We just sit and enjoy a comfortable silence between two old friends.

"Thanks again for the water, but this time I really do need to go. I've got a golf lesson at 11:00 and I don't want to be late." I hand the glass back to Aunt Betty and make my way towards the door.

"Suzanna, I look forward to seeing you Saturday night. And I know Patrick will, too." How does she know Patrick will be happy to see me? It has been four years. Have they talked about me? I don't ask although I think Aunt Betty wants me to. She seems ready to reveal more information, but then thinks better of it.

"Goodbye, Aunt Betty, see you soon." I give her a quick hug and then bound down the steps to start the walk home.

"Bye, Suz. Don't be a stranger!" I hear Aunt Betty yell my way. I turn to see her standing on the steps waving her hand. Straining my eyes against the sunlight, I could swear it is Marie who is smiling and waving goodbye to me.

Chapter Twenty-Five

(Present Day)

By the time I get back to the beach house, I am running late. There is no way I will be able to squeeze in a grocery store run before meeting with my new coach for the summer. I jump in the shower and get dressed quickly. Luckily, I didn't unpack my golf equipment when I arrived yesterday so it is still in the car. I lock the house and bolt down the steps, taking them two at a time. I know exactly where I am going, having played the ocean course several times with my dad and brother. I pull into the parking lot of the club with five minutes to spare. Hauling all my stuff from the car, I make the walk over to the golf shop to meet my new coach. The shop is busy with foursomes getting ready to either start their rounds or finish the back nine. I walk over to the counter to ask where I might find Mr. Dale Moore. Mr. Moore has been contacted by my dad to coach me in preparation for qualifying in Hilton Head later this summer. He worked with some high profile golfers in his younger days, but now is retired and just helps out aspiring golfers such as myself. I think he also works with Coastal Carolina University and their golf teams.

"Hi, I'm Suzanna Caulder and I have an appointment to meet with Mr. Moore. Do you know where I might find him?" I ask the young man manning the counter at the golf shop.

"Oh, hi Suzanna, we've been expecting you," he replies. I am puzzled how he seems to know that I would be here, but I don't have to think too hard. "I'm Drew Moore, Dale's son. I'll be playing against you today while Dad watches. He always says a little competition brings out the best in everyone's game. Hope you don't mind the company today on the course."

I smile thinking that competition is exactly what I need. I always play better against someone else. "That would be great. And it's nice to meet you. When do we get started?" I ask.

"Right now. Dad is lining up a couple of carts for us. Let's go meet him on the putting green and get started. You need anything? Water? Gatorade?" Drew asks.

"No, I'm fine for now. Maybe when we make the turn at nine, I'll get something." I follow Drew towards the putting practice green and am introduced to Mr. Moore.

"Well, hello Suzanna, it's nice to finally meet you. I've heard all about you from your father. However, he failed to mention how pretty you are." That immediately makes me blush a little, although Mr. Moore is just being kind.

"Um, thanks, Mr. Moore." That's the extent of my reply.

"I didn't mean to make you feel uncomfortable, Suzanna. I promise I'll judge just your game from now on and not your looks." Mr. Moore gives me a wink and a smile. "Oh, and call me Dale. Mr. Moore makes me feel old."

"Well, you are old Dad. Stop giving the girl a hard time and let's play!" Drew teases his father, rolling his eyes in my direction. We pack up our bags and head to the first tee. Three and a half hours later, we finish at hole eighteen. Drew is an excellent golfer. I learned that he played for the local university until he graduated a year ago. He is enrolled in graduate courses now and helping with the golf team as an assistant coach. He has the talent to play professionally, but informed me that he would rather further his education than try his hand at a golf career. I don't think this makes his dad too happy, but it is Drew's life and Mr. Moore accepts Drew's decisions. Dale takes notes about my game at every hole and we are going to talk about what he wants to work on with me for improvement over the summer.

"Suzanna, your putting is fantastic, probably the best part of your game. Chipping could use some improvement, but it's acceptable. I'd like to work with your driving skills. I'm worried your distance off the tee could be a deterrent to you during qualifying." I have known that my distance game is weak. I usually make up for it with my putting abilities, sinking ten to twenty foot putts with no problem. "Do you work out?" Dale asks.

"Yes, I actually went for a run this morning," I answer feeling proud of myself for the exercise.

"Cardio is essential to your stamina, but I'd really like to develop more strength to your core and upper body." Great. He'll have me joining a gym this summer to lift weights. Ugh, I hate gyms. "Your dad tells me you are living at the family beach house, located on the inlet, right?"

"Yes, that's my home away from home for the next several months," I answer not quite sure how my living arrangements have anything to do with upper body strength.

"Perfect location to do some outdoor strength training. Ever tried paddle boarding or surfing?" I laugh out loud.

"Um, just once a few years ago and it was a disaster. I couldn't even stand up for two seconds without falling off," I say remembering what a klutz I looked like that day. Chloe had been with me and we decided to try it together. Between our giggles and lack of coordination, we ended up forgoing the paddle board experience in lieu of happy hour at the marsh walk.

"Suzanna, I'm not looking for you get all buffed up. I just want to strengthen your core muscles. Drew here, gives both surfing and paddle board lessons. Think you'll let him teach you? He can come to your place so it won't be too embarrassing," Dale says trying to hide the smirk on his face. Well, paddle boarding beats a gym any day and plus, I like Drew. He was fun on the golf course today and I'd like to get to know him better. He'd make a great golfing buddy this summer. Not to mention he is very easy on the eyes!

"Sure, why not?" I answer. "But Drew may have his work cut out for him!" I laugh. Drew and I exchange numbers while Coach Dale checks his schedule for my next golf session. "Looks like we can meet again next Tuesday, around eleven. Work for you?" I thought that Tuesday would be a day of depression for me, since Wyatt would be flying out for New York early Tuesday morning. What better way to let out my frustrations than by hitting that tiny white ball around.

"Tuesday is perfect. And I'll call Drew to set up a paddle board lesson." We say our goodbyes and I head back to the beach house to wait for Chloe to arrive.

I have just finished my second shower of the day. Typical hygiene behavior living in the southeast. Plus, I must have inherited an extra sweat gland, or two. Most southern women are described as glistening in the hot, humid temperatures. Not me, I flat out sweat like a fully padded linebacker in one hundred degree heat. So, multiple showers are a necessity, especially after exercising and golf. Drying off, I think I hear a car door. Sure enough, a few minutes later, Chloe is banging on the front door. When I open the door, I have to laugh. She is swallowed by bags of clothes, shoes and toiletries. I swear anyone else would have thought she was moving in permanently, which would be fine by me. But, I know better. Chloe is as indecisive as she is pretty. She always over packs, stating that she would rather be prepared to change her mind. I open the door widely so she can enter and start to help her untangle herself from all of her travel gear.

"I don't understand why this stupid beach house is built on stilts, yet no one saw the necessity of adding an elevator!" Chloe huffs.

"Come on in, let me help you." I laugh at her dramatic flair. After three more trips up and down the stairs, we finally have Chloe's car unpacked. I let her unpack her things in her bedroom, because that may take days and I don't have it in me. Luckily, Chloe's mom sent a cooler and bags of food with her that could feed an army. Thank goodness I didn't go to the grocery store this morning. I load the fridge and pantry while Chloe collapses on the couch, exhausted from her drive and multiple trips on the front stairs.

"I'm so glad you're finally here!" I exclaim. I have only been at the beach alone for one night, but I am thankful for the company. Chloe and I have lived together for the past two years and I miss her when she isn't around.

"Me too!" Chloe says still sagged into the couch cushions.

"You hungry? I could throw in one of these casseroles your mom sent." I realize I am actually starving, since I skipped lunch while playing golf. The banana and bagel I ate earlier this morning have already been digested.

"Yeah, let's cook the lasagna tonight. I've got a craving for Italian, plus I bought a couple of bottles of red to wash it down," Chloe says. I preheat the oven and pour us each a glass of wine. After I pry Chloe off the couch, we head out back to enjoy the setting sun across the inlet.

"So, how's everything at home? Nice visit with your parents?" I ask Chloe.

"Sure, things are fine. Mom's all hyped up trying to plan Ashley's wedding. Thank God she finally found a guy Mom and Dad approve of. She went through a ton of frogs to find her prince, that's for sure." We laugh at the expense of Chloe's dim witted sister. She seemed to have a magnetic pull to all bad boys, which drove her parents crazy. But she finally met Ben, who has some tattoos and a few piercings, but covers them up nicely in his three piece suit he wears to work as an investment banker. The perfect blending of Ashley's taste and her parents' approval.

"So, when will Brian arrive? He is still going with you to the party Saturday, right?" Chloe swallows her gulp of wine before answering.

"Yep, he's still going. He'll be here tomorrow by lunch time. We want to get in some beach time this weekend." Chloe doesn't sound all that thrilled about Brian's arrival.

"Hey, is something wrong with you and Brian?"

"God no! We still have fun together, but I think we have decided we may be best suited as friends. You know me girl, I'm nowhere near ready to find my prince charming yet." Chloe isn't one to dwell on relationships. She seems to know right up front what she wants. Until she finds that perfect guy who can deliver, well, she'll be leaving a trail of broken hearts in her wake. I hope Brian hasn't been too caught up in her spell. He is much too nice of a guy for her to throw away to the side after she decides she is done. I guess I'll have to take her word for it that they have mutually decided to take the friendship route.

"How was golf today? You told me you'd be meeting your coach for the summer. Is he hot?" I giggle trying to picture Dale Moore as being hot.

"I guess if you're into retired, old men!"

Chloe narrows her eyes at me, "I'd give it a try, if he's hot. And wealthy!"

"Ewww, you're gross Chloe. He does have a son that's not bad to look at." This seems to peak her interest.

"Oh, do tell." I tell her all about my golf lesson today and playing with Drew. I tell her about Drew being wormed into giving me private paddle board lessons to build my upper body strength. By the end of the conversation, we are doubled over in hysterics remembering our last paddle board experience. Knowing I'll need some moral support to get there, and thinking she'll have a chance to meet Drew, I ask Chloe if she will join me in my humiliation of learning to paddle board.

"Sure, why not? I mean if the guy is cute, I'd humiliate myself, too!"

"Great! I'll call Drew to set something up Saturday during the day. You think Brian will mind?"

"Nah, like I said he knows the deal. We're just friends." I call Drew from my cell when I go inside to put the lasagna in the oven. He answers on the second ring.

"Hello?"

"Hi Drew, this is Suzanna, from golf today." I hear his slight breath over the phone before he speaks.

"Hi Suzanna, good to hear from you. What's up?"

"Well, I have a friend in town and she has agreed to give me moral support to try and conquer the paddle board if she can participate in the lesson also. I was wondering if we could arrange a lesson this Saturday, around noon or after?"

Drew laughs, "Are you really that scared of a twelve foot long board with a paddle that you need a friend to hold your hand?"

"Shut up, now you're just teasing me," I smart back.

"That I am. Um, let me quickly check my appointment book. Can you hold on a second?"

"Sure, no problem." Chloe walks in with an empty wine glass in need of a refill. *Drew*, I mouth silently while she gives me a naughty grin. I roll my eyes at her.

"Suzanna, you there?"

"Yes," returning my attention to the phone call.

"I have some free time around 1:00 Saturday afternoon. Will that work?"

"That would be great. Thanks, Drew," I say as Chloe jumps up and down like a high school cheerleader. I give Drew directions to the house and end the call. And just like that, I have scheduled my first paddle board lesson with Chloe as my witness. I know she'll never let me live this one down.

Chapter Twenty-Six

(Present Day)

Chloe and I both enjoy two helpings of lasagna, bread and yet another few glasses of wine. We are feeling quite full and giddy once dinner is over. Calling it a night, we head into our bedrooms for a good night's sleep. I love Chloe's presence in the beach house, but it doesn't fill the empty place in my heart being away from Wyatt. For the second night in a row, I crawl into a cold, empty bed. I need to bridge the distance between me and Wyatt, so I grab my cell phone. I know he'll still be at work, but I just need to hear his voice. Thinking I will get his voice mail, I am surprised when his phone is answered. But what really takes my breath away is who is on the other end of the line.

"Hello?" a female voice answers.

"Um, I think I might have the wrong number," I stutter utterly shocked.

"Suzanna, is that you? It's Bridgett." Oh hell no! What the fuck is she doing answering Wyatt's phone?

Without an ounce of friendliness, I ask, "Where's Wyatt?"

"He's busy with a customer right now. You want to wait a minute? How's the beach?"

I really don't feel like getting into a conversation with this barfly and I'm pissed that she is answering Wyatt's phone. "Just have him call me when he gets a chance."

"Sure, honey. I'll be sure to give him the message," Bridgett assures me in a sugary voice, which to me is the equivalent of nails scraping down a chalkboard. I don't bother with the formality of a goodbye and quickly end the call. Before I realize what is happening, my head is buried in my pillow while my tears soak the linens. Okay, I realize that Bridgett is a regular customer at the bar where Wyatt works. He admitted she comes around frequently and is relentless in her attempts to flirt with not only him, but the rest of the bartenders. However, what gives her the right to answer his phone? Something just doesn't seem right. Just when I was getting used to this distance thing between us, she comes along and brings back all my insecurities regarding our relationship. I trust Wyatt, I really do. However, I wouldn't put anything past Bridgett in her quest to get what she wants. And even if Wyatt doesn't realize it, I know for a fact that Bridgett wants Wyatt.

A few minutes later, my pity party is interrupted by the ringing of my phone. Looking at the caller ID, I see that Wyatt is returning my call. I try to reign in my crying to sound normal, but I know I fail miserably as soon as I accept the call.

"Wyatt...," I say with a whimper before the choking sobs prevent me from continuing.

"Suz, baby, what's wrong?" he asks immediately concerned.

"I just really miss you and wanted to hear your voice. So I called to get your voicemail, but Bridgett answered and I lost it. Why is she answering your phone?" I don't even try to hide my disgust and hurt at the situation.

"Suz, I'm sorry. I was just wrapping things up, trying to get out of here and left my phone on the bar. I got sidetracked by a customer wanting one last drink. I guess she took it upon herself to answer the call. I'm so sorry, Suzanna. Baby, please don't cry."

"It just hurts that she gets to see you and be near you while I'm missing you every second. The last thing I need is to hear her voice answering your phone and putting all sorts of doubts in my mind. It's hard enough with the distance and it's just going to get harder. I don't think I can deal with this." I don't know why I added that last part. I know I'm not considering letting Wyatt out of my life. But it has taken me four long years to get myself to a point to love and let someone love me back. I'm getting stronger, but right this moment my emotional state is fragile.

"Wait, Suz. Just calm down and think about what you're saying. Listen, I love you, only you. Bridgett is meaningless to me. She's just another desperate, pathetic woman who, obviously, finds it amusing to mess with our happiness. Please baby, don't let her petty attempts ruin the beauty that is happening between us." Wyatt is pleading with me. He patiently waits for me to respond.

"Are you going home now?" I ask.

"Yes, I'm walking out as we speak. Suz, I love you. Please, please tell me you still feel the same way. Have faith in me, in us. Please!" I can't bear to listen any longer to the desperation in his voice.

"I love you, Wyatt. Just call me when you get home." With that I end the call and try to compose myself for our next conversation.

Ten minutes later, my phone buzzes again. I've had a chance to calm down and think things through. Bridgett still gets my blood boiling and I'm angry that Wyatt even put me in that situation, leaving his cell phone within her reach. However, I believe in Wyatt and in us and I never want him to be out of my life. After the third ring, I answer.

"Hey, babe."

"Only you, Suzanna. Only you!" he declares and I think I might love him even more.

"I know and I love you, Wyatt. Just please keep your cell phone away from slutty fingers from now on."

He chuckles and finally breathes a sigh of relief that I hear through the phone. "Suzanna, I promise my phone has lost it privileges to be answered by anyone who has slutty fingers."

I burst out laughing.

"Are you okay, Suz? You don't know how worried I was that you were going to end things with us. I don't know what I'd do without you."

"I spoke in a moment of emotional distress. Wyatt, I never want a life without you in it. Look, it has taken me a long to time to get to this point, but I'm there only because of you. You never gave up on me and loved me the entire time I continued to push everyone away. Then, you beat down my barriers and planted yourself right inside of my heart. I couldn't get rid of you even if I wanted to. It would tear me apart. Just please be patient with me. You know I'm new at this whole relationship thing." I'm trying to reassure him that even though I am still somewhat broken, he has the healing power.

"Baby, you don't know what your words mean to me. I miss you so much and I can't wait until Sunday to see you and wrap you in my arms." I can hear the anticipation in his voice and I feel it throughout my body even though we are just on the phone.

"Oh baby, I miss you, too. I'm counting down the hours until Sunday." We chat for a few minutes and my melancholy mood disappears. I tell him of Chloe's arrival and my golf outing today. I even tell him about Drew and the paddle board lesson. He finds that rather funny, and I laugh with him at myself. Towards the end of the conversation, I start yawning.

"Suz, sounds like you had a busy day and you're tired. Why don't you lay that pretty head of yours down and fall asleep," Wyatt says.

"I wish you were here with me, to help me go to sleep."

Wyatt chuckles, "If I were there right now, you wouldn't be getting any sleep." Just his suggestive comment makes me moan in the phone. "You're making it rather hard for me not to jump in my car right now, drive to the beach and cover you with my body," Wyatt replies in a sexy, breathy voice. My body tingles from head to toe just thinking about his touch. I am about to convince him to make that late night drive, but know I have a full day planned with Chloe tomorrow, which includes a mani/pedi appointment and a full afternoon of beach relaxation. Plus, I'd worry myself into a frenzy about Wyatt driving over two hours this late after a tiring night of work.

"Hold on, Casanova. As much as I would love to wrap my arms around your hard, sexy body, I think it's best we wait until Sunday," I say but hate every word.

"Until Sunday, then. I can hardly wait. Goodnight, Suz. Love you."

"Night, Wyatt, I love you, too." I end the call, cradling it to my chest letting Wyatt's declaration of love send me into a peaceful sleep.

This morning is a carbon copy of yesterday morning, with the bright sunshine making its way through the slits in the blinds waking me up.

I really need to invest in some blackout shades or something that will block out the morning glare. This is the second morning I have awakened at the crack of dawn. Knowing I'll never be able to fall back asleep, I push the covers down to crawl out of the bed. My phone, which I had cradled to my chest the entire night crashes to the floor. Picking it up I notice a text from Wyatt sometime after we ended our emotional conversation.

Wyatt – Remember, only you Suzanna, only you! Yours always, Wyatt

A silly grin is plastered across my face as I make my way into the kitchen to make coffee.

"God, when did you become a morning person?" Chloe hisses trying to locate a bottle of aspirin from the kitchen cabinets.

"Good morning to you, too!" I respond cheerily.

"Ugh, there's nothing good about waking up this early. Has your mom heard of a little invention like blinds, or maybe curtains? And on top of the blasted sun I've a got a wine headache," Chloe snaps at me.

"Guess now's not the best time to invite you for a walk or run, huh?" Chloe gives me her best death stare once she downs a couple of ibuprofen. I hold up my hands to indicate I won't push the matter until later. Maybe coffee will cure her bad mood this morning. The java seems to do the trick and by mid morning we are lacing up our tennis shoes to walk off all the lasagna we consumed last night. I think about Coach Dale and how he wants me to build up my upper body strength. Maybe I'll do some pushups after the walk. I decide to venture south this morning since the northern route will take us towards Patrick's house again. I am avoiding running into Aunt Betty and whatever other family members have descended on the property during the last twenty-four hours. I tell Chloe about my run in with Aunt Betty and how I think it is strange that she is so excited about me attending Patrick's engagement party.

"Stop overanalyzing, Suz. She's probably just glad to get another chance to see you again so soon," Chloe comments between her complaints of having to exercise. She hates to sweat, although Chloe in true southern form never actually sweats. She just glistens. She also rocks her God given curves without ever having to workout. Lucky bitch! "Can't we turn around now? It's so hot and it's not even ten a.m.!"

"What's wrong Chloe? Scared your makeup is going to start running!" I'm laughing because she actually bothered to apply makeup before her exercise. Classic Chloe. Chloe gives me a fist to my shoulder.

"Ouch!" I shout, although it barely hurt. "Okay, Chloe. We'll turn around. Besides you're a slow poke today," I say as I make the turn to head back to the house. After we both shower, we make our way to the mall to get manicures and pedicures. Once our toes and nails are dry, we pick up some sub sandwiches and a bag of ice at the nearby grocery store. We plan to eat our lunch on the beach followed by finishing off a cooler of beer. The weather is nice and warm, making it a perfect beach day. We lie on the beach soaking up some rays for hours, gossiping about everything under the sun. I confess to Chloe how much I miss Wyatt, even though it has only been a couple of days since I left Columbia. Knowing I'll see him Sunday is giving me some comfort, but it makes the separation we face when he leaves for New York that much more unbearable. Chloe tries to reassure me that Wyatt and I have something special and we'll make it through the long distance thing. I am still apprehensive, though. Especially after last night's debacle when Bridgett answered his phone. I fail to let Chloe in on this recent development since I know she'll call and give Wyatt hell. Plus, we worked things out last night with sweet, meaningful words to and from each other and I feel a little better about things today. Unfortunately, the doubt has already been embedded in my mind and my insecurities are rising to the surface. I don't know if any amount of words can cure me.

Soon, the cooler is empty and Chloe and I decide to call it a day. Packing up our things, we make our way back to the beach house to rinse the sand and salt from our bodies. Chloe is busy with her phone, texting nonstop with Brian I assume. His arrival has been delayed due to heavy weekend beach traffic. I have dressed in a floral maxi dress with a coordinating colored cardigan. It is comfortable enough to just lounge around the beach house, but respectable enough if we decide to go grab some dinner once Brian arrives.

"Owww!" Chloe screams as she is pulling her dress over her head. Chloe forgot to reapply sun block earlier this afternoon and her arms and shoulders are pink with sunburn. "Hey, Suz. Do you have any aloe? My skin is on fire!" I look in all the bathrooms and cabinets in the kitchen, but come up empty.

"Sorry Chloe. I don't see any. We probably used it all last year." Chloe turns and pouts. Then, she starts with her famous puppy dog eyed look.

"Suz, would you be a doll and run to the nearest drug store to get some? I'll never be able to sleep until I cool this skin down?" Having been irresponsible enough times in my life with sunscreen, I know she is right. Plus, Chloe in pain can make anyone's life miserable.

"Sure. I'll be right back." I grab my purse and keys and head to the Walgreens a couple of miles away. When I return, I notice Brian's car in the driveway as well as a couple of others that I don't recognize. Maybe some of Brian's friends are also at the beach and wanted to come by to meet Chloe. I grab the recently purchased aloe and walk up the stairs to enter the house. As soon as I cross over the doorway, I am greeted with "Surprise!" Shocked, I look around the room to see the faces of Landon, James, Chloe, Brian, some girl I don't know by name, and my brother, Flynn. Hanging over the window of the kitchen is a homemade banner. It reads "Congrats Suz, on graduation and LPA golf qualifying." Before I can speak, Flynn rushes and grabs me, causing my feet to leave the floor. Suspended in his arms, he swings me around and around, until I think I'll be dizzy.

"Put me down, Flynn!" He does but doesn't stop hugging me.

"Hey sis, sorry I missed your graduation. But I'm here now, so let's get this party started!"

"Oh, Flynn. I'm so glad you're here," I say giving him a peck on the cheek. I turn and find Landon and James in line to give me hugs. It has been years since I've seen either of them, but it feels like old times. "Hey guys," is I all can manage in response before my throat starts to close with raw emotion. Luckily, they don't give me time to shed a tear, sandwiching me between them in an awkward, but sweet hug.

"Suzanna, I'm so happy to see you. And congrats on the golf. You were always better than the rest of us," Landon says with a sweet smile. I can't help but stare at Landon and how he has transformed from lanky high school boy to an all out rough and tough man. He keeps his light brown hair buzzed cut really short. His body is made of steel, with hard muscles shaping his torso and arms. I can see some impression ink peeking out of his shirt sleeve and up the part of his neck uncovered by his collar. I used to tease Landon for being the tough one out of our bunch. Looks like I had him pegged exactly right. But under that rough exterior, he has a soft heart of which you can't help but fall in love.

"Thanks, Landon. Hey, like the ink!" I wink at him and I'm surprised to see him blush. Before I can continue my conversation with Landon, James has to get his two cents in.

"Speak for yourself, loser," James adds. "Really, Suz, we're proud of you. Just remember us peons when you make it big on the pro tour." Now, James hasn't changed a bit. I'm surprised he isn't wearing a bow tie with his button down shirt and khaki shorts. He is the definition of the southern gentleman, both inside and out. James walks away towards the girl who is still standing by the kitchen table. "Suzanna Caulder, I'd like you to meet Lisa. Lisa this is Suzanna, the old, dear friend I was telling you about." I extend my hand to Lisa, but she ignores it and pulls me into a friendly hug, surprising me.

"It's just so nice to finally meet you. James talks nonstop about you being the coolest friend, especially since you're a girl and all." I snort because that sounds just like something James would say. Lisa is just as cute as a button with a personality to match. She is small and petite, like me. Her round face is framed by the most beautiful red, curly hair I have ever seen. Her big green eyes sparkle against her fair skin. I watch as James looks at her with appreciation and I know James has found his soul mate. His mother will be proud to have Lisa as a daughter-in-law. I give Brian a quick hug before I make it over to Chloe who is giving me a look of innocence. However, she fails to pull it off. But, I am being congratulated and celebrating with my family and old friends so there is no way I'll be able to stay mad with her for the surprise. Even though she knows how much I hate surprises! Reaching Chloe, I give her a big hug.

"You are by far the best friend on this entire planet!" I say in her ear. The emotion is back and tears of joy start to run down my cheeks. "Thank you for all of this!" I gesture to the small crowd of guests who are now catching up with each other.

"Suz, you deserve it. All of it. Now, stop those tears. We've got some drinking to do!"

After an hour or so of conversations, we all settled at the kitchen table to eat some appetizers that have magically appeared. Along with being a great actress, Chloe is an exceptional party planner. She will always have a career to fall back on if Hollywood doesn't come calling. The guys start telling stories about me that make us all roll with laughter.

"Remember the time you cleaned my clock with your driver?" James asks. "I've got the scars to prove it!" He lifts his thick hair and reveals the scar at his hairline.

"Well, you should have gotten out of the way. I would have won that round had I been able to get off my tee shot!" I exclaim.

"Hey, James always had a big head. It was impossible not to miss it!" Landon teases. "I just hope your tee shots have improved since then."

"How about the time Suzanna got so mad at Landon, she dumped his entire golf bag in the pond!" I am doubled over laughing thinking of Landon waist deep in that disgusting water trying to salvage his clubs.

"Still think that's funny, huh?" Landon says trying to act perturbed, but failing miserably.

"Learned your lesson, though. You never made Suzanna play from the girl tees again, did you?" Landon just shakes his head.

"No, and she still managed to beat all of us!" I watch the people that surround this table and I feel at home. These are my dearest friends and I have missed them so much. I love that they are back in my life and make a silent promise to keep it that way. I watch as James, Landon and Chloe reminisce about the good ole days. Lisa is enjoying every story and keeps wanting more. Flynn is always interested when it comes to embarrassing me. I catch him several times looking my way, with pride and love in his brotherly eyes. I also catch him stealing glances of Chloe. His eyes tell an entirely different story while they travel up and down her body. Brian is being a great sport, having just met everyone. Chloe is paying him extra attention. I hope it is to make him feel welcome and at ease with her old friends. But secretly I suspect she is gauging Flynn's reaction at her having a date for the weekend.

The food has been replaced with red solo cups. The party is in full swing when we all resort to high school drinking games. We are in a serious game of quarters and I am losing, having consumed at least an entire six pack on my own. It is my turn and I aim my quarter hoping I will miss the center cup. I hope I miss my cup as well, or things will get even fuzzier in my alcohol induced state. Luckily, I land the quarter in Flynn's cup, which means he has to drink it dry.

"Ah ha! Got you Flynn!"

"Hey, don't get cocky. Last I checked, you were losing!" He drains the drink in what looks like only two swallows. My brother could drink all of us under the table.

"Okay, James, your turn," I slur. James is laughing when his quarter narrowly misses my cup and I let out a relieved sigh.

"Whoa, that was close!"

"Yeah, you were never good at this!" Landon teases. "Remember that party after the football game, when we were all playing quarters?"

James is almost in hysterics blurting out, "Oh yeah, the one at the twins house? That was the night Leslie was coming onto to Patrick."

Chloe burst out laughing, "Oh my God, I almost forgot about that. Remember, Suz, your claws came out that night!" I start turning a bright shade of red remembering my uncharacteristic bold behavior that night.

Lisa is practically jumping up and down in her seat. "Ohhhh, do tell!" she giggles.

"Well, Suzanna and Patrick had been carrying on a secret love affair," Chloe starts, but I interrupt immediately.

"Chloe, tone down the dramatics. It was not an affair!"

Chloe dismisses me with a wave of her hand. "So that night we had all been drinking playing a game of quarters when Leslie," she glances over at Landon, but he nods for her to continue. I forgot that Leslie and Landon were now dating. Well, good, maybe someone else at this table will feel as uncomfortable as me. Chloe continues, "Leslie was making a move for Patrick, who had remained allusive from her seductive attempts in the past. Anyway, Leslie was making it known to anyone at the party that she wanted Patrick. During the drinking game, she got a little too touchy feely and Suzanna snapped." Everyone is laughing while Lisa is hanging on Chloe's every word.

"What did you do? Hit her or something?" Lisa asks intrigued.

"No, Lisa. This isn't one of your reality television housewives series. This was high school!" James chuckles teasing Lisa in the most adorable way.

The floor is back to Chloe for the big ending. "No hitting, but she laid the biggest, hottest kiss on Patrick shocking everyone there, even us! Beyond any reasonable PDA!" The hooting and hollering that follows is embarrassing. I am about to hang my head when we are all silenced.

"Best damn kiss I ever received!" All seven heads turn towards the back door to find Patrick standing there flashing his glorious smile. His eyes are locked on mine and I can't bring myself to pull away.

"Hey man. Didn't think you were coming in until tomorrow," James says breaking the uncomfortable silence and giving me a chance to try and find my bearings. James walks over to Patrick to shake his hand, as do Landon and Flynn. When Chloe glances my way and mouths, *Oh my God,* I can't even react. It has been over four years since Patrick was in my beach house. Hell, it has been that long since we have even been in the same room. I look over to the group of guys who are now catching up and take in all of Patrick. He is still just as handsome, if not more so. His hair is just as blond as I remember, cut in long, thick layers that hang down in his eyes. And oh those eyes, still as blue as the sea. I remember how easily I could get lost in those eyes and have to shake my head back and forth to return to reality. He is wearing a white t-shirt that is covered with a blue polo, which only enhances those baby blues. He has on red washed Bermuda shorts, showcasing his long, lean legs. He is wearing Rainbow flip flops, which are the staple summer accessory for both men and women on the southern coast. He is stunning and it takes all I have in me to turn away before everyone catches me gawking. When I do, I notice Lisa eyeing me, but she gives me a quick smile. Not sure if she is saying it's okay, I won't tell anyone that you were looking, or if it is a sympathy smile, like oh, sorry it didn't work out and he's marrying some other chick. Whatever, I am relieved to receive it. I have yet to speak when I hear Flynn being hospitable and asking Patrick to join our fun and games. Patrick makes his way around the table giving Chloe a hug, and being introduced to both Brian and Lisa. Then he is beside me.

"Hey there, beautiful," he says. Act calm, act calm is the mantra I keep repeating in my head. I stand on shaky legs turning towards him. God I hope my voice won't give away the nerves that are racing through my body.

"Hi, Patrick. So good to see you," I say with only the slightest crack escaping. He pulls me into an embrace and by body immediately tenses at his touch. A more awkward hug I'm sure has never been witnessed by our audience around this table. Releasing me from his arms, Patrick takes the seat beside me. Rubbing his hands together he says, "Let's play!" We resume our game of quarters just like it is four years ago and nothing has happened to change the course of our lives.

Most everyone is thoroughly trashed to put it politely. And I am right in the thick of it all. We abandoned our drinking game earlier, turning to cards. But before long no one could tell a spade from a club, so we quit with games altogether. Chloe plugged her iPod into the portable speakers and we moved our party to the back deck. The music thumps as we all dance like we're in our own private club. I take turns dancing with Flynn and Landon, watching them as they imitate silly dance moves from the 1980's like the lawnmower and the sprinkler. Those boys love the attention and don't really mind making complete fools of themselves. While Landon and Flynn go to replenish the cooler from the downstairs fridge, the music changes to a slower song. Chloe and Brian and Lisa and James fill our makeshift dance floor, swaying to the sweet melody. I stand awkwardly against the porch rails and watch until I hear Patrick approach.

"May I have this dance?" he asks extending a hand in my direction. Act calm, act calm keeps replaying in my head.

"Sure, why not?" I say grabbing his hand and following him to the center of the porch to join the other couples. Patrick's arms slide around my waist as I place my hands on his shoulders. We don't say anything for a few moments while we just enjoy the closeness that the dance provides.

My head begins to spin, not quite sure if it is because of Patrick's proximity or the alcohol. I can't fight holding my head up any longer and lay it on Patrick's chest. I think I hear him moan, but can't be sure due to the music and the bristle of the breeze coming off the ocean. I do notice that Patrick's hold around my waist gets a little tighter pulling me even closer into his body. One of his hands starts rubbing my back as we sway to and fro with the melody. My stomach begins to flutter, and, again, I hope it is caused by my alcohol consumption and not Patrick's touch. Towards the end of the song, Patrick takes the chance to finally speak.

"I've missed this, Suzanna. I've missed you." I don't respond because in this moment the alcohol is in war with my body and wants out. Stumbling out of his arms, I throw my hand up to cover my mouth and run inside towards the bathroom. Barely making it to the toilet in time, I heave releasing the contents of my stomach. My eyes water as my stomach constricts bringing up a disgusting colored liquid. I think I can't be more humiliated until Patrick opens the bathroom door to find me hugging the porcelain.

"Sorry," I mumble before another spasm takes over and my head is in the toilet again.

Patrick chuckles, "You were never one to hold your alcohol."

"Don't laugh at me!" I groan. I hear the faucet turn on and Patrick grabbing a wash rag out of the vanity. He walks towards me to pull my hair from my face until I finish puking. When there is nothing left, I turn to him and he gently pats my face with the wet washcloth. The cool temperature of the washcloth feels wonderful.

"You think you can make it to the bedroom, or do I need to carry you?" Patrick asks. I push myself up with my arms, almost falling back into the tub before Patrick catches me. In one swift move, he lifts my legs and back cradling me like a baby and carrying me to my bed. He pulls off my sandals and my sweater, but stops at completely undressing me. Pulling the covers from my made bed, he tucks me in. I want to thank him, but my incoherent brain isn't working properly, so I just begin to pass out. Before falling completely into oblivion, I feel Patrick's lips connect with my cheek, so soft and tender.

"Goodnight Suzanna, sweet dreams." Then, there is nothing but blackness.

Chapter Twenty-Seven

(Present Day)

S omeone's hands are around my throat and I can't breathe or scream. The other hand is traveling up and down my body roughly, grabbing and bruising my skin. I try to think of any way possible to escape this torture, but feel trapped. Taking the opportunity I bite his finger when his grip loosens around my mouth. His hand leaves my mouth immediately, but soon connects with my cheek, a stinging slap across my face. "You dumb bitch!" he yells in my ear, pushing me harder into the wall.

"No, please, no...," I scream before his mouth covers mine hard. I turn my head back and forth until my mouth is free of his assault and yell again. "Stop!" His knee presses between my legs into my privates, the force causing immense pain. My dress has been ripped at the shoulder, his nails scratching my skin. "No, stop, please no!" I scream with everything I have. My dress is being peeled away as I cry, "Noooooooo....Wyatt!"

"Suzanna, Suzanna, wake up!" I hear a voice from outside of my nightmare. Gasping for breath, I am being slightly shaken. I awake to find my brother, Flynn holding my shoulders looking extremely concerned. "Suzanna, you're shaking. And you're cold. What's wrong?" I manage to get my breathing under control as Chloe rushes in behind Flynn.

"Suz, what's wrong?" she asks. Taking inventory of my surroundings, I realize I am in my bedroom at the beach house, with people who love me. The emotions of the nightmare roll over my body until I don't have the strength to sit up on my own. I collapse in Flynn's arms crying softly against his body.

"Suz, baby, what the fuck was that? I thought you were being tortured," he says holding me in his strong arms close to his body.

"I, uh, had a nightmare. I'll be fine. I just need a minute," I whisper loosening my grip around his waist.

"Suzanna, maybe you should talk about it. Talk about it with Flynn," I hear Chloe say from the doorway. I look up to see her sad expression staring back at me. She has been the only one to see these nightmares take me over during sleep. She has been the only one to console me once I am awake. I am forever indebted to her for dealing with her unstable roommate all these years. But, I am not ready to share the ugly details of my senior year with Flynn. Not yet, anyway. I will, however, need him by my side tonight as I go to face my demons while awake.

"Nah, Flynn will just think I'm being silly, having nightmares about that scary movie we watched the other night." I'm avoiding telling Flynn the truth. Chloe narrows her eyes at me letting me know her annoyance at keeping this all to myself. But, she doesn't say anything else about it before she walks out the door.

"You okay now, Sis?" Flynn says hesitantly, not knowing whether he should stay or go.

"Yeah, I'm fine," I respond wanting to end the nightmare conversation for now. "Hey, you wanna be my date tonight for Patrick's engagement party?" I ask hoping he'll say yes. I don't know how I'll survive the party without his brotherly strength beside me.

"You sure you want to put yourself through that? From the looks you two were giving each other last night, I'm not sure either one of you are over each other." Gosh, was I that obvious? And how was he looking at me anyway? My vision had been blurred the majority of the night and I hadn't been aware of the way Patrick looked at me.

"Well, we are over each other. Patrick is engaged and I'm dating, so we have both moved on. Besides, last night was just about two old friends reconnecting after not seeing each other for years," I say trying to sound convincing.

"Whatever you say Sis, but if you need a date, I'm your man!"

"Thank you!" I say hugging him again.

Flynn looks more serious for a minute before asking, "Suz, did Wyatt McBride do anything inappropriate with you? Something you didn't consent to?"

"What?" I say shocked.

"Well, before you were completely awake you screamed his name. And you were terrified. I just thought that he might have tried something with you when you all were younger. I remember him working at the club a lot." Flynn is doing his best to try and explain himself, hoping no one has hurt his sister, but looking for the answers anyway.

"Flynn, Wyatt didn't hurt me. He would never hurt me. Besides, we remained friends all during college and we just recently started dating," I say smiling as thoughts of Wyatt fill my head.

"Oh, really. You and Wyatt, huh?" Now Flynn is teasing me. Flynn knows how guarded I am with my heart after watching things explode with Patrick. He is more than surprised to find out I am dating again. Or maybe he is relieved. It has been four years. He probably was thinking I played for the other team. My thoughts make me laugh out loud as Flynn looks on curiously.

"Listen. Wyatt is a great guy and I'll tell you all about us. But right now, I feel like I've been run over by a MAC truck and a small animal has crawled in my mouth and died. So, do you mind leaving me now so I can get up and change? Gross, I'm still wearing the clothes I threw up in!"

"Yeah, you do stink!" Flynn laughs holding his nose. I push him off my bed towards the door. Before he can leave, I get his attention.

"Flynn, thanks again. For this morning and for being my date tonight." He smiles before shutting the door behind him. I lean back against my headboard, realizing my head is throbbing. Being subjected to another nightmare and waking with a hangover is a lethal combination. Rolling over, I notice a full bottle of unopened water sitting on the nightstand. I don't remember Flynn or Chloe bringing me water in their rush to wake me from my nightmare. But, I wasn't completely awake to notice anything. I grab the bottle ready to remedy the dryness in my mouth. There's a piece of paper stuck to the bottom and it falls into my sheets as I take my first gulp. I pick the paper up and recognize the penmanship.

Suzanna, you're still beautiful, even while hugging the toilet. Sleep well. Drink the water and take the aspirin I left for you. Until we meet again, P

My brain kicks back into gear and I vaguely remember Patrick taking care of me in the bathroom. The memory continues as I see Patrick tucking me in my bed and kissing my cheek. Unconsciously, my finger tips brush across my face where Patrick's lips were. A sensation of warmth fills my body as I relive the feel of Patrick's touch. How will I live through this party tonight? Seeing him again will be more confusing than it already is. Plus, tonight I get the pleasure of meeting Katelyn, his fiancé. That's enough to make me puke again. I've got to think rationally. Patrick invited me to his party as a friend. He wants all his friends to be there. Okay, I can do this friend thing. I have to do this friend thing. Because any other option will be disastrous.

I fold up the note and stash it in my nightstand table drawer. I know holding onto the note seems silly. The note doesn't say much at all. But tossing it is like letting go of the memories of last night and I'm not ready to do that, yet. I trudge into the bathroom, my head throbbing with every step. I wonder when those aspirin that Patrick left for me will take effect. Looking at myself in the mirror, I am horrified at the woman staring back at me. She is a wreck. Matted hair that clings to her face from the throw up and drool left there. There are dark circles under her eyes from a lack of sleep and too much partying. I jump in the shower quickly to escape the image and thoroughly wash away the ugliness. I get dressed in my bikini and cover up and make my way to the kitchen for my java fix. The majority of my house guests are mulling around, all waking in a haze from the morning after affects. All except for Lisa, that is. She looks perky and ready to conquer the day. I imagine Lisa is always that way and I give her a good morning smile.

"Good morning all," I say pouring my first cup of coffee. They all grunt and nod in my direction. I guess it's too early for verbal communication. Lisa joins me at the coffee pot to pour herself another cup.

"Wow, this view in the morning is spectacular!" she says looking out the window over the inlet.

"My favorite part of the house. Want to join me on the back deck?" She nods, bobbing along as I follow her out the door. We sit and enjoy the serenity of the inlet in the morning before it gets crowded with boats and fishermen.

"Thanks for having us this weekend, Suzanna. I know James was really looking forward to seeing you," Lisa says.

"I'm glad you're both here. James is a lucky man." She blushes which I think is adorable.

"So, from what I gathered last night, you and Patrick have a past, yes?" I'm somewhat caught off guard that Lisa would ask such a personal question. But, it was right out there in the open last night as we all retold the Leslie story. Anyway, I feel like Lisa is a part of James, so therefore she's a part of us.

"Yes, we dated until midway through our senior year," I say hoping that's enough. I think she's dropped it because she doesn't speak immediately.

A few moments later she asks, "Can I ask what happened?"

No, you can't I think to myself, but I don't say it. I just respond with a very nonchalant answer. "Life!" That's my final answer on the subject.

"I'm sorry. I shouldn't pry. It's none of my business," Lisa says and I know she's being sincere. But, I'm stunned to hear what else she has to say. "It's just James doesn't like talking about it, the split, that is. I think it really affected him, also. But I saw how Patrick looked at you last night and I don't think things have been resolved, by either of you." Lisa looks out on the inlet while I look at her incredulously.

"He's engaged!" I say a little too loudly. She smiles at me, but with a look of sympathy. Then, she completely changes the subject.

"So, what's on the agenda for today?" It takes me a while to process her question. She's suddenly so cheery, all sad feelings of Patrick and my long, lost love gone.

"Well, you're welcome to go to the beach or hang around this house. No specific plans, just have some fun."

Bouncing up from her chair, Lisa walks towards to the door. "Oh, the beach sounds fun. I'll go get my suit and grab James." And then she's gone, leaving me to stew on her earlier comments about me and Patrick.

Also, I need to apologize to James. She basically just told me that my leaving during senior year was hard on him. I'll need to talk to him and smooth things over. The door swings back open and I think I'm getting ready for my second dose of Lisa. But, Chloe slides in the lounger next to me looking like the lady in my mirror this morning.

"Don't ever let me play quarters again!" she whispers because the normal sound of her voice might split her head open.

I whisper back, "Ditto!" She smiles and that almost takes away from the ugliness her hangover has left her.

"Wow! When I planned the surprise party for you, I didn't know how surprised you'd be," Chloe says. I know she is referring to the surprise guest that made an appearance and found his place back in my heart.

"Yeah, didn't think I'd see Patrick until tonight," I say with a heavy sigh.

Chloe turns and looks at me face to face. "Listen Suz. You don't have to go tonight. I know I urged you to go for closure, but you don't have to put yourself through that." I realize that Chloe is seriously concerned for me. Seeing Patrick and me together last night and then the nightmare this morning, she probably thinks I'm about to lose my freaking mind. She might not be so off track.

"I can handle it," I say trying to sound confident in my decision to attend this stupid party.

"I don't think you can, Suz. And it scares me." Okay, so she really does think I'm a loose cannon. "I saw the way you and Patrick looked at each other last night. Something is off. I just don't want to see you get hurt again."

"Okay, so did we make out or something, because you're the third person this morning that's made a comment about me and Patrick," I say kind of frustrated at the whole situation. Chloe looks back at the inlet like she's meditating.

"I don't know, Suz. I expected you to be all goo-goo eyes for him. Not that you're still into him or anything, just that you didn't get your proper goodbye. But, I didn't expect the feeling to be mutual. I mean, my God, he is engaged!" Hearing the 'e' word again is like a knife slicing my skin open. But, it is the reality and no matter how painful it is to let someone go, it has to be done in order to move on. Plus, I want to move on with Wyatt. So why is this so hard?

"Exactly. He is engaged. And I'm dating a wonderful man who I would like to build a future with someday. So, maybe last night was our goodbye. I'm going to this party as his friend and that's that. Plus, I have a hot date!"

Chloe looks at me mischievously, "You didn't call Wyatt did you? If he comes and sees Patrick undressing you with his eyes, he'll get kicked out of the damn party."

"No, no, Wyatt isn't coming. He has his going away party for work tonight. Flynn is my hot date."

Chloe gives me an evil eye. "Lucky bitch!" I laugh as I walk inside to call Wyatt.

Chapter Twenty-Eight

(Present Day)

Wyatt picks up on the first ring. "Hey, Suzanna. I only have a minute. I'm at my advisor's office signing papers for the internship to count as the last part of my graduate grade. What's up?" I can tell Wyatt is flustered. He has a lot of loose ends to tie up before leaving Tuesday morning.

"Oh, I can call back later, if that's better?" I ask feeling a little disappointed that he doesn't have time for me. I wonder if his job this summer will be as demanding and fear that if so, we won't be talking as much.

"I've got time for you Suzanna, always." My heart does a back flip hearing his words. I briefly tell him about the party last night, of course leaving out the part of the surprise guest. It's not that I'm lying to him, it's just an omission of the truth. Besides, Patrick's presence meant nothing to me. I love Wyatt.

"Well, kudos for Chloe for pulling that off. Tell the guys I said hello." I hear Wyatt's name being called and know it is time to end the call.

"Good luck with your advisor. I'll talk with you later this afternoon."

"Thanks Suz, love you."

"I love you, too," I say, but the call goes dead. I hope he heard me.

Everyone has packed a lunch and cooler and heads over to the beach. I tell them I'll meet them after my paddle board lesson and dare any of them to come and watch. Chloe and Brian stay because Chloe agreed yesterday to be my wing woman. Brian is sticking around to work on a play he is writing. He promises not to watch our lesson from the back porch, but he'll have a straight on view whenever his head is not immersed in his notes. But Brian's cool and won't give me a hard time about my lack of coordination. I hear a rumbling noise and look to see that Drew has arrived in his jeep. I watch as he exits the driver's side and starts to undo the boards that are attached to the roll bar on top of the vehicle. He is dressed in swim trucks and flip flops. He has some surfer decal t-shirt on. His sandy brown hair glistens in the bright sun giving the illusion of highlights. Drew's not a big guy, but is toned and muscular in all the right places. His biceps bulge out of the sleeves of his shirt as he removes the boards from the jeep. I can tell he spends the majority of his time outdoors because his skin is golden. I hate to admit it, but I think I have been enjoying the view of Drew a little too much. Oh well, looking never hurts anyone. Besides he is a prime example of eye candy. Chloe agrees when she steps out on the porch.

"Damn, Suzanna! Why is it you get all the hot guys this summer?" I cringe when Drew looks up at us. Oh God. Did he just hear Chloe's comment and now thinks we are just standing here drooling over him? But, when he flashes his kind smile our way and waves, I don't care anymore whether he heard Chloe or not. The fact is the dude is smoking hot!

"Hello, ladies. Ready to get wet?" He jokes giving us a wink.

Chloe has to grab my shoulder for support before she melts into a puddle. She whispers to me, "I'm already there!" Pushing her to the side and giving her my best 'eww gross' look, I make my way down the front steps managing not to fall, which is a miracle.

"Hi, Drew. I'm ready to be completely humiliated. Follow me and I'll take you towards the backyard to the inlet." I glance at Chloe who is still stunned speechless. Waving my arms to break her Drew trance, I motion for her to come on. She meets us by the dock. After the introductions, Chloe seems to have found her way back to what Chloe does best. She flirts during our entire lesson, using her dramatic flair and southern drawl excessively. Drew doesn't seem to mind, but never gives me any indication that he will pursue something with Chloe. For all I know, he may have a girlfriend. We've barely just met, but I consider him a friend. I could use one of those once my chaotic house guests leave tomorrow.

Drew gives us brief instructions on how to stabilize the board while in the water. "It's all about balance between the board and your body," he says. He demonstrates the correct techniques to use going from the various positions. First lying on your stomach, then kneeling, and finally standing. Chloe and I are both in the water while Drew paddles between us both giving us pointers. I have mastered the kneeling position, but every time I go to stand, I capsize in the water. Chloe isn't much better. She basically gives up after a few spills and is now using the paddle board as a floating lounge chair as she soaks up the sun. We've been going at it for almost an hour and my muscles are tired. Maybe this is good exercise. Brian has been true to his word. I only caught him peering over his laptop a few times to take in the show. He would smile and shake his head before returning to his work. I am getting very frustrated every time I attempt to stand and fall.

"Ugh, this is so hard!" I yell towards Drew who is floating on his paddle board like it isn't in water. It seems to come so natural to him.

"Keep trying Suzanna. You're doing great!" I roll my eyes as I scoot back on the board lying on my stomach. During my next attempt to stand, I hear laughter floating from the backyard. The entire gang has come back from the beach, obviously ignoring my earlier threats. At this point, I don't even care that I have an audience. I just want to be finished with this lesson.

"How's she doing? She a pro yet?" I hear Flynn asking Drew.

Drew chuckles, "Not quite, but she'll get there."

"Come on Suz, show us what you got!" Landon yells from the dock. Determined not to fail again while my peers are watching, I execute the kneeling position with ease. Obnoxious clapping erupts from the dock making me laugh at how easy my stupid friends can be entertained. Holding the paddle perpendicular to my body like Drew taught me, I make it from my knees to my feet in a crouching position. Slowly using the paddle to balance, I stand up without falling. Everyone is hooting and hollering as I concentrate really hard to stand for an extended amount of time.

"That's great, Suz. Once you feel like you are completely balanced, use the oar and start paddling," Drew encourages. Careful not to lean too much one way or the other, I center myself with the board and slowly navigate the paddle into the water. With each thrust of the paddle, I slowly start to move. I am doing it! I am so engrossed in my achievement I don't hear or see the motorboat coming up behind me. When it passes, I still don't acknowledge it until its wake catches up to my board jostling me back into the water. When I resurface, the boat has turned around and is heading my way. Pulling up beside me and my board, Patrick looks down on me with amusement.

"You okay, Suz?" he smirks.

Coughing up water from my lungs I yell, "I was doing great until you decided to tip me over!"

"Sorry," he laughs while offering me his hand so he can pull me into the boat. With little grace, I swing my legs over the side of the boat. He leans down to grab my board and paddle while I collapse in the passenger seat.

"Taking on a new hobby?" he asks.

"Not voluntarily. Coach Moore is trying to improve my long game. Says I need to work on upper body strength. Guess this is the new trendy exercise of elite athletes." Patrick gives the boat some gas and we head towards my dock.

"Who's that?" Patrick asks eyeing Drew who is still on his board padding towards us.

"Oh, that's Drew Moore, Coach Moore's son. In addition to being a grad student, he has been assigned to be my playing partner and fitness coach. Courtesy of his dad!" I watch Patrick as he takes in the presence of Drew. Something flashes in his eyes. Could he be jealous? No, he is engaged I remind myself for the umpteenth time. Drew has made his way to the boat.

"Suzanna, that was great. You did it!" he exclaims, with pride all over his face. He gives me a high five as Patrick looks on, his lips pressed together in a straight line.

"Thanks Drew, you're a great teacher. Oh, and this is Patrick, an old friend." Patrick reaches over the boat to shake Drew's hand.

"Nice to meet you man."

"Likewise," Drew nods. We all turn when we hear a scream from the water, followed by boisterous laughter from the dock. Flynn has snuck in the water, swimming over to Chloe perched atop her board. He flips her over, and she acts like she is extremely put out with him. But, I know different. Chloe relishes any attention Flynn gives her. They are now in a playful fight trying to dunk each other.

"I'm just gonna grab the boards and paddles and start packing up. I'll see you Tuesday for golf and we can schedule your next fitness lesson," Drew says before paddling off.

"Sounds great! See you Tuesday." Patrick watches our interaction with a curious look, but doesn't say anything. It's an odd reaction from Patrick, seeing me and Drew being friendly. Maybe he is just nervous about the party tonight.

Before we get back within earshot of the others I turn to Patrick and ask, "So when does Katelyn arrive for the party?" Just saying her name puts a bad taste in my mouth, but I manage to act calm.

"She's at her family's place in Pawleys. She will arrive about an hour before the party." He doesn't offer any other information and we let the subject of his fiancé drop. Patrick jumps out of the boat first, turning back to offer his hand. I grab his hand and he helps me maneuver my body back to dry land. He doesn't let go of my hand as we walk towards the house, following the rest of our friends. I know this is wrong. Really wrong! But, his touch feels comfortable and I don't pull away. When we make it to the house, Patrick hesitates before going in. He turns his body facing mine and looks into my eyes. I think he is going to say something, but he just looks at me with unreadable emotions flashing across his face. We don't need words, because our eyes are saying everything for the both of us. After a few minutes, I break away looking down at the floor of the porch. Knowing the moment is over Patrick releases my hand and follows me to meet our friends at the beach. I am sad the moment has ended. My goal was to come and find closure, tell Patrick goodbye to what we once were. Now, I'm not so sure I am ready to do that.

I have to take deep cleansing breaths to steady my hand while applying mascara. Nervousness had taken over while I started getting ready for the party. Everyone has come in from the beach waiting their turns for the shower. Leslie arrived a few hours earlier. It was funny seeing her again after all these years, especially since we had just been talking about the infamous party scene last night. But, I can tell Leslie has changed and matured since her high school days. She is kind and sweet towards me, and very gracious for my hospitality this weekend. Her face lights up when Landon is around, and I know she is smitten with him. I can't tell if the feelings are mutual. Landon is attentive, but I see how guarded he is with his emotions, kind of like me. He has always been hard to read. I hope for Leslie's sake that his feelings match hers or else I think she might end up broken hearted. I have given them the downstairs bedroom for the night. James and Lisa are staying in one of the bedrooms across the living area from mine. Their bedroom shares a connecting bathroom with the other bedroom which is occupied this weekend by Chloe and Brian. Flynn is staying in my parent's room. The beach house is full of family and friends. I should be overjoyed, not nervous. But, I can't shake the feeling that this engagement party is a bad idea. I try to calm my nerves by pushing everything else from my mind and concentrating on Wyatt and our reunion tomorrow. I called him before my shower, letting him know I am counting down the hours. He assured me he is doing the same. He will be busy tonight with his own going away party given by his co-workers. I am thankful that he has something to fill his time and not worry about me being so close to Patrick. He was relieved when I told him Flynn will be my date tonight. I'm guessing he could detect the nervousness in my voice when I spoke of the party and is grateful Flynn will be there to support me through it. I secretly wish it would be Wyatt with me tonight. But, I know I have to do this alone. The nerves are still raging when I try to curl my hair. My stick, straight hair is not cooperating anyway. Several times I almost burn the side of my face and hands, once dropping the curling iron completely. I manage enough curls to frame my face, toppling down from a messy up do. I hope the abundant hairspray I applied will be enough to hold the hair in place for the duration of the party. My dress is a cream colored halter, with an open back. It is synched at the waist with a brown silk sash. The lower part of the dress is covered in a sheer chiffon material that flows almost to my ankles. I put on some strappy sandals that have a modest heel. One last look in the full length mirror and I am satisfied with my appearance. Subtle, but sexy. I want to impress Katelyn, Patrick's fiancé since this is the first time we will meet. I'm not sure if she knows anything about the past that Patrick and I share, but I am prepared nonetheless. I walk into the living area, still a bundle of nerves. Most of the guys are already dressed and waiting for their dates to emerge from the bedrooms. James, Flynn and Brian are sitting together on the couch watching a baseball game and having a beer. I have yet to drink any alcohol today, still hurting from my over consumption from last night. But a glass of wine is sure to give me the liquid courage I will need to survive tonight, plus it will also aid in calming my nerves. As I make my way into the kitchen to pour a glass of wine, I am bombarded with whistles from my audience of three whose eyes have left the game and noticed my appearance.

"Wow, Suz you look fantastic!" James says, walking over to join me.

"Thanks, James," I reply reaching with shaky hands for a wine glass. When he notices that I might drop the glass, he reaches over to assist.

"Here, let me help you with that!" He pours the wine and hands me the glass, unsure if I will spill the contents all over my dress. I take a quick gulp and manage not to spill a drop.

"You okay, Suz? You look a little, uh, nervous," James asks with caution. I nod and start making my way to the back deck.

"Yeah, I'll be fine. Want to join me out back? I'd like to talk with you." I remember my conversation with Lisa this morning and have yet to apologize to James about leaving so many years ago. Maybe if I can get this off my chest, some of my nerves will subside. He follows me outdoors and we sit beside each other at the patio table facing the inlet.

"Um, James, I'm sorry," I say releasing a breath I didn't realize I had been holding in.

"What?" he replies somewhat confused.

Finding the courage to continue, I explain. "I'm sorry for leaving years ago, without so much as a goodbye or explanation. You were a wonderful friend, and still are," I smile, "and you didn't deserve that."

James is silent for a moment. I wonder what memories are flashing through his head. Finally, he looks at me and smiles back.

"Suzanna, I don't know why you left and I hate myself for not finding out. Whatever it was, I know it was big. I should have been a better friend, hunted you down and supported you, no matter what. But I let other people influence me, letting me think the worst of you. You owe me no apology. I should be the one apologizing to you." I look at James completely shocked. He has been beating himself up for years thinking he's been a horrible friend when I was the one that left, completely shutting out everyone and not letting anyone other than Chloe in. Tears fill my eyes at how deep our friendship runs and I am so thankful that I have allowed myself to open back up and salvage this relationship.

"Oh James, thank you. But you couldn't have done anything back then, so stop hating yourself for another second. One day, I promise to tell you what happened and why I had to leave. I just can't right now. However, I could kick myself for waiting over four years to get you back in my life!" He laughs causing the tension from earlier to blow away with the ocean breeze. "I'm just glad you're here now," I say.

"Me, too. Now, let's not get too mushy. Your tears will ruin your makeup and we'll never make it to the party. Lisa will be pissed if she knew I made you cry. She already adores you." I think of Lisa and how lucky she is to find such a sweet man like James. I need to tell her so later.

"I adore her, too. And James, she is one lucky woman! She hurts you, and I'll hunt her down and beat her with my driver!"

"Glad you've got my back," he laughs as we make our way back inside to join the others who are now all dressed and ready to go.

"Always," I say, giving James a friendly hug. I glance over and see Lisa looking our way. She isn't giving me the evil eye like she is jealous. She seems to know that James and I are back on track to a friendship that will last a lifetime. I smile back, hoping that lifetime will include her also.

Chapter Twenty-Nine

(Present Day)

Everyone reloads their drinks and we leave for the party. The weather is perfect, a warm breeze coming in off the ocean. Since the Jones' beach house, where the party is taking place, is just a few blocks north of us, we decide to walk to the party. Plus, everyone has been drinking and we don't want to risk getting a DUI. Chloe and I walk together towards the back of the pack.

"Suzanna, you look beautiful," she says her smile giving me encouragement. She is the only one from this group who knows how anxious I am about tonight, and that it all doesn't have to do with Patrick.

"Well, you look sexy as hell! Poor Brian, he'll be the envy of the party with you on his arm," I tell Chloe. She does look stunning, as usual.

"Just friends, Suz, remember?" She really doesn't care what Brian thinks. Her attention is on my brother, who cleans up quite nicely. I will be the envy of every girl there, including Chloe, with Flynn flanking my side. We loop our arms together, as we have been doing since grade school and continue walking.

Chloe whispers so just I can hear. "Suz, you need me at anytime tonight, don't worry. I won't be too far away." I nod, seeing the concern in her eyes. I squeeze her arm in a gesture of thanks. The support of my best friend will be needed tonight more than ever. She feels the shiver that runs through my body as we approach the house. Stopping before coupling off for our entrance, she gives me a quick hug.

"Suz, I love you. You are so strong and you can do this." I don't feel strong. I want to turn around and run home. I feel Flynn approach and he grabs my other arm.

"Ready, Sis?" he asks. He and Chloe share a look between each other that I can't read. It isn't a passionate look like I have seen between them many other times. This look is like an unspoken vow between them to protect me tonight. I take a deep breath and try to exhale the fear that my body is filled with.

"I'm ready. Let's do this." Chloe pats my shoulder before joining Brian up front. Flynn holds my arm tightly, supporting my weak knees as we follow the others up the stairs and into the party.

The Jones' beach house is beautiful, but tonight it is magnificent. Fresh flowers are everywhere, lining the railings of the multiple porches and scattered throughout the house. There are a few guests inside mingling as we make our way towards the rear of the house to go through the receiving line. Mr. and Mrs. Jones are first in line as we approach. James, Landon and Chloe are all greeted with hugs as they enter and introduce their dates. When Flynn and I approach, Mrs. Jones smiles brightly.

"Suzanna and Flynn, you two are a sight for sore eyes. My, how you two have grown into such lovely adults. I know your parents are so proud. Just sorry they weren't able to make it tonight." She gives us each a hug.

"Everything is beautiful, Mr. and Mrs. Jones. Thanks for having us tonight." Okay, I can do this.

"Well, I'm so glad you're both here." Next to greet us is Aunt Betty. Her excitement over seeing us all alerts the entire crowd of our arrival. "I thought I wouldn't live to see the day. All my babies all grown up and so pretty." Landon and James laugh.

"We would prefer, handsome, Aunt B," James says jokingly. She pinches both of his cheeks like she had so many times when we were younger.

"You are pretty, and that's that." James flushes with embarrassment, rubbing his cheeks as if she caused him pain. "Now you all get out there and have a good time, but don't go too far. I will be armed with my camera and need a group shot of the Fabulous Five." We all sigh in unison. Aunt B and her camera are a constant. She was always snapping pictures for the scrapbooks she made for Patrick since he was a child. The line moves slowly and I am the last one to receive one of Aunt B's hugs. "Suz, you're trembling," she whispers as she holds me in an embrace. I know we are getting close to the end of the line where the guests of honor are welcoming everyone. The wine from earlier is not doing its job, and I am anxious again. Where the hell is the bar? I need another drink and fast.

"She's probably just chilled from our walk here," Flynn says coming to my rescue. Aunt Betty releases me from her hug, looking at me through narrowed eyes. I don't think she believes Flynn for one second, but the line behind us is filling up with more guests trying to enter the party and she doesn't have time to second guess him.

"You're probably right, Flynn. Now take your pretty sister and get her a drink."

"We're on our way," he replies flashing Aunt Betty his gorgeous smile that even a woman her age isn't immune to. I roll my eyes and pull Flynn forward. I am ready to get to that bar, now. But I have a few more people to greet on my destination. We meet Katelyn's parents next. They are nice and friendly to us all. I have a feeling if Katelyn does know my identity, she has not told her parents. The lady next in line, I have never met. I am surprised when she introduces herself as Patrick's dad's girlfriend. Her name is Ruth and is pleasant enough. While we introduce ourselves, Patrick's dad, Jim, comes to stand beside her, with a fresh liquor drink in his hands. Obviously, some things haven't changed. My body goes rigid, and I struggle to breathe. Flynn immediately notices my anxiety level has escalated and he moves us through the line fast, not even speaking to Jim as he settles back in his spot. I watch as Chloe glances back, looking me over and giving Flynn a nod before settling back into Brian's arm. I have a sneaking suspicion that they have talked earlier, but I am not sure how much she has divulged. I don't have time to elaborate because I am suddenly standing in front of Patrick and his fiancé Katelyn. I watch as Flynn shakes Patrick's hand while he introduces Katelyn to my brother.

"Nice to meet you, Katelyn. And this is my sister Suzanna." I am still looking at Patrick when Flynn nudges me.

"Suzanna, this is Katelyn."

"Oh, hi, it's nice to meet you. Congratulations. This is a lovely party." I am rambling, nervous words escaping. Patrick chuckles under his breath causing me to stop before I make more of a fool of myself.

"Well, it's nice to meet you, Suzanna," Katelyn replies.

Patrick finally speaks. "Suzanna is the friend I was telling you about who is qualifying this summer for the pro tour." I notice Patrick's use of the word 'friend' and feel a little relieved and disappointed at the same time. Has he not told her about us? Maybe he is referring to our new relationship as friends. I can't tell from Patrick's poker face.

"That's right, how exciting. Well, good luck to you," Katelyn replies with all sincerity.

"Thanks," I say focusing my eyes on Katelyn and not Patrick. She is beautiful. With her long, dark hair that matches her dark eyes. She is taller than me by a few inches, which isn't shocking since I never grew out of my runt size. She is also more voluptuous, her body filling out her cocktail dress in all the right places. Studying her physique I notice that she sports a couple of tattoos that haven't been hidden with her strappy number. The tats seem fitting on her, with her sensual, exotic style. I can see how Patrick is drawn in by her beauty, but I sense that Katelyn has a dark side that is waiting to be unleashed. I start to feel insecure of my petite frame and lack of curves until I notice Patrick's eyes roam over my body briefly, taking in my appearance. Before things get more uncomfortable, Flynn pulls me slightly towards him.

"We're going to head to the bar and let you greet the rest of your guests. We'll see you both later." I don't say anything as I just walk away letting Flynn lead us to the bar. We mingle with a few hometown friends before meeting back up with the rest of the gang getting their drinks filled. Chloe rushes to my side, handing me a glass of wine I haven't yet ordered. Beyond thankful, I take a huge un-lady like gulp downing half the glass. If this weekend doesn't end soon, I'll more than likely be on the verge of a drinking problem.

"I thought you might need that," Chloe whispers. "How'd it go?" she asks with concern.

"I was a blubbering idiot. Thank God Flynn was there to rescue me from myself. I think Patrick got a kick out of it." Chloe doesn't find it funny, but only replies with a "hmmmmm." An hour later, most guests have arrived and the party is in full swing. People are drinking, talking and dancing and I find myself having a good time with my friends. I am sharing a dance with Landon when I see Patrick again. I haven't seen him since our arrival, figuring he has been busy parading Katelyn around and making introductions. The majority of the people in attendance are here for him. I watch as he makes his way through the crowd of people, stopping briefly to say hello to a few. By the time he approaches me and Landon, the song has ended and the band is starting up with another slower tempo song. Patrick lays his hand on Landon's shoulder.

"Mind if I take the next dance?" Landon glances over my way making sure I am okay to dance with Patrick. Even Landon seems to take on the protector of Suzanna title tonight. I give him a slight nod before he turns to face Patrick.

"Yeah man, but just one. There are a number of guys waiting to dance with the prettiest girl at your party." I blush at Landon's comment, which is so very unlike him. Patrick is paying no attention to Landon, drinking me in like a cool glass of water. Our threesome on the dance floor will get awkward if one of us doesn't leave soon. Landon reluctantly starts to walk away, but not before giving me one last look as if he is letting me know he'll be there if needed. Patrick wraps his arms around my waist loosely while I place my hands on his shoulders. It is like déjà vu of last night's dance, except tonight we keep a comfortable distance between our bodies. As we sway to the music, I feel like I need to say something to appease the uneasy feeling between us.

"Katelyn's nice and beautiful," I say, suddenly regretting bringing her into our brief time together.

"Yes, she is. But, Landon was right. You, Suz, are the prettiest girl here." Wow, he just gave me a one up on his fiancé. I don't know what to make of Patrick's compliment.

"You guys are just biased, having known me all my life. Katelyn is the belle of this ball and you are a lucky man." Patrick looks at me with a smirk.

"You were never good at receiving compliments, were you?" I smile shyly, before looking away. The song ends and I want to exit the dance floor, but Patrick's arms are still around my waist. I take this moment to look back up at his face and our eyes meet, just as they had earlier today after my lesson. This time I see sadness there that I hadn't been able to recognize earlier. If I am right, this is his goodbye. The goodbye to our past. I don't notice the band has started the next song, and other people are dancing around us as we stand there, saying goodbye without uttering a word. Finality sinks in and I realize that the boy who was my first love, my first everything, is letting me go. And I have to let him go, also. That's why I am here, anyway, right? Yes, that's why I am suffering through this stupid engagement party to finally find closure on that part of my life. As a few tears escape my eyes, I reach up and brush my fingers across Patrick's cheek, our gaze never breaking. With barely a whisper, I manage to end this before I crumble into a sobbing mess on the dance floor.

"Goodbye, Patrick." I turn and walk away, closing that door of my life.

I make it into the guest bathroom before the flood gates open and I cry for what Patrick and I will never be. I know I don't have time for the full on sobbing I will do later in the privacy of my bed, but I have to release this emotion before I explode. Touching up my face and hoping no one will notice, I finally make my way out of the bathroom. Luckily no one else has been waiting to use the facilities. I am making my way down the hallway to get back to the party and my friends when I freeze, my feet planted under me like they are cemented to the floor. Standing at the end of the hallway is Jim, Patrick's father. He gives me a stern look before closing the gap between us. I try to sidestep him but he blocks my path. My breath is stuck in my throat allowing nothing to escape.

"Suzanna, I'm surprised to see you here tonight," he says in a low voice, causing me to tremble. "Don't think you can come prancing back into our lives, messing things up for him and me. I'd hate for someone to get hurt." I look around darting my eyes anywhere, but towards him. I am pretty sure he has just threatened me, but he isn't very specific.

Finding my voice, I say, "I'm here as his friend only," hoping that his bully dad will get out of my way so I can escape. He still doesn't budge, just stands there sloshing his drinking around in his glass, pinning me with his evil stare.

"Good, because if I see you looking at my son again the way you did on that dance floor, I'll make sure my version of the story is more damning to you than to me." I gasp, terrified of the man in front of me and what he can possibly do to ruin any loving memories Patrick will hold onto of me, of us. Feeling a sudden surge of fear, my body instantly starts to run down the hallway. But before I make it completely by Jim, he grabs my arm pulling me to an abrupt halt. "I think it's time for you to leave," he growls. Before he can push me away, Chloe and Flynn come around the corner. They see Jim's tight squeeze on my arm and the glowering look on his face. Then they see me, shaking violently now with fear all over my face. Before Jim realizes they are there, Flynn covers the distance like a cat, and pushes Jim in the chest. Jim releases my arm as he staggers back, spilling his drink in the process. Flynn, with his fists clenched, is going in for a fight, hatred pulsing off his entire body. His punch lands on Jim's midsection, sending him sliding across the hallway on his rear end.

"Don't you ever lay a hand on my sister again, you low life drunk!" Flynn yells while Chloe wraps her arms around me, trying to shelter me from the violence that is taking place. A few of the guests have heard the commotion and are now witnesses to the horrible event.

"Suzanna, you okay?" Flynn asks never taking his eyes off Jim who is still on the ground.

"No, but let's go, I just want to get out of here." I answer as best I can considering the effort it takes to just breathe. With Chloe on one side of me and Flynn on the other, we make our way to the front of the house, ignoring the stares and whispers of others. We are almost out the front door before I hear a panicked Patrick come running towards us.

"Suzanna, what's wrong? What the hell just happened? Someone told me Flynn just took out my dad." I can't even begin to explain, especially at this time and place. Hopefully, we can escape and the engagement party will not be completely ruined. I don't explain, just turn and walk out the door, while Flynn and Chloe follow. I hear Patrick calling my name from the front porch, but I never turn around, just keep walking from the nightmare that is becoming my life.

The walk back to our beach house is quiet, no one saying a word. When I get home, I go to my bedroom and undress, throwing on a pair of pajama pants, a tank top, and hoodie. I slip on my flip flops and meet Flynn and Chloe on the back deck where they are whispering to each other. When they stop as I appear, I know they are talking about me. Flynn has to know the truth, and though I suspect Chloe of telling him bits and pieces, he needs to hear the entire story from me. I sit down in the chaise lounge at Flynn's feet. With all the courage I can muster, I turn looking at Flynn.

"I need to tell you a story." He doesn't say anything, just waits patiently for me to begin. Chloe shifts to get up, thinking she will give us some private time. But I grab her leg, urging her to stay. I need all the support and strength she so willingly gives me. She relaxes back in her chair, nodding for me to start. The memories rush through my head, causing me great pain, but I manage to verbalize that awful night that changed my life and continues to haunt me now.

Chapter Thirty

(December Senior Year of High School)

It is the country club's annual Christmas party. Our parents have been dragging us to this thing for years. We are finally of age that we actually enjoy it, having more time to spend with each other, and getting all dressed up. Chloe and I enjoy the idea of getting dressed up, although the guys hate having to wear suits and ties. We have to cling to our parents for the obligatory period of time, talking to their friends while they show us off and gush about our accomplishments. Once that is over, the parents mingle amongst themselves enjoying drinking and dancing. The younger children are picked up by babysitters or nannies so the parents can party into the wee hours of the night. Since we are all seniors in high school, everyone except Chloe, we obviously don't need a babysitter or nanny. We decide we'll make our own party at our favorite golf hole, like we've been doing all year. Wyatt secretly packs us a cooler, promising to meet us if he gets a break or our parents start getting curious about our whereabouts, whichever comes first. All five of us, Chloe, James, Landon, Patrick and I meet up at the golf shop and make our way to the seventeenth hole, our secret party place. I left my coat in the lounge earlier when I arrived and I am freezing. The December weather has been mild, but the night time air is cold and I am wearing a sleeveless cocktail dress. I start to go back to retrieve my coat, but Patrick gives me his suit jacket to keep me warm. After an hour or more of beer and lively banter among the five of us, the temperature is getting unbearable. Plus, it is getting late and I'm sure the party has died down. We all trudge back to the club house together, Patrick and I bringing up the rear.

"You look beautiful tonight, Suz," he says, kissing the tender spot below my ear. We are barely able to walk, our arms entangled as we cuddle with each other for warmth. "I wish we could be together tonight, just you and me," Patrick continues to whisper.

"Me too," I say in agreement. It has been weeks since Patrick and I made love, finding little time to be alone. I want to be with him so badly. His arms around me, the whispering in my ear, he's kisses on my neck, all of it is driving me crazy with desire no eighteen year old should feel. But I don't know how we can manage some alone time, unless...

"Let's go back to our spot, on the course. I'll say I forgot my phone or something," I suggest.

"But Suz, its freezing!" Stopping him to get more distance between us and the rest of the gang, I turn him to face me, feeling desperate to get that alone time.

"I'll keep you warm. Please, Patrick, I need you." I am begging now, and I can tell he wants this as badly as me. I press my lips to his and kiss him deeply, urging him to agree with my proposal. When we break our kiss, Patrick gives me a wicked smile before turning to the others.

"Hey guys, I think I left my phone. Suz and I are going back to get it. We'll meet up with y'all a little later." Before they can respond, Patrick is pulling me back towards the course into the darkness. When we arrive, we are both needy and horny. Our kisses become hard and forceful, hands exploring each others' bodies. Patrick lays me down on the cold grass, covering me with his body. His hands are running up and down my thighs inching closer and closer to the throbbing place between my legs. My hands are all over him, running up and down his back, across his shoulders to his chest and down his stomach muscles. My fingers inch to the waistband of his pants slipping inside towards his boxers.

"God, Suzanna," he moans as I unbuckle his belt, unbutton his pants and start unzipping him. He manages to pull my dress up around my waist, while his hand skims along the edge of my panties.

"Patrick, please," I beg again. I need him inside of me, now. He leans up from my body and balances on his knees while I pull his pants and boxers down his thighs, releasing his manhood that is ready for me. Hungrily, he pulls my panties down as I arch up to meet him. Pushing me back down, he kisses me forcefully, as our bodies rub together.

"Suz, you feel so good." I am wiggling beneath him, trying to position myself so he can enter. Using his hand as a guide, he centers himself at my entrance before plunging in.

"Ohhhhh," I moan as he slides in and out of my body. His thrusts become faster and his breathing becomes ragged. I want to keep him inside me forever pulling him deeper as my hands grip his ass. I wrap my legs around his torso, making our bodies one. My body has never responded so quickly and I begin to feel that tingle that starts in my toes and races up my body until it stops at my core and rages to a burning fire, right before I explode. Patrick feels when I tighten around him, finishing his release a few moments after several more hard thrusts inside me. This, by far, has been the best sex we have ever experienced together. I lie back against the cold hard earth, completely spent, while Patrick relaxes on top of me. After a few moments of post coital ecstasy, we are brought back to reality by the beeping of my cell phone, alerting me of an incoming text.

"We better check that, make sure no one is sending out a search party," I say. Patrick kisses me quickly on the lips before getting up and redressing his lower body. He offers his hand and pulls me to a standing position. "Where is my underwear?" I ask looking around in the darkness. Patrick pulls them from his pocket.

"I was hoping I could keep them, a little reminder of this night!" he laughs.

"Give me those, you perv!" Grabbing them from his hand, I slide on my panties and press my dress down with my hands. I hope all the parents have left the club because I'm sure my appearance screams, 'I just had sex'. Patrick checks the text.

"That was Chloe. They are waiting for us in the parking lot. They want to go to some party Landon knows about." Patrick relays the content after reading her text.

"Oh, okay, text her back that we're on the way." He does and we walk hand in hand back to the club house. The party has died down, most guests in the process of leaving. Patrick and I check each oth-ers' appearances, giggling at what we have just done, before walking through the club to the front parking lot. We almost make it to the front exit before I realize I left my coat in the lounge.

"I need to go get my coat. Go with James and Landon and tell Chloe to wait for me. She'll have directions to the party and we can meet you there."

"You sure, Suz? I don't want to leave you." Giving him a quick kiss before pushing him away, I smile.

"Go, we'll be right behind you." I turn to go back into the club and Patrick leaves to go get in the car. The staff is making their way out, after working the party. Most of the cleanup is being done in the ball-room on the other side of the lounge. The lighting is dimmed, but not completely dark. I slip into the lounge to retrieve my coat from the back of the chair at the corner table. Reaching out to grab it, I am startled by footsteps behind me. On edge anyway, in an almost deserted club late at night, I whip around to find Patrick's father, Jim, standing in front of me. His eyes are glassed over from the multiple liquor drinks he has undoubtedly consumed tonight.

"Well, well if it isn't the beautiful Miss Caulder," he says with a slur.

"Um, hi Mr. Miles, I was just getting my coat."

"I see... going somewhere?" he asks coming closer into my personal space.

"Yes, Chloe's waiting for me now, so I've really got to go," I say quickly grabbing my coat to walk away. But before I can make an escape, Jim grabs me pushing me backwards against the wall. I am so stunned I can't even scream. He glares down at me, his alcohol laced breath roll-ing across my face.

"You know Suzanna, Patrick seems to have found a good thing," his eyes roaming my body from head to toe, "a really good thing. Maybe if I had a little taste of what's his, I can forget his mother like he seems to have done so easily. You look like a good distraction at the moment." Oh God, what is he planning to do to me? And when did he become so angry and bitter towards my relationship with Patrick? When Marie was alive, he seemed to support the fact that Patrick and I were dating.

I squirm against the wall trying to break free from his grasp, but his man sized body is no match for my petite frame. He starts kissing the sides of my face while his hands roam up and down my sides. I scream but only the first part escapes before one of his hands clasps over my mouth, shutting me up.

"Don't scream, Suzanna, or this will get a lot worse for you," he whispers, while stabbing his tongue in my ear. The pressure of his body becomes almost unbearable, pinning me even further into the wall causing my back to ache in pain. His hands are harsh against my breasts where he begins to fondle me. I can barely breathe, but know I have to do something to stop him or he will take his assault to another level. When I hear the straps of my dress being ripped from my body, I take the only chance I have and bite a finger of the hand that is still over my mouth. He pulls back, releasing his hand jerking the finger from my teeth.

I scream, "No, stop, please stop!" before he slaps me hard across the face causing my vision to blur.

"You fucking little bitch!" he growls jabbing his knee between my legs. I am dazed from his slap, but manage to hear the sound of his hands fumbling with his belt. I am about to be raped by the father of my boyfriend and there is nothing I can do.

With one last breathe, I begin to plead, "Please, stop. Don't do this, Nooooooooo!" And suddenly he isn't there, and my body goes limp falling down the wall to the floor.

"Keep your hands off of her, you drunk bastard!" Wyatt yells while slinging Jim to the other side of the room. In his drunken state, Jim staggers unbalanced crashing into a table and landing on the floor. Wyatt rushes to my side, scoops me up like a baby, grabs my coat and whisks me out of the lounge. Chloe, who has been waiting patiently, meets us in the hallway.

"Wyatt, what are you doing?" Wyatt never stops walking and Chloe turns to follow him back out the front of the country club.

"Get in the car and start driving, now!" Wyatt barks at Chloe while he places me in the back seat sliding in beside me. Chloe, for once, takes his directions without reason and drives out of the parking lot.

"Where are we going and what happened to Suzanna?" Chloe demands. Wyatt gives Chloe directions to his sister's house, which is empty since she happens to be out of town this weekend. Wyatt helps me walk through the door of his sister's house, Chloe following closely behind. Wyatt wraps me in a blanket as I sit on the couch while Chloe stares in silence. Patience is not Chloe's strong suit, but she waits knowing the explanation is going to be bad.

"Suzanna, can you tell Chloe what happened?" Wyatt asks. I shake my head, unable to speak yet. "Do you want me to tell her?" I look at Chloe, concern coloring her beautiful face and nod yes. Wyatt tells Chloe what he found Jim doing to me when he walked into the lounge earlier tonight. Chloe rushes to my side, hugging me tightly.

"Oh my God, Suz! I'm so sorry." Through her coat pocket, I can feel her phone vibrating nonstop. I know it is probably the guys wondering what the holdup is. As if she can read my mind, Chloe asks, "You want me to call Patrick?"

Almost before she can finish the question, I shout, "No!"

"Suzanna, he's blowing up my phone now wondering where the hell we are. I've got to tell him something."

"He can't know what happened tonight. It would kill him. Jim is the only parent he has left and I can't take that away from him."

Wyatt looks over with widened eyes, "So you're not pressing charges? Suzanna, he was going to rape you!"

I cry as I hear the word, and realize how close I came to being a rape victim. "I can't!" I whisper. "Patrick can never know. Please, don't tell him." Wyatt and Chloe exchange a look. They both think I am making a huge mistake, but are willing to follow my wishes. Chloe texts Patrick letting him know that her parents nixed the idea of a late night party and have demanded she make curfew tonight. She only tells him that I am with her, spending the night and that I left my phone at the club. She promises I'll call him tomorrow. All three of us spend the night at Wyatt's sister's house, in her living room, never needing the comforts of a bed. None of us get much sleep that night, Wyatt and Chloe too concerned for me and me, not wanting to shut my eyes, fearful of the face I'll see in the dark. The next morning I beg Chloe to come with me to the beach. We concoct this Christmas shopping spree that our parents believe, and we leave for the beach that morning. While at the beach, I contact the junior golf academy and beg them for acceptance into the program. The academy is a private school for aspiring teen golfers across the country. It is very prestigious and expensive, but if I can guarantee acceptance, I know my parents will let me attend. My high school coach must manage to pull some major strings because by the end of the weekend, I have been accepted and will start in January. Patrick and I text back and forth briefly over the weekend, but I am very vague about my whereabouts and plans, only telling him that Chloe and I are shopping out of town. When we return Sunday, I plead with my parents to let me go finish my high school career attending the golf academy, faking problems between me and Patrick, but never telling them the truth. Reluctantly, they agree only because Dad figures it will be good for my golf game and will prove easy to get a scholarship to college. Chloe is heartbroken that we will not be going to the same school, but completely understands and holds back her emotions. The only obstacle now is Patrick. A week after the incident, I have yet to see Patrick, making up silly excuses that I am busy helping Mom with preparations for Christmas. The night before Christmas Eve, I finally agree to see him one last time before I leave, breaking both our hearts. He picks me up to go to dinner, but before we enter the restaurant, I talk with him in his car. I tell him that I have chosen my golf career over our relationship, and I don't want to continue a long distance romance. He is stunned, begging me that we can make this work. But I refuse to listen to anything he suggests, knowing if I do I might rethink the whole thing and spill my guts. I have to let him go and protect him from the ugly truth. We never eat dinner that night. He takes me back home an hour after our breakup and just drives away, leaving me a sobbing mess for the rest of the night. I leave the day after Christmas and never come back to take up permanent residency again in my hometown. The occasional family get-togethers for birthdays or holidays are celebrated either at the beach or Columbia, once I move there. There are only a few times I travel back to Florence, and most of them involve Chloe. She is the best friend I have and if I am going to salvage anything from this disaster it is her. Luckily, she agrees to spend our time together at her home or mine, never once asking me to go out in public. I am ecstatic when she decides to attend the same university I chose a year earlier. We are finally able to be together again. Wyatt moves to Columbia the same year as Chloe and starts working on his graduate degree. They had kept in touch at the club, so naturally they did the same in Columbia. Wyatt picks up our friendship without blinking an eye, and we never talk about his heroic measures until just recently when we started our romantic involvement.

Chapter Thirty-One

(Present Day)

As the memories rush back, I realize I have told Flynn everything, except the golf course part between me and Patrick which is too much information for my little brother to handle. What I am giving him is enough to handle, without the knowledge of his sister's sexual escapades. I realize when I finish talking that I have been crying. Flynn reaches up wiping a tear from my eye, and hugs me harder than he ever has, which only brings on a fresh batch of tears. I glance over at Chloe and notice she is also crying. I'm sure her tears have more to do with me finally sharing this part of my life with a family member, and not so much to do with the horrid details.

"I'm so sorry, Suz," Flynn says as he rubs my back. "I should have killed him tonight!" he growls trying to control the anger just beneath the surface.

"Suzanna, what happened tonight? What did he say?" Chloe asks. I tell them of Jim's threats against me, saying if I have any other intentions than friendship with Patrick that he will make up his own version of the story. And that version will not be kind to me.

"You have got to be kidding me!" Chloe says in exasperation.

"I'm really gonna kill him now!" Flynn jumps up ready to punch something.

"Guys, he's a drunk and a jerk, and it's over. Plus, Patrick and I are just friends. He's engaged to Katelyn and I'm in love with Wyatt." Flynn turns back and looks at me, jaws flapped open. I have managed to shock him twice tonight.

"You're in love with Wyatt? I thought you guys just starting dating!" he asks flabbergasted.

"Well, yes. Look, I know it seems fast, but we maintained a friendship for years, and just recently took it to a new level," I answer smiling at the thought of seeing him tomorrow. "That's why I'm leaving first thing in the morning. I'm spending the next few nights with him before I take him to the airport Tuesday morning to catch his flight. He was offered a very prestigious internship in New York where he'll be spending the summer." It is like I am slapping Flynn in the face with all the new information I am giving him in a rapid pace.

"Okay, sis, I think that's about all I can take tonight. Whoa, who are you?" he laughs. "When you get back on Tuesday we are going to sit down and have a good long chat. But right now, I think I hear our house guests returning from the party." Coming over to give me one last hug, he whispers, "I love you, sis."

"Love you too, little bro." I walk inside the house and wait for the other house guests to arrive while Chloe and Flynn whisper to each other behind me. Landon and Leslie walk through the front door, followed by James and Lisa, and finally Brian. Thank goodness they remembered to gather up Brian and bring him home. I had completely forgotten he was even there.

"Dude, we heard you decked Mr. Miles?" James says. Flynn and I exchange glances before he answers.

"Yeah, I may have overreacted. But doesn't he know better than to insult my sister's golf game?"

James laughs, "You are an overprotective brother, even though you are a year younger. Hate to see how protective you get with an actual girlfriend." Everyone laughs knowing Flynn's womanizing history.

"That's a good one, me and an actual woman I could call a girlfriend. How long do they have to hang around to earn that title?"

Chloe slaps his arm. "You're a pig, Flynn Caulder!"

A couple of hours later, everyone has turned in for the night. Before they are all tucked in, I say my goodbyes since I am leaving in the morning for Columbia. I don't want anyone getting up early on my behalf, especially after a weekend of heavy partying. I am in my bedroom finishing packing my overnight bag, thinking back on this day. Wow, what a day. It feels like it has been a month long with everything that happened today. I should be exhausted, but I can't go to sleep. Maybe it is my anticipation of finally seeing Wyatt after our five days apart. Or maybe it is my brain trying to make sense of the two moments I spent with Patrick and our heartfelt goodbyes. Then again, it could be the drama that transpired between Jim and me, causing Flynn to come to my rescue. I was finally truthful with Flynn about that horrible night over four years ago. It felt good to finally share that secret with someone other than Chloe and Wyatt. Tossing and turning for more than an hour, I give up trying to sleep around midnight. I grab a bottle of water from the fridge and walk out to rocking chairs on the front porch. It is quiet out, and I can hear the waves breaking from across the street. The sound is therapeutic as I keep the rhythm with my rocking chair. I am lost in thought when I hear the sound of faint footsteps coming up the stairwell. I'm about to run into the house and bolt lock the door before I see the blond head of hair that belongs to my first love. Patrick appears on the landing, still wearing his suit from the party minus the tie. His jacket is unbuttoned, as are the top few buttons of his un-tucked shirt. His hair is windblown due to the ocean breeze. He looks stunning.

"Hey," he says, bringing my eyes back to his face.

"Hi," I reply like it is so natural he would show up after midnight on my porch.

"May I join you?" he asks. I pat the rocking chair next to me as he walks over and takes a seat.

"I couldn't sleep. What's your excuse?" I ask.

"Same. Plus, I wanted to make sure you were okay."

"Yeah, I'm fine. Sorry if Flynn ruined your party. He tends to be a bit overprotective where his sister is concerned." I don't offer any other explanation and he doesn't ask.

"Well, my dad's a jerk, especially when he drinks, which is quite often. I'm sure he deserved it." Patrick looks sad having to say such things about his only living parent. Thank goodness he only knows about the drinking and not the rest of the things his dad is capable of.

"I'm sorry, about your dad, Patrick. I guess he never really got over your mother's passing."

"He hasn't, but that's no excuse to drink himself into a stupor every night," he says with traces of anger in his voice. "But I didn't walk all the way down here to talk about my dad."

Huh?

"Suzanna," he pauses trying to find the right words, "I need to ask you something." I have no idea where this is going, but I know it might involve a deep conversation.

"Yes?" I prompt him to spit it out.

Taking a deep breath he asks, "What did I do?"

What did I do? I'm not following. Seeing my obvious look of confusion, he offers more details.

"When you left, what did I do to make you leave?" His question is like a punch to the gut, causing a loss of breath. Seeing the apprehension on his face, it dawns on me that he could have been blaming himself for me leaving four years ago.

"Nothing!" I say with more force than intended. He doesn't look convinced as he sits in the rocker slouched over resting his elbows on his thighs.

He glances over my way before asking, "Did I, um, was I too forceful, when we, um, were on the golf course? I know it was frantic, and um, passionate. I hope I didn't..."

"Stop!" I say, not wanting to let him ruin the best memory of that night. "Patrick, you never hurt me. Us, that night, well, that was intense, yes, but don't ever think that it isn't a very special memory for me." I watch as some of the tension eases from Patrick's body.

"It was special for me, too," he grins. I feel a warm blush run up my neck and through my cheeks. I quickly look back towards the ocean to avoid his gaze.

"Suz?" I hear him say between the creaks from my rocking chair.

"Yeah?"

"So, why did you leave?" he asks. Even after all these years, I still can't tell him the truth.

"You know, the golf academy. I wanted to go to the academy to concentrate on golf." I watch as he leans back in his rocker, trying to digest my false statement.

"So, what you're telling me is that you chose golf over your family, friends, school, and *me*. That's what you're telling me?" he says incredulously. I can hear the doubt in his tone, but I nod anyway trying to confirm another lie. We sit there in silence, nothing but the waves of the ocean crashing against the shore.

"Well, I guess I got my answer. I better head back to the house," Patrick says as he stands up from the rocker. I stand up with him with intentions of walking him to the door. But then he turns to face me, both of us frozen in front of each other.

Patrick slowly lifts his hand and gently brushes it across my face. Involuntarily, I lean into his touch. "So, let me ask you this Suz. When you drive your tee shot perfectly down the middle of the fairway does it make you feel anywhere close to the way my touch makes you feel?" I know in this instance that my traitorous body has given me away and Patrick is fully aware of the affect he has on me. But, I still don't answer because my ability to speak has been paralyzed. Patrick continues grilling me with questions. "And when you chip out of the bunker, your ball landing inches away from the cup, does it cause you to tremble like you do when our bodies are pressed together?" He asks me this as he simultaneously wraps his arm around my waist and pulls me against him, not a millimeter of separation between us. And right on cue, my body trembles. "One last question Suz,...when you sink the winning putt from ten feet out for the victory, does it make you feel anything like this?" Before I can think of an answer our lips are locked and we begin kissing slowly, but passionately. Thank goodness his arm is still firmly around my waist or else I'd be falling to the floor. Suddenly, the kiss ends and Patrick pulls away looking in my eyes with so much intensity, I fear what he'll say next.

"Suzanna, I don't believe that golf was your reason for leaving. I know what I felt when I was with you, and I'm pretty sure you felt the same. I could never have just left that behind." His words sting and my guilt begins to rise to the surface, bringing with it a knot, trapped in my throat. "But whatever your reason for leaving me behind, well, I hope it was worth it." A tear escapes my eye and trickles down my cheek before Patrick gently wipes it away with his thumb. The pain of missing him for the last four years triggers more tears until I am crying.

"I'm so sorry. Please forgive me," I beg as he wraps his arms around me and I sob into his chest.

"Suzanna, please don't cry. I'm not blaming you for anything. I just don't understand leaving me when I love you, I mean, I loved you.." I pull back to look for the confirmation of his slip up. It was a slip up, right? No way can he still love me years later, after I broke his heart. He cups my face in his hands and leans in so our foreheads are touching. "I love you, Suz. I never stopped."

I gasp at his declaration, but don't know how to respond. His lips press ever so slightly against mine, warm and soft. It is as if he is asking permission to continue. This is what I have wanted since the day I left him, and now after years of separation, he is kissing me, again. I lean in pressing my hands to his chest, then sliding them up and around his neck. His response is immediate and our kiss deepens. There are so many things running through my mind, his engagement and Wyatt, but I push them down and cherish this moment. This moment I have been clinging to since the day I walked out of his life. Jim took this away from us, and if just for this night, I am reclaiming what is mine. Passion ignites in me as my hands run up Patrick's neck and my fingers tangle in his thick blonde hair, pulling him in closer. No longer paying just my mouth attention, Patrick kisses every inch of my face, almost as if he can't make up for the four years lost without touching me. His kisses inch along my jaw line, up my cheek and end near my ear, making me shiver when he finds the sensitive spot right below my ear. I hear him whisper between each kiss.

"Was"....kiss.

"It"...kiss.

"Worth"....kiss.

"It"...kiss.

Then he is back to my mouth, pleasuring me with his tongue. I respond giving him everything I have in this one kiss, hoping that it can answer his question without needing words. Because right now, I don't know if anything was worth giving up Patrick and the way I feel in his arms.

Suddenly, the head lights of a slow moving approaching car beams, illuminating the porch. Our lips break away from each other as we catch our breaths and watch the car continue its slow moving path down the road. The tourists are always arriving at all hours of the night, trying to find their weekly rental in the dark. I am grateful for the interruption, pushing Patrick away, realizing what I have just done.

"Um, Patrick, I'm sorry. This is wrong. You're engaged!" I say breathless still trying to find my bearings from that kiss.

"I know, and I'm sorry. I guess I got carried away talking about the past." He holds his head down in defeat. Two months ago, I would have begged him to try again, begged him to leave Katelyn for me. But I think about Wyatt and my happiness. Patrick is in the past and that's where he needs to stay. I walk slowly on unsteady legs to the door, still a little shocked from Patrick's revelation and that kiss. Before entering the house, I turn as Patrick is about to descend the stairs.

"Patrick?" He turns and waits for me to continue. "Just because I left, it didn't mean I ever stopped loving you. Goodnight, Patrick." I close the door on tonight. Tomorrow morning I will open this door again, to my future, which belongs to Wyatt now.

Chapter Thirty-Two

(Present Day)

After a restless night of sleep, I wake early. I'd like to attribute my lack of sleep to the excitement of seeing Wyatt, but I'd only be kidding myself. All I can think about is last night and Patrick's last words whispered between kisses in my ear. Was it worth it? The conviction I felt in my decision to leave four years ago is wavering. What if I made a mistake? I believed at the time that Patrick needed his dad and that by removing myself from his life, then they could go back to being a normal family unit. Obviously, with the interaction I had with Jim at the engagement party, and the angry words of Patrick referring to his father's drinking, things didn't get back to normal, even after I left. Did I make a mistake, causing Patrick years of suffering without me and an alcoholic father to contend with? Ugh, just more unanswered questions that I don't need. I can still smell Patrick's scent and the feel of his lips on mine. I remember how my body automatically melted into his even after all those years apart. It's as if we fit perfectly together. Maybe I should have told Patrick the truth about his dad years ago. No, that was not even an option. Not only would Patrick have hated his dad, not to mention probably tried to kill or at least cause him major bodily harm, but he would have had to suffer the embarrassment from our community had I gone public with assault charges. Basically, I took the only option I felt I had at the time, which only caused both of us pain at the time and still does to this day.

Shaking my head, I try to push all thoughts of Patrick away and focus on today. I'm excited about seeing Wyatt. I need to see Wyatt. Even though it will be for only a short time, Wyatt will bring my wandering 'what if' mind back to the present and then I can focus all my attention on the man who brought me back from the dark side. The man who taught me how to love again and who loves me unconditionally, faults and all. I dress quickly and I am ready to leave by 8:30. I'm about to make it out the door when Chloe walks into the kitchen, stretching and yawning.

"Oh, hey Chloe. I'm just about to leave." She walks over to me and gives me a big hug.

With her arms around me, giving me the support she always does, my emotions go into overdrive and I begin to cry. So much of what happened last night weighs heavily on my mind. I'm unable to contain it any longer.

"Hey, what's all this?" Chloe asks gently wiping away my tears.

"It's just been an emotional weekend and I'm both nervous and excited about seeing Wyatt. Plus, I know I'm going to have to deal with saying goodbye, again, this time for longer. I guess I'm feeling a little weak at the moment."

"Suzanna, you're stronger than you give yourself credit for. Look at what you did last night. You walked into the engagement party of your first, true love. Not only that, you put yourself in the position to have to deal with Patrick's asshole father again. You did all that looking like a million bucks and you handled yourself with grace. You are selfless and strong and you can handle saying a temporary goodbye to Wyatt. Because, Suz, it is just temporary. Wyatt loves you and you love him."

Chloe gives me her reassuring smile while I gather myself. "Thanks, Chloe. You make it all sound so easy." I want to tell Chloe about what happened last night between me and Patrick, but I think it's best if I leave that piece of information out of this conversation. First, because I don't want to talk about it this morning and ruin any excitement that I have reserved for seeing Wyatt. Second, I don't need to be detained any longer. Knowing Chloe, she'll have plenty to say on the Patrick matter and I just really need to get in that car and leave to go see Wyatt. So, I plaster on a fake smile, grabbing my bags as I open the door.

"Have fun, Suz. I'll be here when you return Tuesday morning." I return her hug, knowing how much I'll need her Tuesday after Wyatt leaves for New York. I know I'll come back a depressed mess.

"Bye, Chloe. I'll see you Tuesday."

Since I left early, I missed most of the tourist traffic so the drive is easy. I arrive in Columbia around 10:30. I have barely pulled the car into the parking lot before I jump out and sprint across the parking lot, reaching the steps and climbing them two at a time. I am out of breath when I finally make it in front of Wyatt's door. Trying to calm myself, I take three deep breaths before knocking on the door. I assume that Wyatt is just as excited to see me as I am to see him, so I'm disappointed when I have to knock two more times before he opens the door. He stands in front of me wearing a pair of draw string pajama pants and wrinkled grey t-shirt. His wavy brown hair is sticking all over his head, and he looks adorable. Before he even has time to react, I rush him like an SEC linebacker, wrapping my hands around his neck in a tight embrace. I am so busy planting kisses across his cheek and down his neck I almost don't notice that he has yet to return my welcome. When I don't feel his arms around my waist I pull back to see that he is avoiding looking in my eyes.

"Wyatt, hey, are you still asleep?" I ask hoping that is the case. But when Wyatt only responds by removing my hands from around his neck, I know he is wide awake.

"Suzanna, I think we need to talk," he says motioning for me to take a seat. Panic is starting to set in as I walk with weak knees to take my seat at the kitchen table.

"Wyatt, is something wrong? Is everything okay with your family, the internship?" I am nervously rambling.

"Suzanna, I need to tell you that I don't think I can do this," he says not looking me in the eyes.

"Wyatt, you're brilliant. You deserve this opportunity. You're going be great_"

"Not the job, Suz. I can't do this," motioning between me and him, "you and me. I've thought about it and I don't think a long distance relationship is going to work." I can't believe what I am hearing. Had our five days away from each been too hard for him? I sit in stunned silence trying to make sense of what I have just heard. "Suzanna, I think it's best if you just leave and not make this harder for both of us," he says as he pushes up from his seat and starts heading to the door to escort me out.

"Wyatt, I don't understand. We've talked about this and decided we wanted to make it work," I plead for any type of understanding.

"I've changed my mind. I think this is for the best, so now, if you'll just leave." His voice is cold and he still can't look me in the eye. I know I can't stay where I'm not wanted. Tears sting my eyes while my heart breaks. I walk slowly to where Wyatt is standing at the door to usher me out like yesterday's news. I finally make it to the door, pausing in front of Wyatt.

"I can't believe you're doing this. I love you," I cry. I think Wyatt is ready to cave and rethink his decision, but I never get to find out. In the exact same moment I declare my love, I hear some movement coming from Wyatt's bedroom. I turn to look down the hallway, but don't see anything. Turning back to Wyatt I ask, "Is someone here?" He doesn't answer verbally, but the way he drops his head in shame tells me all I need to know. I storm down the hallway to see for myself. I push the door open to find my worst nightmare. Lying in Wyatt's bed is none other than Bridgett, completely naked. She turns once she hears the door open and has the audacity to look shocked to see me.

"Oh, Suzanna, I, um, thought you were at the beach." I just stand there hand over my mouth, trying to trap the scream that wants out. It finally dawns on me and I realize that it is over between me and Wyatt. I have been so dumb to think that I could find love again, and not get hurt. I mean really, what did Wyatt and I have anyway? It had only been a month since we starting dating, and obviously it wasn't as exclusive as I had thought. Anger floods my body, not at Bridgett or Wyatt, but at myself. I am angry that I opened my heart once again just to be betrayed. Both times I had been forced to walk away. I turn and walk slowly down the hallway towards the door where Wyatt is still standing. As I make my exit, walking right beside him, he reaches out to grab my arm and stop me.

"It's not what _"

"Goodbye, Wyatt," I say with a calm voice that shows no emotion. My heart is cold and beginning to freeze over. My walls are being built back up and I swear that I will not let anyone break them down again. Wyatt looks at me one last time and I see all sorts of emotions swimming in his beautiful, brown eyes. He opens his mouth to start to explain, but then closes it. We stand in silence, face to face, memorizing each other one last time. Then he lets me go and I walk down the stairs and out of his life.

Chapter Thirty-Three

(Wyatt)

I *didn't mean to try to stop her, but I couldn't just let her walk away. I wanted to tell her I had not slept with Bridgett, no matter how bad it looked. But she didn't let me. She just looked at me with an expressionless face and told me goodbye. My heart broke in that instance, watching the love of my life walk away from me. When I devised the plan to let her go, I didn't know it would be this hard. But I will never play second fiddle in her love life. The kiss I saw last night on the porch of her beach house devastated me. She and Patrick, again. I wanted to surprise her and spend some time at the beach with her since my flight had been postponed until Thursday. My going away party kept me from leaving Columbia until after 10pm. So it was after midnight by the time I arrived in Garden City. I was familiar with the area, having vacationed there as a child. Plus, Suzanna had told me the location of her family's beach home. The road was dark so I had to drive painfully slow, looking at every house that matched her description. I was also looking for her car, which would be a dead give-away I had picked the correct house. When I saw her standing on the front porch my heart skipped a beat, and I couldn't wait to put my arms around her. But then I saw Patrick, standing in front of her, caressing her face and then lowering his mouth to her for a kiss. And she kissed him back. I was shocked but couldn't look away. Then they seemed to notice my approaching car, and pulled away to glance towards the road. I accelerated and looked straight ahead, passing the house and Suzanna. I knew I would have to let her go, for now at least. But I didn't want her to know that it was because of the kiss. If she ever came back to me, I wanted her to come on her own, not out of guilt.*

The drive back to Columbia was miserable. Knowing I wouldn't get a bit of sleep, I headed to the bar that my coworkers often visited after the restaurant. I was in need of a stiff drink to numb my emotions. When I arrived, they were surprised to see me, but never asked why I had come back. Probably because they could see it written all over my face. Plus, they were all quite drunk at this point. Bridgett, especially. She had still been hanging around the bar, making nice with the bartenders. When she saw me, she stumbled over to make her move. I could have banged her right then and there, but she was drunk, and she wasn't Suzanna. I did the honorable thing and took her drunk ass to my place to sleep it off. I slept, or tried to sleep, on the couch. But all I could think about was Suzanna and watching her kiss Patrick. My heart was broken. I thought I wanted her to hurt as much as I was. But seeing her today, when she thought I had slept with Bridgett, about did me in. The pain etched across her face, caused by me, was unbearable. I had hurt her and I knew I may never get her back. So yes, I grabbed her arm, to try to explain. Even after all that happened last night and this morning, just touching her warmed by body. I was ready to tell her the truth. But then she uttered those two words, shattering my heart into more pieces..."goodbye Wyatt". It wasn't goodbye for now or goodbye for the summer. No, the way she looked at me when she whispered those words, it meant goodbye forever.

Acknowledgements

On January 1, 2013, I got this crazy idea that I was going to write a book. When I told my husband, he just shrugged his shoulders and went on to his office muttering something like, *yeah, sure you are*. Now a year later, I am published and he is the first person I have to thank. Although, there wasn't too much encouragement or support at the beginning, he eventually saw that I was serious about this project. He didn't mind that after working a ten hour day he had to come home to make dinner for the family. He didn't complain too much that the laundry basket was overflowing or that the dishes were piled high in the sink. He just let me write and finish what I set out to accomplish. Months later, after several proofs, he finally agreed to read the finished product and was happily surprised with what I had produced. His compliment of *"Hey babe, this is really good!"* will forever be one of my favorite memories. So I'd like to thank my husband for his financial contribution and emotional support throughout this process. Your accolades mean more to me than you know.

Thank you to my children, who were proud of me before I wrote the first word. And now, they can't wait to introduce their mother as not only a math teacher, but also an author. They survived on microwave dinners and peanut butter and jelly sandwiches and never complained when I had to finish a chapter before playing with them. You are both an inspiration for me and everything I do is for you.

A big thank you goes out to Ellis, my neighbor and friend. You agreed to read my book for editing purposes and did a fabulous job. But the fact that you got so enthralled in the book and the characters lead me to believe that others would as well. I remember it wasn't two hours after giving you the book that I received a text from you singing my praises. That put a huge grin on my face and gave me the encouragement I needed to continue my dream of getting published. Your only complaint was that when you finished reading the book, you wanted more. Well Ellis, more is on the way and you'll be one of the first to get a sneak peek of how Suzanna's story ends.

Thank you also to my dear friend Lisa, who I am nicknaming the "Comma Queen". You were one of the first people I thought of when I needed help with editing. You never hesitated telling me how proud you were of me before reading the first word. Your constant texts during your reading were hilarious, especially whenever you were getting to a spicy part. It is a blessing that we both share the love of reading but more than that, I am blessed to call you my friend.

Thank you to my sales consultant and creative team at CreateSpace. You have helped make this possible. Even with the technology cloud that hangs over my head, you walked me through the process with patience. You returned my many phone calls and answered all my numerous questions. I appreciate you making the publishing experience a little less scary.

Last, but definitely not least, a humongous thank you goes out to my hairdresser, my neighbor, but most importantly my close friend, Bethany. Not once did you ever doubt my ability to write a book. You encouraged me from the first typed word. You were the first person to read the very raw, unedited version. Never once did you shy away from giving your opinions about the storyline or the characters. I'll never forget the day I had a conference call with the publisher while you were coloring my hair. You were there from the very beginning of this process to the very end. Your enthusiasm rivals mine about this book being published. I have always taken your input very seriously and applied it to the finished product. I feel like this is as much yours as it is mine. I hope I have made you proud.

Thank you to everyone who reads this book. For a part-time teacher and full-time wife and mother, it is nice to escape reality for just a while within the pages of a book. I hope I have provided you with that same escape. Happy reading!

About the Author

Virginia C. Hart resides in her beloved state of South Carolina, where she was born and raised. Married for thirteen lucky years, she and her husband have two children, a fourteen-year-old dog, and a brand new kitten. After graduating from Francis Marion University with a bachelor's degree in accounting, followed by a master's degree in education, Hart has been teaching part-time at the local technical college for nearly a decade.

When she's not teaching or chauffeuring her kids around, Hart is likely to be found typing away at a new book, furiously reading yet another book, or visiting her favorite South Carolina coastal spots.

Inspired to write her own romantic fiction when she was reintroduced to her love of reading a few years ago, *Beneath the Lie*, the first book in her first series, is where it all begins.

Made in the USA
Columbia, SC
02 September 2017